Pony Trials

Full of Running #3

pony trials

GRACE WILKINSON

Also by the author

Comet in Summer

Confetti Horses

Eventing Bay

The Loxwood Series

chapter 1

'Don't be a lunatic,' I warn Otto, unfastening the leather halter and letting it slide from his nose. For a moment, the gelding doesn't move, ears pricked as he takes in the still frost-covered paddock, looking the epitome of good manners. I step backwards, knowing what comes next, and then it does. Otto shakes his head, as though only just realising he's free, squeals, spins on his hocks, and takes off.

The light bay pony gallops across the field, kicking up his heels and launching into a series of bucks. I wince as his shoes click dangerously with every stride, crossing my fingers he keeps all four on.

At the far end of the field, Otto comes to a standstill and shakes his body like a dog that has just been bathed, his turnout rug making a flapping sound. He stares at the land around him, as though seeing the post-and-rail fields for the first time, and neighs at the grazing broodmares in the distance. He gets no response, he never does, but he's pleased with himself, and finally lowers his head with a sigh to start snatching at the short grass.

'Charming pony,' I say, smiling at his antics. This has been his daily routine for all of the years he's been here, and yet Otto takes off across the field every morning as though he's never done so before, always under the impression that he's taken his handler by surprise.

I pull the gate closed and fasten the head collar to one of the aluminium rails. It's eleven in the morning, but the air is still crisp enough to believe it were hours earlier. I shiver, stuffing my pink hands in my coat pockets. It was only once I reached the stables earlier this morning that I remembered I'd forgotten my gloves in the house, and even the cold wasn't enough for me to go all the way back to get them. My toes are freezing, my boots get stuck with every step, and my breeches are flecked with mud. *I am so done with winter.*

From the paddock beside Otto's, Fendi lifts her head to glance at me as I pass her, looking as laid-back as she always does. Her navy blue turnout rug is covered in mud, and wet clumps are stuck to strands of flaxen mane that poke out from her neck cover, behind the ears. I cluck to the pony and utter a greeting, but the chestnut mare lowers her head again, ignoring me. Typical. If there were ever a horse understandable and straightforward enough to explain with a manual, it would be Fendi. She's not one to get easily distracted, and rarely bothers showing affection. She's a worker, a pony who just likes to do her job. *And yet Sophia still managed to mess her up*, I think, and the thought is taken over by another. *Sophia.*

'Mia,' I call as I walk back into the yard, heading for Doris's stable. The yard - *our yard,* as my sisters, my mother, and I refer to it to avoid confusion - is modest compared to the others. Internal partitions have been assembled beneath an open agricultural building, creating a row of six stables that adjoin a high security tack room, a wash stall, and a tie-up point complete with a solarium. Opposite the row of boxes, some fifty feet away, is another open building, where bales of hay and shavings are stacked neatly beneath the tin roof, beside pieces of equipment like a hay steamer and spare wheelbarrows, and farther along from which is a feed room consisting of metal bins above which hangs a whiteboard.

My stables - Otto and Fendi's stables - are already mucked out, with big banks of shavings and well-swept doorways. Otto's tack is scattered miscellaneously outside his box, where I tied him up before and after our ride, as I took him straight to the paddock before having time to tidy everything away, but it'll have to wait another minute. *Castle on the Hill* blasts from the radio, probably the fifth Ed Sheeran song I've heard today, because Suffolk isn't exactly famous for producing pop stars, and the local radio stations certainly give him - and what is possibly the only hit song ever written about the county - plenty of airtime.

'What?' Mia says.

I reach the stable door and lean against the iron doorway as I look into it. Doris stands tied up, pulling at a net of steamed hay with a bored expression, while my little sister, Mia, is on her knees in the shavings, scrubbing at a manure stain on the grey pony's hock. If it were any other horse, I'd tell Mia not to be so careless, but Doris, who has carted all three of us around our first events, is as safe as they come.

'*Yes,*' I correct automatically, because my mum's strong ideas about manners rub off on you after a while.

Mia rolls her eyes and straightens up, clean shavings covering her beige jodhpurs. 'India.'

'Fine,' I say, letting it go and moving on. 'Have you seen Sophia yet?' I walk up to Doris and rest a hand on her clipped body as I wait for Mia to respond.

My sister shakes her head, the scattering of freckles on her nose accentuated by a recent suntan, her long, tangled hair swinging.

This doesn't exactly come as a surprise, as she wasn't here ten minutes ago, but still I struggle to hide my annoyance. 'She still hasn't been out at all?'

Mia shakes her head again. 'No. Not that I've seen, anyway.'

I sigh loudly and step out of the stable again, carrying on down the row. I pass Mia's other pony, glancing into the box long enough to see that he has been mucked out and cared for, before reaching the fifth stable, where kind, dark eyes stare into my blue ones.

Dammit, Sophia. My older sister getting on my nerves is nothing new, and I ignore it most of the time, but it gets hard when there is a horse involved.

Sophia and I have always fought occasionally. When we were younger, it was just usual sibling bickering. Nothing abnormal, easy to ignore. Growing up with horses, we both started riding at a young age, going from showing to Pony Club classes, and naturally we became competitive with each other.

When Sophia decided she wanted to event more seriously, our parents - or, our mum, to be precise - did what anyone with a large bank account and an inflated sense of their child's ability does: she decided to buy her daughter one of the best event ponies in the country. Then she bought another one, for good measure. Suddenly Fendigo and Lakota - FEI event ponies; European medal-winning ponies - were stabled in our yard, and Sophia was ecstatic.

At first, it seemed like things were going to go all right. The ponies competed and went double clear, picking up placings. The ponies were happy. Mum was happy. Sophia was happy.

But then things started to go wrong.

Because what Mum and Sophia failed to see was that Sophia couldn't ride these ponies. Couldn't ride them well, anyway. They started picking up refusals, until neither was getting around a course at all. Fendi, the more experienced of the two ponies, lasted longer, but even she went wrong eventually.

Trainers were blamed, ponies were blamed, previous riders were blamed - my mum even hired Sophia a sports psychologist, whose instructions of blocking out negativity at shows basically meant not being corrected, and ignoring your coach is hardly going to help your riding progress. What was simply a loss of confidence on the horses' part, which should have been easily enough fixed, was blown out of proportion and turned into a ridiculous issue. Of course the only person not blamed, by herself or our parents, was the one holding the reins. There was no mystery to uncover, no secret remedy, just a girl who didn't ride well enough to ride the ponies she owned. But neither she nor Mum would hear any of that. I didn't say anything - what did I know? - but other people did. Trainers and riders. But it wasn't accepted, and Mum continued to search for a solution for a non-existent problem.

When Sophia turned sixteen an event season ago, achieving none of the pony success that had been hoped, Otto and Fendi were passed to me, if for no other reason than them not possibly being able to earn back their original sale prices. Nothing to lose, no expectations. But I don't think anybody - myself included - expected us to triumph. I'd *hoped*, wished, imagined that I'd be able to ride them, that I could train and work hard and learn to master them, because the well-schooled ponies were still in there somewhere, but it actually happening was still unexpected. Not that everything was perfect. After one full season, I could get both ponies around metre-high courses without being eliminated, but we still had occasional blips. Both ponies had lost confidence and muscle with Sophia, and it was nothing that could be regained overnight. But it *could* be regained. And I am determined to succeed.

Simple.

Except not, because of course, ageing out of ponies, Sophia needed a new horse. So our parents bought a horse that had been on a Junior European team. And so far, everything has gone smoothly. Mason is honest and forgiving, and keeps jumping even when Sophia buries him into fences.

And here he is, staring back at me.

Still not looked after.

'Hey, Mase,' I say, letting myself into the stable. The dark bay gelding turns towards me, and I hold my hands out to show him that I don't have treats. I fed him this morning, when I fed the others, because if I hadn't, he'd still be waiting for his breakfast, and standing around in a stable all morning is bad enough without being starving, too. I slide my hand beneath his heavy combo rug, the one he's spent the minus-five night in, and feel his shoulder warm with sweat. 'I'm going to kill her.'

We have a full-time groom, but she has most weekends off outside of the event season, which is when it falls to me and my sisters to look after our own horses, something Sophia has never been good at.

When I close Mason's stable door, after swapping his heavy rug for a lighter one, I put my gear away, then write down what each of my ponies worked on today in the diary in the tack room, and when I step back out the door, Mum is walking into the yard, our two cocker spaniels at her heels. Her highlighted, shoulder-length hair is tied back, face made-up, and she's wearing a fur-trimmed riding coat, jeans, and walking boots.

I head straight for her. 'Have you seen Sophia?'

Mum stops in her tracks and turns her head slowly, from left to right, as though Sophia is possibly beside her and she hasn't noticed. 'She isn't out here?'

I shake my head. As much as my mum gets on my nerves a lot of the time, especially where Sophia is involved, she's also quite an easy person to have on side. 'I haven't seen her, and neither has Mia. I fed them all this morning, and we've both mucked out ours, but Mason hasn't been done, and I just changed his rug because he had the heavy one on and was sweating like a pig.' I can hear Sophia's voice in my head calling me a telltale, but I don't care.

Mum frowns and raises her hands to her temples. 'She must be in bed, then, because I haven't seen her.' She lets out a long sigh and winces, like this twenty second conversation has given her a migraine. 'Can you go get her?'

I shake my head. 'I'm not getting involved. Just letting you know because it's not fair on Mason,' I snap. If I spoke to my mother this way about anything else, she'd go mental and yell at me for being so rude, but where horses are concerned - so long as I don't criticise Sophia's riding - anything goes. 'I'll be back in a minute. Otto and Fendi are all done. I'm going to see the foals.'

It's what every pony-mad child dreams of. Living on a hundred-acre farm, with horses grazing in the post-and-rail paddocks, foals everywhere. And I suppose it is all that, but it's also not quite as picturesque as the image that comes to mind.

'Hey, Middie,' I say.

Midnight Moneymaker looks up from her hay, alert. I walk closer to the stable door and stifle a squeal as I peer beyond it, at the little body and long legs nestled in the straw.

Middie is an old-hand - this is her sixth foal - and I slide the bolt across the door, letting myself in. Like many of the older mares, she isn't foal proud, and is only too happy to let you fuss over her little one.

'Hey, cutie,' I say, kneeling down beside the bay colt. He lifts his head shakily, his body still uncoordinated the way a newborn foal's always is, and then lowers it to the straw again. Jealous of the attention her baby is getting, Middie turns towards me, lowering her nose to rest it on my thigh. I smile at the brown mare, scratch her head. 'Clever mum.'

It's the end of January, and the colt is the first foal of the year. It's ridiculous, to have frost on the ground and ice covering the water troughs and yet be foaling, but that's how it is. I once heard Dad say that he doesn't breed racehorses, he breeds Thoroughbreds that will make money at the sales, and I suppose his words are true. Everyone wants a January foal, a January colt. Colts generally make more money than fillies due to their breeding potential should they be successful, so that one is obvious, but the early birth date is something else. Foal sales take place in December, which means any foal born in June will be up against those with winter birthdays, and one that is five or six months younger than the others around it will never stand out. The Thoroughbred stud season does not correlate with a mare's natural cycle, and we have to keep them in lit-up barns for weeks before they're covered to artificially bring them into season. Many believe early births don't put horses at an advantage in the long run - if anything, it's the opposite, with many believing that the strongest foals, the ones that make the best racehorses, are those born when the air is warm and the grass is lush, but it's not an idea that has reached bidders at the sales rings. Not to say we've never had late foals sell well, because we have, but rarely younger than yearlings. The best horse we've ever bred, Intrico, was born in May, and we only kept and raced him because he wasn't mature enough as a foal or as a yearling to go to the sales, which ended up being a serious strike of luck, because he won the July cup and stands at stud today as one of the most desirable stallions in the country.

'You're the lucky January colt,' I say to the foal before straightening up again. At this time of day, the barn is almost empty. All the mares have been turned out, with just Middie and the new arrival sheltered from the cold weather, and the stables have been mucked out, the deep straw beds ready for the mares to come back in at two o'clock. *Take note, Sophia.* My older sister comes to see and photograph the first few foals of the year, when we all still find foals cute and irresistible, but the novelty always wears off by April.

I leave the mare and foal to walk down the aisle, towards the open double doors, peering absently into each stable, calmed by the sight of the tidy beds of straw so golden I really could imagine

Rumplestiltskin spinning it into the real thing. There's just something about a well-kept barn that feeds my soul. In a couple of hours, the building will be abuzz with movement, as the mares come in from the paddocks and the daily vet round starts. We don't have a teaser pony, mainly because Mum has always been adamant she doesn't want a stallion on the property, that the yearling colts are bad enough, which means we rely solely on scans to tell us when each mare is ready to be covered. The afternoons are always busy, as is early morning, but for now, everything is peaceful.

Rolling paddocks surround me, these ones framed with Keepsafe fencing for foals, and dotted with grazing horses - mostly bays, all mares due to foal in the next few months. There are two more barns on the property, and the three combined bring the stable total to sixty, excluding the six reserved for our eventers. I love this place. I love my ponies, and I love eventing, but this... this is something else. The stud is where I feel at home.

In the nearest paddock, a bay mare comes up to the fence, and, seeing me, she whickers. The sound never fails to make my heart flutter, and I grin as I walk up to greet her.

'Hey, Pearl.'

Pearl whickers again, and I lean forward to prop my elbows on the fence, resting my head against hers. A fine white blaze runs down her head, veering off to the left before it reaches her nose. In many ways, she's ordinary. She wasn't the greatest racehorse, and she hasn't the greatest pedigree, but in my eyes, she's one of the standout mares. She has it all - brain, heart, and courage. But bidders don't look for those things, and as a consequence her foals have made little over the years. Most studs would have ditched her, but Pearl is a useful mare - easy to handle, good at looking after other mares and foals in a herd - and so she stays. One year, some time ago, she had a colt that I fell for, hook, line, and sinker. He was beautiful, and smart, and affectionate, but he went to the sales, made a disappointing price due to his sire going out of fashion, and that was that. I cried, and my parents argued that I was always getting too attached to the foals and yearlings, but that one was different. And I'll never see him again.

'You looking after that baby, Pearlie?' I ask the mare, rubbing her ears. Two years ago, she delivered a nice-enough filly, but the birth wasn't an easy one, and already being May, it was decided that the mare would have a rest year. I saw it as a chance. Studs open February fifteenth for covering, and that was the intention. Pearl would be covered early, put to a reasonable stallion, and finally, *maybe*, she'd have that coveted early colt. She *is* having a colt, we know that much from the sixty day scan, but unfortunately she didn't take first time, or second, which meant she was covered a third, and her due date isn't until the end of March. But still, an early-spring colt is nothing to complain about. The stud fee was the highest Dad has ever spent on Pearl, for a first season sire already creating a buzz, and I know she won't get this privilege again, not unless the foal's good. This is it, her one shot.

None of Pearl's foals has been successful. She's had a few pick up some placings, but nothing more, and at fourteen years of age, she won't get many more shots at producing a winner. That's my dream: that Pearl will breed a winner. A Group horse, one that will go on to stand as a stallion and put Pearl on the map, not only upping the value of her future offspring but giving her a legacy. I want Pearl to matter. Her two-year-old, her last foal due to run, was bought by a trainer Dad knows, and she did a tendon while being backed at the end of last year, ending a racing career that never started. This next foal needs to be good. It'll be two or three years until the colt starts racing, but at least if he comes out well, if he's straight and goes on to fetch a good price at the foal sales later this year, Dad will be more inclined to invest in higher stud fees. We kept breeding rights in Intrico after we sold him, which means we get to send mares to him for free rather than pay thirty-five grand a piece, but he's too closely related to Pearl to make the combination a good match. So this foal has to be good, because whichever stallion she goes to next, Dad will have to pay full whack for, and he's not going to invest highly if the colt comes out wonky.

'Eight weeks,' I whisper. Eight weeks until she's due. But every mare is different, and learning each horse's habits is important, and in all the years she's been here, Pearl has always foaled two weeks late, which means it will most likely be ten. Ten weeks. It feels like a long time now, but I know it will pass in the blink of an eye - or the stride of a Thoroughbred.

I glance over my shoulder, looking at the grand listed house in the distance, on the other side of which is a newly-surfaced arena, and, even farther along, a stable yard. In the quiet, I can just make out Mum's voice, and the unmistakable one that answers. Sophia. She must have finally decided to grace the world with her presence, then.

I turn back to Pearl. 'Ten weeks. So long as I don't kill Sophia in that time.'

'There's more if anyone wants seconds,' Mum says, setting her cutlery down on her almost-empty plate. It doesn't matter what the meal is, but she always leaves a forkful.

'I'll have some,' I say, standing up from the table, the chair legs screeching across the tiled floor as I push my seat back. Sophia groans like my action is the most irritating thing in the world a person could do, while Mia is busy fussing over the dogs as her food gets cold on her plate, and Dad is holding his phone in one hand and a fork in another.

I wordlessly spoon another helping of lasagna onto my plate, listening to the mundane silence at the table behind me and wondering how long it'll be until Mum cracks and speaks up. Her family's inability to have a dinner conversation is something she complains about frequently.

'Mia, honey, eat up your dinner,' Mum says as I sit back down, reaching a hand across the table to touch her youngest's arm.

Mia stops stroking Troika and looks down at her plate, sticking out her lower lip and tucking her straight hair behind her ears. It's no wonder people are often surprised to hear she is as old as twelve, I think, because she wears the facial expressions of a toddler. 'But I'm full.'

'You can't be full,' Mum says reasonably, 'because you've barely eaten anything.'

Mia shrugs and starts prodding her lasagna with her fork, and Mum gives up, eyes shifting to another family member. 'Are you around this evening, Arthur?' she asks Dad. He came back from the Cape Yearling Sales in South Africa this week, having flown over for only three days, and in the four days he's been home, he's probably been in the house about four hours.

Dad frowns at his phone, clearly preoccupied with whatever he's doing. 'Uh, sorry, Cads, what was that?'

I brace myself for Mum's loud sigh, which she emits on cue. 'Are you around this evening?' she asks again. 'It would be nice if we could all have some family time before everything gets hectic.'

Hectic is an understated way of describing breeding season. There are always pregnant mares to check, foals to keep an eye on, vicious first-time dams to handle, mares to scan and take to be covered, and, the spanner in the works, the fact that most of this will be done on no sleep thanks to horses' preference for foaling at night.

To his credit, Dad makes an effort to put his phone down, and I glance at the screen to see the Racing Post website. 'I'm not sure, Caddie. Earl thinks the Resolute mare is going to go tonight, so I'll see how that-'

'Final Resolution is foaling tonight?' I interrupt, which earns me a glare from Mum.

Dad nods slowly, sucking in his cheeks and running a hand

through his pale hair. 'Looks like she might. Started dripping milk this morning and hasn't eaten up her evening feed.'

'Can I do a round of foal watch?' This is another beginning of season novelty, because in a few months' time the thought of staying awake to stare at camera footage will be less preferable to getting root canal, but for now it's still fun. In the height of breeding season, Dad can go weeks without making it to his bed, and much like a doctor on call, you learn to nap whenever and wherever you can.

'No, you can't,' Mum says, cutting off Dad who was about to say the contrary.

I slump back in my seat. 'Why not?'

'You've got Merritt coming tomorrow.' She sits up straighter and glances at Sophia across the table. 'How were the horses today? Ready for a lesson?'

'What time's Merritt coming?' I ask, hoping Mum hasn't already told me, and also saving us all from an argument because I know for a fact that Sophia ended up not working Mason today.

'Ten. And she can do all five horses, but you have to be ready because she needs to leave by three. Which one of you is going to be ready first?'

'I don't mind,' I say.

Sophia doesn't respond.

Mia is ignoring her dinner again and playing with the roan spaniel beneath the table.

'Right, well, that's helpful,' Mum says.

'When would you rather ride, Soph?' I ask, because there is only one of us who will complain about the order.

Sophia shrugs. 'Don't care. Doesn't matter.'

'Well so long as you sort it out amongst yourselves before Merritt gets here,' Mum says, staring intently at Mia's plate of food as she speaks. Despite being slim, Mum has been on a so-called diet for as long as I can remember, and I swear she's wishing she could finish off Mia's meal.

I try again. 'I don't mind riding one first. I could turn Otto out early and have Fendi ready for ten, then turn her out and bring him in while someone's riding in the next session.'

'Mia,' Mum warns, and my sister straightens in her seat unhappily. 'I don't mind what order you do things in,' she goes on, responding to me. 'Just make sure you have it sorted.'

'Do you want to ride first, Mia?' I ask.

'Don't mind,' Mia says, shrugging.

'Oh for God's sake,' Sophia snaps loudly, slamming her fork down on the table. 'Why do we have to keep discussing this? What does the order we ride in matter?'

'Sophia,' Mum says, much in the same tone she gave Mia a warning a moment ago.

Sophia ignores her and continues talking to me. 'Do you never just *shut up!* Seriously, what does it matter?'

'Soph,' Dad says firmly.

'I'm only trying to help,' I say.

'India's only trying to help,' Mum repeats. 'There's no problem.'

'I just don't know why she always has to go on about things,' Sophia says as though I'm not sitting right here, picking up her fork.

'That's enough, Sophia,' Dad says.

'You can ride first if you want,' I offer.

Sophia throws her cutlery down again. 'I don't care about riding first! I just don't get why you have to keep discussing things that don't matter.'

'Sophia, that's enough,' Mum says, standing up from the table with her plate in hand. 'The only one causing a problem here is you.' As much as Mum tiptoes around Sophia where her riding is concerned, she has a zero-tolerance policy when it comes to manners and behaviour in the house, which applies to dinner time outbursts. Sophia can be perfectly civil, and very nice to other people, but she's in a foul mood at the moment, due in part to Mum saying we can't go skiing during the half-term holidays. We own a chalet in the French Alps, and Sophia hasn't taken the news that we won't be going next month very well. Even though Mum's main argument for us not going is that we just came back from a New Year holiday in St Lucia earlier this month. 'And for goodness' sake, Mia, eat your dinner.'

Mia looks down at her plate as though she were noticing the food for the first time. 'But I'm not hungry,' she says brightly. She pauses. 'Can I have a yoghurt?'

Mum sighs. 'You don't need to ask me if you can have a - wait, no, you just said you weren't hungry.'

'I'm not hungry enough to eat lasagna but I'm hungry enough to eat a yoghurt.'

'Fine, whatever.' Mum places her plate on top of the dishwasher, flicks the kettle on, and sits back down at the table. 'I give up.'

We all sit wordlessly for the remainder of the meal, the silence broken only by the loud sound of Mia's spoon scraping against the inside of a yoghurt pot. And then two more.

chapter 2

Fendi's eyes are closed as I fasten her throat lash and tuck the strap into its keepers. I straighten her flaxen forelock and lay a hand against her neck, resting my weight against her. 'You're gonna need to wake up a bit more before Merritt gets here, Fendigo.'

'India,' Mia calls, appearing in the doorway. 'Have you seen my tail brush?'

I shake my head. 'Take mine, if you want.'

Mia bends to retrieve the item from my grooming box, shivering when she stands. 'It's absolutely freezing,' she says, stepping into the shavings.

'It is,' I agree, and I glance towards the house.

In view of Sophia's reluctance to pick a riding slot, Mia and I are alternating the first four, so that Sophia can't interfere with our lessons. Which means she doesn't need to have Mason ready until two, but it would be nice if she made an appearance before then. I fed and hayed this morning, with Mia's help, but as usual Sophia was nowhere to be seen. She did do the bare essentials yesterday, staying in the yard long enough to muck out, fill a haynet, and turn Mason out, but she was so late that the brown gelding only got a couple of hours in the paddock before coming back in. He didn't even get worked, and now he's going into a jumping lesson today. 'I hope Soph at least turns Mason out this morning before riding,' I say.

Mia follows my gaze to the house, then looks back at me. 'Why doesn't Sophia like looking after her horses?'

Why indeed. Because she's lazy? Because Mum spoils her? Because she doesn't like horses, just winning? Because she *did* like horses, but her failures with Fendi and Otto have knocked the passion out of her? 'I don't know,' I tell Mia honestly.

'I love riding,' Mia begins, 'but I also *love* looking after Doris and Harvey. I'll *always* look after my horses, even when I'm going round Badminton.'

'Good. Don't forget that.'

Mia holds up the tail brush. 'I need to go wash Doris's tail. It's *filthy.*'

I nod. 'You go do that.' Merritt isn't a stickler for immaculate turnout at home by any means, but that doesn't matter to Mia. She always makes sure her ponies are well-presented before riding, which isn't as cute as it sounds when I'm waiting for her to go hacking on a freezing winter evening and she's trying to get every clump of mud out of her pony's mane.

The hay steamer alarm sounds, the loud, constant buzzing more annoying than any other alarm I've ever heard, and I sprint to switch it off, not only to silence the noise as quickly as possibly, but because leaving the machine on when the canister is out of water is how you bust it.

'Are you going to be good, Fen?' I ask my little mare when I return, scratching her neck. She's a bright chestnut in summer, but having just been clipped again a week ago, her coat is now hazelnut-coloured, in contrast to her fluffy red legs.

I hear Merritt's car before I see it, and I shrug out of my heavy coat, swapping it for a fleece-lined waistcoat. My hat is on the floor, and I pull it over my hair, tugging my plait free from the gilet. I tighten Fendi's girth and remove the folded-over rug I left on the mare's haunches so she didn't get cold waiting.

'Morning all,' Merritt calls as she walks into the yard, rubbing her hands against each other. When Otto and Fendi began going wrong, my parents started going through trainers at a ridiculous speed. Pony Club instructors, four-star riders, team trainers… but of course, the person on the ground was never the problem, and Mum didn't want to hear the truth.

Luckily for me, Merritt came along just a short while before Otto and Fendi were handed to me, because I'm sure she'd have been driven away if she'd had to deal with Sophia on the two ponies for any longer, and I couldn't love her more. Merritt's past sixty now, but she's never slowed down. She evented to Advanced level thirty years ago, switched to show jumping after she had kids, and competed all the way to one-sixty before hanging up her show boots just a couple of years ago. Merritt is of average height, with shoulder-length grey hair, a physical strength that would scare a bouncer, only takes her sunglasses off when it's raining, and drinks black coffee like the world is running out of the stuff.

'Morning, Merritt,' Mia says.

'Good morning, Mia.' For her no-nonsense ways, Merritt is quite soft outside of an arena, and she has a big fan in Mia - and vice versa. And so far, she's the only person who has managed to put up with Sophia - well, except for our dressage trainer, Edmund, but sitting pretty for flatwork on schoolmasters has never been a problem for Soph, so that isn't a discipline she struggles with. 'How's Doris?' she asks, glancing at the grey mare tied in the wash stall, a fleece over her clipped body.

Mia giggles. 'Good. So's Harvey.'

'Good, that's what we like to hear.'

'The Nespresso machine's on,' I say to Merritt.

'Oh, bless you,' she says, rubbing her hands together again as she scurries into the tack room. I hear the rumble of the coffee machine, and then Merritt is back in the yard as it runs. 'How are you, my dear? One, two - where's the third?'

'She's still asleep,' Mia yells before I can respond.

Merritt raises her eyebrows at me. 'Is she, now?'

'The princess needs her beauty sleep,' I say.

Merritt pulls a face. 'How's she been?'

'I dunno, she's barely been in the yard,' I say, then feel a twinge of guilt at not having Sophia's back. 'I mean, everything's going all right, though. I think.'

I lead Fendi out of her stable as Merritt gets her coffee from the tack room, bending to pick up my schooling whip from the concrete, and then halt the pony and pull down the stirrups of my close-contact saddle now we're through the stable doorway. The mare is in good condition, if a little heavier than she is during the competition season. She's a naturally chunky pony, and it's only when she's running at events that she starts to slim down, regardless of how much work she does in between. Not that she is unjustifiably heavy, because food is not something she deprives herself of.

'She's looking good,' Merritt says as she re-emerges, coffee cup in hand.

'She's a bit chunky,' I admit.

Merritt shakes her head. 'No problem with that at this time of year.' She eyes the chestnut up and down, then shakes her head again. 'No problem at all. Right, let's get going.'

Even in these freezing temperatures, the arena doesn't freeze. The expensive surface is springy beneath Fendi's feet as she trots around in circles.

'Good. More inside leg there, make her bend through her ribcage. Good. And go wide and keep her straight down the long side.'

I sit up and push Fendi with my left leg, carrying on down the long side of the school, and glance briefly in the arena mirrors to check my position. The mare is light in the hand, her neck elastic, head carriage still. She's an easy pony to ride, but she doesn't come through from behind, doesn't overtrack, doesn't really bend her hocks, unless she has to.

'Okay, give her a breather and then come down the line in trot.'

I ease Fendi back to walk, making the transition count, and seek out the fence. There's always a grid set up in the middle of the school, and only the first jump is set, a sixty centimetre upright, with placing poles both before and after it. Fendi ducks her head to rub her nose against her knee, and I cluck to her.

'Here,' Merritt says, holding out a short whip, and I swap it for the schooling stick.

'Thanks.'

I push the mare into a trot, collecting her and adding more leg as Merritt tells me to increase the stride. The mare moves with grace, naturally balanced, and I turn her up the centre line, towards the poles. Fendi stays in a rhythm all the way to the placing pole, and I barely have to adjust her as she easily clears the upright, staying straight on landing.

'Good. And again.'

For the next twenty minutes, Merritt sets exercises, and Fendi and I navigate them. The little mare is on form, rideable into every fence and also bold. With Sophia, by the time they were handed to me, the ponies refused every other jump. Sophia can't see a stride, which she could have maybe got away with if she'd ridden positively, but she didn't. Instead she hooked, pulling on the reins and burying her ride into the foot of the fence. Otto and Fendi kept jumping for a while - Fendi for longer - but soon they lost confidence and started slamming on the brakes.

My eye for a stride isn't perfect, but I'm aware of it. I don't often put the ponies in trouble, and even if I do I still make sure to ride positively, to kick on in that last stride and try, not for one moment, to let the possibility of a refusal cross my mind, because Otto and Fendi both react strongly to hesitation. I listen to Merritt and try my hardest to improve my riding, to iron out my faults, and give the ponies confidence. But confidence is a lot easier to lose than it is to build, and as easy as it was for the ponies to lose, it will be that much harder to regain. At competitions especially, I still can't count on either pony not to throw in a stop if I make a mistake. There's no magic solution, no mystery of how to solve the problem, but only repetition. Miles on the clock.

Fendi jumps into the line, and I sit up on landing, balancing her for the two strides to the next element. The thing with Fendi is that if you ask her to jump a fifty-centimetre fence, she'll jump one centimetre above it. If you ask her to jump an eighty-centimetre fence, she'll jump one centimetre above it. If you point her at a metre-thirty upright, she'll jump one centimetre above it. She isn't capped, has no limit that anyone has found, but she does only what is necessary, and nothing more. Which makes her an easy horse to jump, because her bascules are rarely unseating. It still amazes me that Sophia wasn't able to ride her. And I really believe that even if my sister hadn't ridden well and just sat back as a passenger Fendi would have jumped everything put in front of her, because she was honest and confident in her ability, but Sophia *did* interfere. Though she isn't a typical mare, Fendi does still have an independent streak, which means not responding well to being too controlled, especially when the rider is wrong. And after so many dodgy strides, and being caught in the mouth through the air and on every landing, she finally, justifiably, threw her toys out the pram.

The chestnut mare powers forward, and I sit up again, making sure to lower my hands because Merritt often warns me I lift them. A blue-and-white oxer looms, set only at a metre, and I look straight ahead, not letting the obstacle affect the rhythm Fendi and I have. The take-off spot comes naturally, and I lean forward as

Fendi launches into the air, front feet tucked, and lands with her head up, carrying on in perfect cadence.

'That's the one,' Merritt says, and I pat Fendi as I bring her back to walk. My cheeks are flushed, my body is warm beneath my waistcoat, and a smile breaks across my face as I pat the pony enthusiastically.

Merritt walks back to the stables beside Fendi, empty coffee cup in her hand about to be filled again, and I smile down at the mare as she walks.

Mum is standing with Mia in the yard when we step onto the concrete, and her smile grows when she sees us round the corner. 'Morning, Merritt,' she says brightly.

'How're you, Caddie?' Merritt asks, making a beeline towards her. 'They were great,' she adds, nodding at me and Fendi, and I look away to hide the grin on my face. 'Really good. She did great on the flat, really got Fen using her hind end, and they jumped great, too.'

Mum smiles at me. 'Brilliant. I'm so pleased. Coffee, Mer?'

'Yes, please.' Merritt passes Mum her mug and moves towards Doris. 'You ready, Mia?'

While I lead a rugged Fendi to the paddock, I keep my eyes on the distant sand school and watch the outline of a grey pony move around it, Merritt's voice calling out corrections. In two event seasons, when I age out of ponies, Fendi and Otto will probably finish their careers with Mia, unless I do so well that our parents decide to make a quick buck and sell them, but if they do go to Mia, I think she'll do just fine with them. There are plenty of twelve-year-olds eventing who are better riders - more professional, more effective - but Mia has the right attitude. She's unafraid, accepts criticism, and works hard at what Merritt tells her even when her coach isn't around. Mia is more competitive than Sophia and I were at her age, but she doesn't let her love of winning affect or override her love of looking after her ponies. You can guarantee that even if she's up until midnight after a successful event, gloating about her results and admiring elaborate rosettes, she'll still be in the yard at dawn the next morning to feed and muck out.

The grey mare is trotting in circles, tracking up with a still head carriage, while Mia is sitting tall in the saddle, looking straight ahead, long ponytail bouncing against her coat. Doris isn't the flashiest pony in the world, not now that age is starting to catch up with her, the same way Mia isn't the most amazing rider, but those are the kinds of combinations that always succeed in the long run: quiet, humble, determined. The kind of combination that makes it to the top of the leader board before anyone else notices they're even in contention.

I take my time getting Otto ready, knowing I have at least forty-five minutes until our lesson. The bay pony stands tied up outside his stable with a net of steamed hay, and I swap his turnout rug for a light stable one. While he tugs at the forage, I make myself a cup of coffee in the tack room and carry it out with a packet of digestives, pausing in the doorway to look back behind me. The tack room is immaculately kept, thanks to our groom Bree. There are no fewer than ten saddles, whose combined purchase price could buy a pretty decent eventer, because Mum's idea of ridiculous is ponies having to share tack at an event, and not a kid having fifteen thousand pounds' worth of saddles - almost four grand a saddle, and two saddles per horse. Robbers could probably get into the house with relative ease, but suffice to say that getting past the tack room security system would require a seriously well-planned heist.

Bridles are hung neatly, and drawers of boots are labelled with the horses' names, white stickers scrawled on in black biro. Built-in shelves are stacked with rugs and clean saddle pads, and rosettes hang along a string above the sink.

It never escapes my attention how lucky we all are, but I can't say the same about someone else.

When Otto is tacked up, a fleece over his quarters, I tidy up the yard while I wait for Merritt to return. Mia had Doris tied up earlier and the mare's head collar is on the floor, hanging from the rope. I pick up the leather halter, running my thumb over the brass nameplate in which the words *PILLOW TALK* are engraved, and hang it on the stable door, moving on down the aisle. Mason still has hay, happily pulling at his net, but as Sophia has yet to come out, his stable is filthy. He stares at me through the bars of his stable, his eyes soft, as though saying, *Really, it's okay, don't worry, I'm fine,* and I lean over the half door to talk to him.

'I'm sorry, bud,' I say. 'But if it's any consolation, I'm sure Sophia'll give up in a few months when she finishes her A-levels and go off on a gap year or something. Then I'll look after you or you'll go to someone who will. Okay?'

Sophia still hasn't made an appearance when Mia rides Doris back to the yard, all smiles as Mum and Merritt walk alongside her, and I don't need to ask to know that the lesson has gone well. All of Mia's lessons go well, really, because even when they don't, she doesn't carry the defeat around. It's Sophia who's unpredictable. When she's riding, Mia and I are always prepared for the potential tornado of wrath and sulk that could come out of the arena. If something goes wrong, then a black hole might as well open up and swallow us all whole, because it's like the end of the world. Even leading up to a lesson Mum will be anxious, dreading what may come, but yet it never occurs to her to blame Sophia for the consequences.

'Sophia out yet, India?' Mum asks, and I have a feeling the smile on her face from Mia's lesson is about to disappear.

'Haven't seen her today,' I say, glancing at Merritt, who raises her eyebrows and looks away. What she doesn't say about Sophia's behaviour she sure makes up for in facial expressions. 'I obviously fed Mason and everything,' I go on, 'but he hasn't been mucked out, and he's probably starting to get warm in that rug.'

Mum sighs. 'I'll change the rug.'

'I'd change the owner,' Merritt quips quietly as she passes me on her way to the coffee machine.

The sun has taken the edge off the winter chill, and it's almost warm when I finish riding Otto. For his plain and chunky appearance, Otto is actually a spicy ride and a flashy mover once he gets going. When Sophia failed with him, Mum was convinced it was because Alex, Otto's former rider who was still young at the time, hadn't put the basics in, but if anything he's better schooled than Fendi, because he hasn't had as many riders on his back. Almost a year ago, at the first event of the season, I started talking to Alex, and she's been discretely helping me ever since. Mum fell out with her after Otto started stopping, when Alex wasn't so quiet about how she thought Sophia rode, and finds her arrogant, rude, and brazen - which she sort of is. But she can certainly ride, and Otto never went wrong for her.

'That was much better than last time,' Merritt tells me as I bring Otto to a halt in front of her. 'He was much softer, and he wasn't fighting you on the approach so much. You rode better, too.'

'Thank you.'

Mia has Harvey ready when I swing off Otto. The dun gelding is chunkier than Doris - well, to be fair, he's chunkier than most ponies - and rounder in his way of going, but just as well-schooled, though he's a more challenging ride. The dun used to be mine, the only pony I've had that didn't go to Sophia first, and is similar to Otto in character, but with an even more stubborn streak, and more scope than he knows what to do with. His mane and tail are twice as thick as those of the other ponies, absent of a single grey or white hair despite being in his mid-teens, and always silky. With Mia dressed in her best jodhpurs and Kingsland waistcoat, and Harvey immaculately turned out, the two look like they've just jumped out of an equestrian catalogue.

Sophia isn't in the yard, but neither is Mum, and I can only imagine that the latter has gone to rouse her. Mia and Merritt head back to the school, and I look after Otto, untacking him and spongeing his girth and saddle patch. I lead him to the feed room, where he stands in the doorway while I retrieve a carrot, then chuck a rug over his back and carry on to the field. The bay pony goes through his usual gallop and buck routine before lowering his head and rolling, which is when I leave him. In the other paddocks, Fendi and Doris are grazing, both calm in the midday air.

Back in the yard, Mason neighs when he sees me, kicking the stable door as he paws the ground. The horses are all used to being alone in the yard, never allowed to get attached to one another, but when it's one o'clock and they have yet to leave their box, it's understandable that they start to fuss.

I've put all my tack away, washed boots, and skipped out Fendi's stable when Sophia finally decides to make an appearance.

'I fed him,' I tell her coldly, sweeping the front edge of the shavings into an even line and swinging the door closed.

Sophia pauses in her tracks, glancing at me with a scowl. Her dark hair has been straightened and pulled back in a low ponytail, and she's wearing riding clothes she always refuses to do stable chores in for fear of ruining them. 'What's that supposed to mean?' she snaps.

I walk past her and balance the broom on my barrow, wheeling it around to the side of the building. 'Nothing. Just telling you I fed Mason. Mason is your horse, by the way, in case you've forgotten.' I pick up the bucket we use as a skip and empty the mud I picked out of Otto's feet into the barrow.

'Last I checked, the two ponies you're riding were mine, too, so maybe you should be grateful.'

'At least I-' *At least I can ride them.* The words are there, on the tip of my tongue, but I can't bring myself to say them. As much as Sophia drives me mad, as much as I hate Mum's reluctance to criticise her, and as much as I resent my sister for wrecking Otto and Fendi, actually telling her, saying to her face that she can't ride to save her life, isn't something I can do. I think I can, and sometimes want to, but my conscience always kicks in and overrides my words.

And I think Sophia knows what I'm thinking, too. She's holding my stare, blue eyes made even bluer by the turquoise jacket she's wearing, and it's almost like she's daring me to say the words. But luckily another voice interrupts.

'All these horses belong to me, actually,' Mum says, obviously having overheard our discussion as she strides across the concrete, carrying a freezer bag of sandwiches I presume she's taking to Merritt. 'India, mind your own business. Sophia, go start getting Mason ready, and maybe thank your sister for feeding him.'

Thank me Sophia does not, but she does head for her horse's stable, and Mum shoots me a warning glare before heading off to the arena to take Merritt some lunch. And because I've finished putting away all my tack, and to avoid any more run-ins with Sophia, I follow.

'What is she doing?' Mum mutters, looking at the time on her phone.

'I can push it to ten-past, but I can't leave any later,' Merritt warns her.

'I know, don't worry. Just do what you have time for.'

'I can see her,' I say, standing up from the jump filler.

Mia rode Harvey out of the arena twenty minutes ago, and since then we've just been waiting for Sophia to arrive. Mia and I know how to get our ponies ready quickly when Merritt is pressed for time, but Sophia doesn't share that skill. It's also why Merritt is careful not to head back to the yard for a coffee refill when my older sister is next to ride, because Sophia takes it as a chance to waste another ten minutes doing who-knows-what - it certainly isn't groom or put anything away.

But finally, I see Mason's brown body walking down the limestone track from the stables, Sophia riding him on a long rein, clearly in no rush. Mia is walking beside them, and even on foot she's faster than the sport horse.

'SOPH!' Mum calls, waving her hands. 'COME ON! YOU KNOW MERRITT DOESN'T HAVE LONG!'

Yelling at Sophia before a lesson is risky, and not something Mum would ever let anyone else do, so she must be pretty angry. And my sister isn't happy, because I can see her face scrunch up from here, making her look even moodier than usual, and she pushes Mason into a trot until she reaches the arena.

'What's your problem?' she snaps, and as Mum once again repeats how Merritt needs to leave by three, my eyes fall on Mason's bridle. *Typical,* I think.

For Christmas, Sophia got a new bridle, which she'd been asking for because Mason's was starting to get worn, supposedly. It has diamanté crystals along the browband and cost an arm and a leg. Mum made a point of not letting Sophia use it until it had been oiled, something my sister only got around to doing this week. She's had the bridle for over a month, and *of course* she decides to fit it now, when she's already running late.

'It's fine, we'll do what we have time for,' Merritt says. 'Start walking him.'

As Mason walks on a circle, and Mia comes to sit beside me with a Tupperware box of flapjacks she passes around, I can see the bridle doesn't fit properly. Plenty would accept the bit as low as it is, and the noseband that loose, but not Merritt, and I wonder how long it'll take her to say something.

I'm not left wondering for long.

'Your bridle's too long,' Merritt says, beckoning Sophia towards her.

'Is that the new one?' Mum asks, and I see her expression

change as she realises, like me, why Sophia was late.

'Blingy,' Merritt says, 'but pointless if it doesn't fit.'

'It fits fine,' Sophia says tartly, halting Mason in front of Merritt.

Merritt is unaffected by her tone. 'Um, no, it doesn't. The bit's hanging in his mouth.'

'It's fine,' Sophia says again. I glance at Mum, and she looks furious. In her eyes, any one of us speaking rudely reflects badly on her parenting, and she can't handle it.

'No, it's not fine,' Merritt says sharply, and she goes on again before Sophia can disagree. 'It's hanging in his mouth, it's not doing a thing.' She slides her hand beneath the crank noseband, which passes easily, and scoffs as she does the same thing to the flash. 'Where's his usual one?'

'Back at the yard,' Mia answers for Sophia.

'It looks fi-'

'Sophia,' Mum warns through gritted teeth.

'Is there a hole punch here?' Merritt asks, and we all shake our heads.

Smoke almost comes out of Sophia's ears. 'I'm not punching holes in a new-'

'Mia, you can run get the bridle, can't you?' Mum interrupts in a clear, firm voice, cutting Sophia off, and Mia sighs loudly, but she nonetheless gets up, balances the Tupperware box of flapjacks on a jump filler, and starts jogging across the sand surface. 'You can warm up in that for now, Sophia.'

'There's nothing wrong with-'

'Last I checked,' Merritt interrupts, 'you haven't been around an Advanced track. Go on, get him moving until Mia gets back.' I don't know if Sophia wants to scream or cry, but she clicks her tongue and moves Mason out onto a circle. When she's away, Merritt turns back to us and blows out her cheeks, raising her hands to her head. 'Sorry for snapping at her, but-'

'No, no, that's fine,' Mum says, shaking her head and taking a step closer to Mer. 'Spoiled rotten, she is. I think she's nervous, though.'

Merritt makes a sort of tutting noise that makes me think she doesn't agree with the latter statement.

Mia returns shortly with the bridle, and the change is made, Sophia still muttering all the while that the new one fits, by which point there's only twenty minutes left until Merritt needs to leave, as if the lesson needed a reason to go badly. Odds are Sophia would've been in a foul mood anyway, but the bridle incident has pushed her over the edge, and she spends the whole time doing the opposite of whatever Merritt says, and taking her annoyance out on Mason.

'Stop see-sawing the reins. More leg, more leg. Let him lengthen his neck, don't just jerk his mouth every time you're annoyed.'

When Sophia is annoyed, she turns into a rumbling ball of sulk and irritation, and Merritt knows that as well as the rest of us do. Mason is confused, not understanding why his rider keeps lashing out at him for no reason, and I almost wish I could knock my sister off his back and take her place.

'Look,' Merritt says quietly to Mum, turning away from Sophia who is still fighting her horse on a circle. 'I don't know what you want me to do here. She's not listening to a word I'm saying. She's just getting mad at him, and it's not the horse's fault... I know time's tight which doesn't help... If it were up to me I'd want to give her a serious earful.'

'No, no, don't worry,' Mum says quickly, as always turning into a nervous wreck at the thought of Sophia being criticised on horseback. 'Just... see if it can end on a good note, and I'll talk to her later.'

I slip the knot through the ring and pull it down, levering the hay to the top, then tie the rope to the haynet. Horses to bring in, evening feeds to prepare, and that's the day done.

Stepping out of the stable, I glance down the aisle, towards Mason's box, and frown. Behind me, Mum is paying Merritt through her car window, and I wait for the vehicle to drive off before heading towards her. 'Mum!'

'You rode great today,' she says with a big smile. I think she gets more excited about good riding lessons than any of us do.

'Okay, but where's Sophia?'

'Turning Mason out, isn't she?'

'She *was*,' I say, 'but I don't know what she's doing now, and she hasn't mucked out yet. And it's already half-three.'

On weekends, Sophia has a habit of not mucking out, of putting it off again and again until it gets so late that somebody else - usually Mum - caves and does it themselves because it isn't going to get done otherwise.

'Just let me deal with it,' Mum says. 'Please,' she adds, fixing her eyes on me. 'I think Sophia's been got at enough for today.'

When Sophia does reappear, having gone to the house for a snack and a rest, and Mum mentions Mason's stable, Sophia conveniently remembers she hasn't done her homework, that she has a thousand-word essay due tomorrow. To Mum's credit, she stays firm and points out that we all have to schedule the horses around school and homework, but Sophia starts going on about how important the grade is and Mum lets the argument go as my sister retreats to the house to start her essay.

'Do you want me to get a couple Bedmax?' I offer, watching as Mum forks dank shavings into a barrow. Mucking out is bad enough when a horse has only been in overnight, but close to twenty-four hours, without even being skipped out…

Mum rests her hands on the shavings fork handle, kicks at the rubber matting, looks up at me, and forces a tight smile. 'Thank you, India, that'd be great.'

chapter 3

Siren is sweating when I lead her down the ramp, and I scratch her neck as I mumble words of reassurance. 'It's okay,' I say. 'You're just on a date.'

Dad pulls a noseband-less bridle on over the mare's halter, and I unclip the rope as he takes the reins and straightens her forelock. 'A bloody expensive date,' he mutters quietly.

'How're you doing, Arthur?' the lad who gave us the all clear to unload asks as we walk Siren behind him. Farther away, beyond the covering pen, I hear a stallion neigh. 'Getting busy yet?'

'Not bad, John, not bad. We've had five foals, and so far all good.'

'Buy any more the other week?'

Dad chats to John about the fillies he bought at the Tattersalls February Sale earlier this month as they lead Siren to the covering pen, some winners and some unraced, all needing to be covered. I wasn't trusted to spend too long in the bidding ring, seeing as the last time I did, I came back with Siren, but I did see every one of Dad's purchases, and some I like more than others. There's a small mare who resembles Pearl that was my favourite at first glance, and a big gangly filly I didn't like at all. All four mares have been turned out in the isolation paddock at home, now waiting to be covered, and I've barely seen them since they arrived.

I hand over Siren's passport and clean swab reports from the lab, then walk to the viewing area, well-accustomed to the protocol. The stud farms work with an efficiency that could put military bases to shame. Sometimes it's only ten minutes from the moment you pull into the parking lot until you're already driving back home with a covered mare. There are only so many covering slots a day, and if you miss yours then you won't get another. Every minute is accounted for, and handlers and horses remain in their lorry until told otherwise.

There's a pen in the covering ring for foals, seeing as most mares are covered just weeks after giving birth, but thankfully we don't have that hassle with Siren.

From my vantage point, I watch the chestnut mare, her eyes out on stalks and her ears pricked as her hind legs are strapped into boots to protect the stallion, and I think how glad I am we got her. She was entered in the Tattersalls December Breeding Stock Sale in Newmarket, a last-day lot that wasn't consigned through a big name, and few bidders were present. I liked her from the moment I saw her walk around the parade ring, liked her chunky build and the calm attitude with which she took in her surroundings. While she has good breeding, Siren's pedigree isn't popular. The Thoroughbred breeding industry comes down to fashion, which stuns all of us who are breeding horses and watch average foals with good pedigrees sell for fortunes while beautifully put-together horses from unfashionable lines go for peanuts. Siren comes from a family of winners, a descendant of some of horse racing's biggest names, and she's lovely to look at, but the sales ring was empty. Minimum bid was eight hundred guineas that day, a guinea only 5p more than a pound, which the auctioneer had finally managed to tempt somebody into bidding, but it was still too cheap for such a nice horse, and I couldn't let her go.

Somehow, while the auctioneer was trying to entice a new bidder in the last few seconds before lowering his gavel, my arm found itself shooting up into the air from my spot beside Dad in the bidding ring, and Siren came home. He pretended to be annoyed, but I knew he liked her really, and saw the same thing I did: a well put together mare with a nice pedigree, and who, at almost four years old, still had a lot of foals left in her.

Siren covered today!!! I text Freya and Sybil on the way home. They were with me at Tattersalls, also saw the pretty mare in the parade ring, and were both shocked when I actually got Dad to buy her - or, agreed to buy her on his behalf. When you grow up on a stud, when horses are a business, you forget that others tend not to acquire them so casually. I know Freya better than I know Sybil, especially as we've got closer over the winter at training clinics with the European Pony Team trainer, but I feel just as familiar with Sybil in the short time we've been friends. Freya is reserved, often coming across as quite serious and shy, much more than Sybil does, and as a consequence I don't feel like I know Sybil any less.

'What're you doing?' Dad asks, glancing at me.

I throw the phone down on the middle seat of the small horsebox and shake my head. 'Nothing. Just telling Freya and Sybil that Siren's been covered.'

Dad nods, keeping his eyes on the road.

'Any mares looking like they might go tonight?' I ask him.

'Two have waxed up.'

I straighten in my seat. 'Which ones?'

'Bubble and Medusa.'

'Can I stay up?'

'You've got school tomorrow,' he reminds me.

'Just until ten, then,' I say. I slept terribly last night, because just as I was settling into bed, I was struck by the thought that I hadn't turned off the hay steamer, which I probably had, but I couldn't remember doing so, and once a thought like that enters your head, you can't ignore it. So I got up, went downstairs, pulled on boots and a coat, clipped a lead to Alice's collar so I had a dog on my side if ever I were to run into a weapon-bearing robber outside, and trekked to the yard, where, of course, the machine was off, but I had to check or I'd never have slept. I still didn't sleep, though, and once I don't sleep one night, the next is always worse, so I may as well put insomnia to good use. 'Please?'

Dad takes his eyes off the road just long enough to look at me. 'It's not like I can stop you. You'll only watch in your room, anyway.'

I grin. Each foaling barn has a viewing room for a night watchman to stay in, with camera screens, sofas, and a TV, but all the cameras can be accessed via devices, too. Even when I know somebody else is watching, I often pull the footage up on my iPad and watch the night vision image of a mare moving around her box. If I can't sleep, I'll grab the tablet and stare at a sleeping mare until I do.

My phone beeps, and I pick it up to see a response from Sybil. I'm not surprised - Freya rarely has her phone on her, and it can take days for her to notice a message. **Yay! We'll have to come round next year and watch it be born!!! Any foals this year yet?? Xx**

Yes! Five so far, a few more due this week! Come see them sometime if u want!

Yes yes yes!!!

'What're you smiling at?' says Dad.

'My friend Sybil wants to come see the foals sometime,' I tell him.

He smiles crookedly. 'Funny how other people find 'em cute.'

I glance at him, and think of all the stress we endure, all the kicks we've received, all the sleepless nights, and we both start laughing.

Some mares - usually the older ones - like to foal at the perfectly reasonable evening time of seven p.m. The foal chooses the day, the mare chooses the time - that's what we say, and a lot of the experienced mares like to foal not long after being given an evening feed they won't eat up. Bubble is one of them.

'You're so good,' I tell the mare, watching as she licks her foal. Dad is here, and Earl, the sixty-year-old yard manager who lives and breathes the stud and has a cheeky sense of humour. One time, a couple of years ago, Dad and I came out to find the wealthy owners of a broodmare pulling away, and Dad hurried over to Earl.

'Was that the Archibalds?' he said. 'We sent that mare to graze over in Bury.'

'I showed them another one,' Earl said with a shrug. 'They can't tell the difference.'

We all laughed then, and when I pondered aloud why was it that those who can afford to own horses know nothing about them, Earl said it was *because* they didn't spend time with horses that they could afford to.

Dainty Steps, nicknamed Bubble due to her rotund figure, is a staff favourite, and with good reason. Not only was she a reasonable racehorse herself, and the dam of numerous winners, but she is the sweetest mare you'll ever meet, and an excellent mum. She is a dark bay, her coat a carpet of dapples in summer, with a white star in the centre of her head and a blaze farther down her nose.

'Good old Bubble,' Earl says, pulling off his plastic gloves.

Dad lets himself out of the stable, wincing as he straightens up. He places his hands on his lower back and rocks back onto his heels. 'If only they were all like her,' he says.

'For every Bubble there is a Medusa,' I recite. The other mare due tonight won a listed race, or else there's no way we'd go through the agony of dealing with her each year. She's extremely foal proud, and trying to get near her baby for the first week of its life always results in flesh being torn by teeth and various bruises. This will be her sixth foal, and so far four of the other five have resulted in trips to A&E. I was in the stable aisle last year, talking to one of the vets as she scanned a different mare in the stocks, when I heard the sound of a horse lungeing, followed by a cry, and turned around just in time to see one of our new stud hands fly out of a stable and onto the concrete. Medusa had launched at him with her teeth, grabbed hold of his coat, and thrown him into the air. The stud hand escaped with only a few bruises, though he gave in his notice later that day. The mare's stable name is Medusa for a reason.

Once Bubble is on her feet, Dad passes me the milker, and I get a full bottle of milk high in colostrum off Bubble, which I feed to the filly before we head inside, leaving Earl to watch the cameras until the night man arrives. Most mares foal without difficulty, but we can never risk the next one being the one that doesn't, and there is always someone around.

Everyone else has already eaten when we go inside, but there are two plates waiting on the kitchen table, beside a big stew pot, and the house smells like treacle. I think Dad and I both drool.

'Everything all right?' Mum asks, walking in from the snug at the sound of the back door opening and closing, an empty wine glass in her hand.

Dad nods.

'Bubble had a filly,' I say, unwrapping a tartan scarf from my neck and shrugging out of my big coat, dumping both onto a chair. I head for the sink, coating my hands in Swarfega and holding them beneath running water.

'And it all went well? The foal look all right?'

'Yeah, looks straight,' Dad says, and as I dry my hands to lift the lid off the stew pot he adds, 'This smells great, Cads.'

'Nothing much,' Mum says, sitting down at an empty space at the table, her eyes following Dad's movements as he serves himself a helping of dinner, and then doing the same as I serve mine. 'You've got someone on night watch tonight, yeah?'

Dad nods, not speaking until he swallows his mouthful of stew. 'Yes, but Medusa looks like she's gonna go, so I'll need to help.'

Mum groans. 'Oh, that mare. I wish you'd sell her already.'

'She's the devil reincarnated,' I say with my mouth full.

'Too good to sell,' Dad says with a shrug.

'Did Bubble have her foal?' Mia calls as she runs into the room, dressed in pyjamas and fluffy socks. She makes a beeline towards the dog beds, which lie beneath a framed photograph of a chestnut racehorse crossing the finish line with his nose in front - Intrico, our horse of a lifetime, racing in Tricklemoon's light blue silks - and sits down between Troika and Alice, resting her chin on her knees.

I nod. 'Yep.'

'What colour is it?'

'Only bay.'

'Oh.' Mia stares at Dad and me eating dinner, and jumps to her feet. 'Do we have any dessert?'

'You've already had dessert, Mia,' Mum says tiredly.

'Oh. I forgot. Do we have any *more* dessert?'

'Not until Dad and India have some,' Mum replies.

'You can have mine, Mia,' Dad says, and Mia squeals as she hurries to serve herself another helping of treacle pudding, while Mum mumbles a complaint about her having not touched her dinner but eaten her weight in sugar this evening.

'What's going on?' comes Sophia's voice as she walks into the room. Troika jumps up from her bed to greet my sister, and Sophia bends to ruffle her head.

'Bubble had her foal,' I say.

Sophia's face lights up - she's not interested in the mares and foals as a general rule, other than photographing them, but even she considers Bubble to be part of the family. 'Filly?'

I nod.

'Bay?'

I nod again.

'Oh.' She sticks out her lower lip, then looses a breath. 'Is it cute?'

'It's *correct*,' Dad says, the only thing that matters to him. Every other foal is born with *something* not quite right - over at the knee, varus, just plain bad - but Bubble's looked, well, correct.

'It is cute,' I tell Sophia. 'White face, like Fendi.'

Sophia pulls a glass from the cupboard and fills it with water from the fridge dispenser, spins around, takes a sip, and starts walking again. 'I'll have to come see it tomorrow.' And with that she heads back to the TV room.

'I love treacle,' Mia announces as she sits back down at the table and pours a large quantity of double cream over the top of her pudding.

'We noticed,' I say.

We all eat in silence for a while, too hungry to make conversation, but the stillness is interrupted by the ringing of Dad's phone, and his cursing as he searches his pockets to answer it. Be it early morning or late at night, his phone never stops ringing. Even outside of breeding season the work never ends, because just as we all start to recover from the hassle, there are sales to prepare for.

'Earl?' Dad sighs. 'Yeah, all right. Be right there.'

I'm already standing up. 'Medusa?'

Dad nods. 'Medusa.'

'You're heading back out?' says Mum.

'Earl can already see the bag,' Dad says, which means *yes*.

'I'm coming,' I tell Dad, pulling my coat back on.

'No, India, you've got school tomorrow,' Mum says.

'It's not even eight. And I won't be long. And I'll go do night check too,' I add, a task that Mum is usually responsible for. 'They might need another pair of hands.' I look her in the eye. 'Please?'

Mum relents. 'You've got until nine. But I don't want *you* going near that mare.'

'I won't,' I assure her. 'Promise.'

'Bring me the blue spray, India, will you?' Dad says, crouched with Earl beside Medusa and the strong colt.

I grab the bottle of antiseptic from the foaling box by the door and step into the straw, handing it to Dad. While Earl stays at Medusa's head, Dad sprays the foal's umbilical cord, which makes him wriggle, and Medusa moves in response, kicking out with a hind leg.

'And the bottle now.'

Dad passes me back the spray and I chuck it down in the aisle, taking a bottle from a bucket of warm water, the colostrum now defrosted. Colostrum is the first milk a mare produces, and essential for newborn foals, and while they usually source it themselves without need for interference, we often bottle-feed them the first lot just to be safe.. Most mares we milk right away, here and then, which is easier, but milking Medusa is definitely *not* an option. We keep extra bottles of colostrum in the freezer for the foals whose dams don't produce a lot of, but it also helps us out when it comes to mares like this. Medusa won't let us anywhere near her or the foal once she's up, so we have to act while we can, and act quickly.

Like his mother, the colt - Medusa's fourth colt in a row, part of the reason she is such a valuable broodmare, because even if it's the stallion that is supposed to dictate the gender, we've had mares that have only ever thrown fillies and vice versa - is as strong as an ox, and he drinks the entire bottle in under two minutes, which has us all laughing, and we manage to bag up the afterbirth and get out of the stable before Medusa stands back up.

'Why is it the bitches of mares that have the best foals?' says Earl. 'All those bloody slow mares we have that are gentle.'

'Good racehorses are rubbish mothers and vice versa,' I point out, which isn't strictly true, but is often the case. A racehorse needs to be tough, ruthless, totally self-assured - not qualities that make for caring parents. Every rule has its exception - like kind Bubble, who was a successful racehorse and now a successful mother, and of course evil Medusa who also excels at both. But then, most of the *really* good racehorses aren't super tricky, but tough, confident, rarely fazed, and *those* ones, the ones you never think to worry about beforehand, are the useless mothers. That's one of the reasons Bubble and Pearl are so useful - we turn them out with first-time dams, and they show them how to look after a foal, and if the others still don't learn, then they look after them themselves. It's not uncommon to find Bubble sharing her feed with three other foals that aren't hers because their own dams have refused to let them anywhere near theirs.

I smile as I watch Medusa stand and sniff the black colt, before she looks up at us and pins her ears, suddenly throwing herself at the stable door and threatening to attack us. This is typical Medusa, but the action is so violent it still catches us all off guard, and we leap back, but once she returns to her foal, and we're a safe distance away, we laugh.

'The joy of breeding,' Dad says, his face lit up and his cheeks flushed from the shock.

I look ahead, at the mare and foal standing in the straw, at the other mares in the aisle. It's two degrees at a push, and we're all wrapped up in coats, the open barn doors giving way to a night sky. Earl and Dad are still wearing long plastic gloves, and there's the distinct smell of afterbirth in the air. Tonight, after the night watchman arrives, we'll all get some sleep, but often, since most mares foal after ten p.m., we don't get to sleep at all.

And then tomorrow, and the next day, and the weeks after that, we'll have to deal with psychotic Medusa, and the bites and kicks that will come with her. Because foaling is the easy part. There's getting the foal checked by the vet tomorrow, getting the two turned out in the paddock, the small matter of having Medusa covered again in a few weeks, the lead up to which involves many vet checks and scans. And the foal's first farrier visit, which is always a workout for us, and weaning, and then prepping for sales…

But the excitement of leading a foal out onto concrete for the first time and seeing how perfect its conformation is. Seeing straight legs and short pasterns and a stubborn character that promises a fighter. Seeing them gallop around the nursery paddock for the first time with balance and grit, and knowing you have a future winner on your hands.

'The joy of breeding, indeed,' I say, and I mean every word.

chapter 4

The blue roan cocker spaniel whines as she watches me, wriggling with excitement as she attempts to remain sitting. I strap on the final transport boot before turning to look at her.

'What?' *Wriggle, wriggle, wriggle.* 'What is it, Troi?' Troika continues to whine excitedly, her nails scratching against the concrete as she moves from side to side, waiting for me to give her a signal, to give her permission to jump up, and I tap my knees, which sends her into a frenzy, and she throws herself into my arms. 'What's got into you, dog?' I ruffle her neck, then push her back onto the ground. 'You want to go cross country schooling?'

Troika jumps up again, and Otto turns his head and starts pawing the ground, annoyed the dog is getting the attention instead of him. The dog scratches at my jodhpurs and I keep my left arm around her, leaning to the right to scratch Otto's shoulder with the other, and the pony stretches his neck out towards me, lowering his nose to my folded knees. 'I swear, Otis, you have an ego the size of Africa.'

'Much like his former rider,' Mum says as she steps up beside me, and I start to grin, almost laugh at her joke, but then I realise she isn't talking about Sophia, she's talking about Alex, and I keep my mouth shut. 'Right,' she goes on, not noticing my hesitation, 'you ready?'

I nod, pushing Troika down to the floor before standing up. 'Yep. I haven't bandaged his tail, but I think he's fine.'

'He doesn't sit back on himself, does he?' Mum agrees. 'And it's not far. Is Soph ready?'

'I don't know,' I say. I *do* know that she hadn't even loaded her tack a few minutes ago, let alone started getting Mason ready, but I don't say this. Let Mum discover that for herself.

Ten minutes later than planned, the horsebox is bumping down the driveway, with Mason and Otto in the back. Sophia is reclined on the sofa in the living compartment, looking up at her phone, while I'm slumped in the passenger seat, leaning against the window. Troika is in the middle seat, tongue lolling out the side of her mouth as she looks out the windscreen, and Mum is driving, short blond hair contained beneath a woolly hat.

'I can't believe we're already back out cross country-ing,' Mum says, shaking her head. 'Feels like the season only just ended. It's so exciting. You two excited?'

Sophia is silent in the back, so I take it upon myself to answer. 'Ask again in a couple hours.'

'Isn't that Freya's lorry?' Mum says as we drive into the cross country venue, pulling up beside a tiny horsebox. The horses respond to the change in terrain by moving in the back, Troika jumps up at the window, and Sophia stands in the living compartment. There's another big horsebox on the opposite side of us, the ramp down and travel boots thrown miscellaneously across it.

'Looks like it,' I say, though the only horse I can see on the course from here is a lumpy piebald.

Mum is beaming. 'Oh, how fun!'

We're late, but luckily Merritt appears to be, too, and Sophia and I set about methodically unloading and tacking up Mason and Otto. Mum stands between the two horses, holding lead ropes as we fasten boots and lay numnahs on backs. It isn't until Otto is suited and booted, and I'm pulling on my body protector, that I spy a chestnut pony walking across the cross country course, heading this way.

'Hello, you two,' Mum calls, grinning, and I hear Troika bark inside the lorry at her raised voice.

'Hello,' Freya's mum, Nell, says as she walks beside her daughter's pony. Mum would never admit it, but if Freya didn't event and her family didn't have an FEI pony, I don't imagine my mum would like Nell, not because she isn't nice but because she is nothing like Mum and her friends. Nell is quiet, her hair rarely brushed and her face never made up, she doesn't have a cleaner, and she actually has a day job, as opposed to being a full-time event mum. But Freya is an amazing rider, and Leo just as amazing a pony, so Mum is always happy to speak to the Fitzgeralds. 'Everyone rushing out onto the course while it's dry enough for the venue to open?'

'Exactly!' Mum says, passing Mason's lead rope to Sophia in order to step closer to Nell, which my sister looks unimpressed by. 'But how are *you* guys? How are you and Leo getting on, Freya?'

I pull down Otto's stirrups and turn him around to face everyone. Although my two ponies are every bit as talented, even I have to admit that they're nowhere near as flashy as Leo. The chestnut pony stands square, delicately-curved ears pricked as Freya swings out of the saddle. Where Fendi and Otto look like ponies, with chunky bodies and naughty expressions, Leo looks like a little horse. If he could just be enlarged, he'd be the most beautiful quintessential event horse. Like most eventers this time of year, his coat is clipped, his legs a darker shade of red than the rest of his body. His tack is clean, mane and tail pulled and trimmed, body well-muscled, and his expression is happy and relaxed. I wonder what - if anything - Sophia thinks of seeing Freya being bought an FEI pony, one that was even on a European team the same year as Otto and Fendi, and succeeding the way Sophia was supposed to. Though comparing Freya to my sister seems ridiculous, because even if she's found herself in a similar situation, the two characters couldn't be more different.

'Good, thank you,' Freya says politely and robotically, running up her stirrups. The kit she wears is clean, but not new or fancy. Her navy blue jodhpurs have faded from many washes, her chaps are too short, reaching only an inch below the knee, and have broken clasps, riding boots splitting along the edges, the fleece beneath her body protector covered in bobbles. Her dark red hair is in a ponytail down her back, and looks even longer than it did the last time I saw her. Though neither the chattiest nor the most confident, Freya is one of those people I've always liked, and have always defended when heard spoken ill of. Some people I know on the pony circuit think she's full of herself now she has a top pony, but I don't know how somebody can talk to Freya, if only for a minute, and not see how perfectly aligned her moral compass is.

'Just giving Leo a tune up before pony training next week,' Nell says, but not in the boasting way most parents speak of their children attending team training clinics. 'Are you doing the same thing?'

'Exactly,' Mum says. 'Merritt's meeting us here to give the girls a jump.'

'That's great,' Nell says warmly. 'And how's Mia?'

Mum smiles, and I know she's pleased Nell's remembered to ask about Mia when she's only met her a handful of times. And by name, too. 'She's good. Drives me potty, but she's good. She's at a birthday party today, or else she'd have come, too. I can't believe how quickly the season's come around again.'

'I know! We were just saying that…'

Nell and Mum continue chatting, while Sophia unhappily tacks up Mason without help, and as Merritt still isn't here, I move Otto closer to Leo to talk to Freya while she untacks.

'He's looking good,' I tell her.

She offers me a small smile. 'Thanks. So does Otto.'

'I saw your entries online,' I say. Entries open some six weeks before an event, and we try to get in as quickly as possible, and even then there's no guarantee of not being balloted. Each horse gets three *Priority* tickets to use throughout the season, to assure they can't be balloted, but we don't want to use them up this early.

'Yeah, I've got him in a 100 to start, then an U18N, and have tentatively entered him for Aldon Pony Trial.'

'That's great!'

Freya nods and smiles, showing more excitement than she usually does. 'Fingers crossed. How about you?'

'Same plan,' I say excitedly. 'Start at BE100 like last year, and then complete an U18N before aiming for all the Pony Trials.' It's taken me this long to get Otto and Fendi - and myself - going around 90 and 100 tracks confidently, but Merritt has said not only does she reckon we'll be able to move up a class this season, but move up a class quickly. 'Do you want to do Brand Hall Pony Champs?'

Freya lifts her saddle from Leo's back, sliding the undone girth onto her shoulder. 'Yeah, hopefully. I mean, it'd be nice, but that's a way away yet. I'm not gonna get ahead of myself.'

'Right,' I say, looking down. Freya has got to be the most - and only - sensible rider I know.

'How are the foals?'

I perk up, glad to speak about something I know. 'Good,' I say, as Freya removes Leo's bridle and slides on his head collar, the nameplate engraved with his show name, *BATTERSEA*. 'We have ten now, and another twenty-something due. You'll have to come see them! I spoke to Sybil the other day and she really wants to see them, too.'

Freya nods. 'Sure. That'd be nice.'

'Great,' I say. 'I'll check with Mum later what days Merritt's booked for, then send you and Sybil a message.'

'Is that Merritt?' Freya asks, nodding at something behind me, and I turn to see Merritt's car cruising up the driveway.

'Yep.' I tighten Otto's girth and fasten my hat. Sophia is still putting on Mason's bridle, and I subtly nod in her direction so only Freya can see. 'Wish me luck.'

Otto is trotting around like a bullet on springs. His body is flexed, both tense and elastic at the same time, and he's flicking his toes as though he were coming down the centre line of a dressage test and trying to get a judge's attention.

'Oh, look at him,' Merritt says in mock admiration. 'Precious.'

I laugh. 'He's full of himself.'

Merritt holds up her hands. 'Hey, he's allowed to have the ego of an Advanced horse if he wants to act like one.'

'Look, Nell's waving,' Mum says, holding Troika on a lead beside Merritt, and she waves at Freya and her mum as their lorry trundles down the drive. Otto raises his head and lets out a high-pitched neigh, to which Leo responds with a whicker that echoes through the horsebox windows.

'Silly pony,' I mutter. I wonder if he recognises Leo whenever he sees him, whether he remembers the years of attending the same training clinics, travelling abroad in the same lorry to compete at Europeans, galloping a lap of honour with him when they won the team gold. I know that Alex and Leni, Otto and Leo's former respective riders, are close friends, so the ponies must have seen a lot of each other at events, too.

'Right,' Merritt says, 'get these horses paying attention. India, try altering his stride, make sure he's moving because *you* want him to and not the other way round. Practise shortening and lengthening him. And Mason looks half asleep. Just because we're cross country schooling, doesn't mean you forget what we do at home. Come on, get him working. He's not tracking up, so shorten your reins, sit up, and ride him. You're not a passenger.'

I glance at Mum long enough to see her look away, clearly not impressed by Merritt's harsh comments so early in a session. But then when I look back, Merritt has stepped closer to her, whispering something, and Mum nods, so I figure everything's all right.

Ignoring Sophia's moody face as she trots circles around me, I focus on Otto and interpreting the instructions Merritt gave me. Because she's right - though he's moving correctly, working from behind and with impulsion, he's doing so because *he* has decided to, not because he's listening to me. And when I ask for something different, when I ask Otto to shorten his stride and move in a more collected frame, he responds by surging forward and running away from my leg. Typical. Although he's well-schooled, Otto can also be lazy, eager to avoid anything he considers work, and because he's cheeky, he'll always test me to see if I'm serious.

Yes, yes I am.

I sit up taller and lower my rising so that I have more control, adding more pressure with my legs and focussing on riding Otto straight, on feeling every footfall. With a snort of his nose, the pony obliges, shortening his stride and bending his hocks beneath him. And once he maintains this, I ask for the opposite. I squeeze with my legs and urge him on, forward, and the bay gelding responds, moving into an extended trot, flicking his toes while staying in a correct outline, and I bring him back to a collected pace again before changing rein.

'Yes, India,' Merritt praises, and I smile to myself at her tone of approval. 'Exactly. Perfect. Keep doing what you're doing.'

Euphoria fills my chest, the way it always does not necessarily when I get praise, but when I know I've achieved something, when I know I've ridden a movement correctly and understood the corrections I've been told to apply. I bite my lip to contain my smile as Otto listens just as well on the left rein as he did on the right, floating across the turf, and as we pass Sophia and Mason, and my sister sees my expression, she glares at me.

'That's loads better, Soph,' Merritt says after a while. 'Now just try to ask for more within that frame. That trot's fine for a test, but now you need more energy, because you can't come into a fence like that. Good. Good girl. All right, give them both a canter on each rein, then we'll start jumping.'

I touch Otto behind the girth with my outside leg and he leaps forward with exuberance, tugging at the reins and threatening to buck, before settling into a rhythm, and I laugh at him.

'Someone's keen,' Merritt shouts.

Mason shares none of his friend's naughtiness, remaining in a cadenced stride, Sophia perched effortlessly in a two-point seat.

Merritt walks to a group of three logs, each one different in size, and taps the middle one with her boot. 'Okay, whenever either of you is ready, come trot over this.'

Mason is cantering away from Merritt, and Sophia turns back in her saddle to look at the fences. 'Which one?' she asks

'Middle one,' Merritt says, as Mum pulls on Troika's lead to guide the dog towards the smallest fence, where they both stand out of the way.

I bring Otto back to a trot and circle him near Mason. 'Do you-' *Do you want to go first,* I was going to ask, but Sophia turns to the fence before I can finish my question, and I keep Otto on his circle while the brown sport horse carries on towards the log.

Mason is moving nicely, his top line soft and his stride fluid, but he's also not moving with much impulsion, no punch, not like a horse that is about to go cross country.

'More leg, keep coming,' Merritt says, eyes on the horse as he approaches the jump. That's the thing with Merritt - she can sometimes sound harsh when she shouts out corrections, but it's only because she's looking at what the horse needs, not scrutinising your own position. 'Leg. Lower your hands.'

The brown gelding sits back on his haunches and bascules over the fence, ducking his head on landing with a flick of his tail, wavering for a stride, and Sophia taps him firmly with the whip on the shoulder.

'What was that for?' cries Merritt. And when Sophia doesn't respond she shouts again. 'Hey?'

'He wasn't listening,' she snaps.

'He jumped perfectly. He just jiggled on landing because he's excited to be back out after so long. Come straight back and do it again, without telling him off this time.'

Of course, when he turns towards the fence again, Mason lights up more, and anticipating a tap on the shoulder, he breaks into a canter three strides from the fence. They could have continued, meeting the small log easily on a forward stride, but Sophia wasn't expecting the horse to accelerate, and she responds by tugging at his mouth, breaking Mason's rhythm and forcing him to chip in an extra stride, which results in a less than perfect jump. I hear Mum's sharp intake of breath, then Sophia's cry of annoyance as she pulls Mason up on landing, clonking him in the teeth and making him throw his head up.

'No, no, no,' Merritt says sharply, and if it were anyone else but my drama queen sister on-board, I'm sure she'd yell. 'Don't take your anger with yourself out on him.'

'I'm *not* angry with myself,' Sophia says.

'Well, you should be, that was your fault,' Merritt retorts. 'Lengthen your reins and get him back onto a circle. India, go.'

Blocking my sister's face of fury and the image of Mason having his head ripped off from my mind, I widen Otto's circle until the jump is in his trajectory. The pony raises his head at the sight of the obstacle, but instead of trying to hold him back the way Sophia did Mason, I take a check on the outside rein, steadying him for a stride, and release, still riding forward. To his credit, Otto stays in trot until the last two strides, when the excitement of jumping a natural fence becomes just too much and he breaks into a canter. Four months since the last time a horse has been cross country is not the time to punish enthusiasm and hold them back, so I just sit tight and let him find the forward stride he wants, laughing as the pony starts bunny-hopping on landing.

Merritt laughs. 'I love him. Okay, good. Do it once more, then Sophia come back again and then we'll do it coming from the other way.'

Otto is calmer the second time over the fence, still just as excited to be on a cross country course but not taking off on landing, and I start circling him on the other rein while Merritt focusses on Sophia.

'Don't grab hold of his mouth. Let him move. These fences are tiny, let him draw you in and choose the stride.'

By some miracle Sophia manages to take Mason over the log a few times without ripping his head off, and after we jump it coming from the other way, we move on to a different group of jumps.

'Pop the first little house in trot then if that's good carry on to the second in canter.'

Sophia doesn't try to go first this time, so I push Otto on ahead, making sure the pony is moving with impulsion as we trot to the first house. Otto slows his stride as we come into the fence, painted white and spookier than a log, and for a moment I hesitate, afraid he's going to slam on the brakes, a lasting effect of Sophia's habit of pulling horses' heads off on take-off, but I get over myself and keep riding. Otto clears the obstacle, but the jump isn't as smooth as the others we've done, due to my moment of hesitation, and I sit up on landing and urge him on, keeping the next fence framed between his ears.

'Better over the second half,' Merritt says, pausing to seek out my gaze. 'You know what you did wrong, don't you?'

I nod. 'I know, I hesitated and stopped riding.'

'Yep. Okay, then. Sophia.'

The new fence naturally slows Mason enough that he doesn't give Sophia an excuse to pull him in the mouth, and as they land in canter he carries on to the next element, taking control and jumping from far out, which leaves Sophia behind the movement, and she lands in the saddle with a thump.

'I didn't ask him for that one,' she grumbles, gathering her reins.

'It was the only stride he had,' Merritt counters. 'And it was only long because you didn't ride towards it. And again.'

I halt Otto as Sophia repeats the exercise, watching intently, while Mum hovers beside Merritt and starts biting one of her cuticles, something she only does when she's nervous.

The late afternoon sun is shining directly into my eyes, the last bit of light before darkness descends always blinding. Mason looks beautiful, his coat shining like tempered dark chocolate and his thick tail silky. Sophia looks well-balanced in the saddle, but I can see the things she's doing that are wrong. Her hands are see-sawing, pulling Mason's head into a false outline, and I wince at his expression.

'Let him move, more energy.'

Sophia buries Mason into the first element, and it's only Merritt's raised voice on landing that prompts her to move forward, and they jump the second little house cleanly.

'Much better over the second,' Merrit says. 'You've got to stop pulling on the approach to the first, though,' Merritt goes on when Sophia comes to a halt beside me.

'But he's rushing,' Sophia says.

'He's not rushing, and when he did it was only because you were pulling. And if he does, then entering into a pulling battle isn't going to fix anything. Small movements, not a dead pull. But you got it right over the second part. You just need to find a rhythm. Right, and again.'

This time, I keep riding Otto right to the base of the jump, never losing concentration, and he jumps much better as a consequence. Merritt is complimentary, and I pat Otto's neck as I bring him back to stand beside her while Sophia goes. The earlier jump was enough for Mason to now know that he needs more impulsion, more speed to make the distance easy, and as he accelerates his pace, all while staying in a round, balanced frame, Sophia doesn't pull him in the mouth, just adjusts him a few strides out, and they clear the fence perfectly, meeting the next on a correct distance.

'Yes,' Merritt praises. 'That's what I want to see every time. Do it once more to prove it's not a fluke, then we'll go find something else.'

'Okay, so to finish off, you're going to jump the pheasant feeder, the bank down into the water and out over the house, then the corner, the triple of brushes, and finish off by going over the parallel of logs. The smaller one,' Merritt adds, nodding at the group of fences in the distance. 'India.'

Otto is rubbing his nose against his knee, and I click my tongue to pull away his attention, squeezing him forward. We've been practising the fences individually for the past half an hour, so it's nothing we haven't already done.

The bay pony strikes off into a forward canter, breathing heavily with anticipation. I stand in the stirrups and plant my hands on his neck, in his thick mane, and urge him on, between hand and leg, moving with the speed and impulsion a fourteen-two pony needs to clear a solid obstacle only twenty inches smaller than him. The sky has clouded over in the time we've been on course, and there's now a breeze in the air so sharp that my eyes water every time I start riding at a faster speed. But it doesn't matter, because this is the first time I've been cross country in four months, the first time I've brought Otto back out since our first full event season together, and I didn't know if he'd come out as well as he finished last year.

And he's even better.

The pheasant feeder runs uphill, back towards Mason, and Otto accelerates as we come out of the turn, neck solid as he powers forward, martingale preventing him from chucking his head. I lower my seat to the saddle and steady him with the outside rein, all the while making sure I keep my leg on, making sure I stay positive. We see the same take-off spot, and Otto flies, jumping with more scope than you'd think possible for a pony of his build. I scratch his withers on landing and look left, towards the water, and sit up to turn him. Otto has never been slowed by water and jumps straight down the bank, ears seeking out the next fence as we carry on through the complex and soar over the house.

The corner is farther up the course, taking Otto away from his friend, and the pony slows as he realises this, testing me, and I click my tongue and tap his neck with the whip. *Don't stop riding,* I hear Merritt's voice in my mind, and Otto responds, forgetting about Mason and looking for the next jump. The corner is an isolated fence, and as this isn't an event, there are no flags, which makes it daunting, on its own in an open field. I get Otto onto a correct line from ten strides out, making sure he knows where he's going, though I don't see the best stride to the fence and it's up to him to jump us out of trouble. The pony keeps going, unaffected, and I pat him in thanks as we continue to the brushes.

Otto locks on to combinations as a whole, never jumping the first without also analysing the other jumps, and this one is no exception. As soon as he sees the first brush, Otto takes into account the second and third, too, and I barely have to steer as he powers through the line, jumping on springs.

The parallel of logs is slightly downhill, and I sit up before it, moving my fingers on the reins to make sure Otto is with me, to make sure he is paying attention. I shake the reins, quickly and briefly, shaking him off my hands and lifting him up in a small, precise movement. He flickers an ear and shifts his balance onto his hocks, listening to me, and I squeeze my legs against his sides, letting him know I'm with him, too. The fence is a metre-twenty wide, and I ride strongly, revving Otto up. The pony gets strong, pulling at the reins, but I'm not about to start pulling back, and I go with him as he takes off on a long stride and flies over the parallel. The landing jolts me, the reins sliding from my hands, but I regain them quickly and pat Otto's neck, amazed how amazing that jump felt. He jumped so big, with so much scope...

'Well. Done,' Merritt shouts, sharply speaking each word as its own sentence. 'Super. Really super.' She pauses as I trot over to her, letting the reins out and patting Otto on the neck.

When I bring him to a halt, the pony stretches his nose out, barely blowing, and looks around as if to say, "What? Those jumps are too easy."

'I know the stride to the corner wasn't great-' I begin.

Merritt interrupts, shaking her head. 'Doesn't matter. You're never going to be right every time. No one is. And you stayed really straight to it and let him read the line early on, and that's what matters. Everything else was great.' She looks around at the fences, recalling them in her mind. 'The triple of brushes, I loved that.'

'It was all him,' I say, blowing as I clap his neck - horses aren't the only ones who lose fitness during the winter break.

'But you didn't interfere. And, sure, the last one was a bit long, but it was the only stride you had, there's no way you could've added one, and he jumped amazingly. You did everything right before the fence, you prepared him and got him listening but you didn't kill the rhythm. Well done, that'll do him. Super, super. Keep riding like that and you really will be hitting all the Pony Trials. Okay, Sophia you go.'

'Well done,' Mum says giddily to me as Sophia starts warming Mason up, patting Otto on the neck. She's never not been nice to any of the ponies, but when they do well her affection towards them certainly grows. 'You both looked amazing!'

I smile, mind whirling with what Merritt said. Only one more BE100, to start off the season, and she thinks we'll be ready for Novice and Pony Trials. Maybe I *will* make it to Brand Hall Pony Championships, go to the Haras du Pin in France for the international pony event, or maybe even be selected for the European team…

Merritt turns to Mum as Sophia canters Mason. 'Really good,' she says again, giving her a nod. 'No, I'm pleased with this one.'

I wonder if *this one* refers to me or Otto, though I think I know.

Mason comes in slowly to the pheasant feeder, his stride flat, and taps the top of it with his hind legs.

'More energy,' Merritt yells. 'You don't have to go fast, but you need impulsion. Bouncy canter. Bouncy canter,' she repeats, loudly letting a breath out through her nose as Sophia carries on to the water. Merritt turns to Mum. 'You can see that, can't you? It's not about going flat out or anything, but she needs pace.'

'Yes, yes,' Mum says, though she still looks unsure about Merritt speaking so firmly to Sophia, her earlier smile faded.

Troika jumps up at my left stirrup as Mason turns to the water, something Otto is well used to, and I lean down, hanging off his side, to lift the dog into my arms, unclipping her lead. Carrying the puppies around while we were riding was something both my sisters and I did with Alice and Troika when we first got them, and while the older dog either doesn't remember or is sensible enough now to know that on a horse isn't her place, the same can't be said about Troi, and she still jumps onto a horse any chance she gets.

Otto shifts beneath me as the spaniel rests her front paws on his neck, but I scold Troika and tell her to settle, which she does quickly, leaning back against me, and the pony settles, too.

Water splashes as Mason canters through the complex, and Merritt looks at me after he and Sophia clear the house and start galloping up the field. 'Oh, Troi,' she says lovingly, and the dog's tongue lolls as she soaks up the attention.

'Good,' Merritt calls in approval as Sophia hits the corner on a perfect stride, but from having done it myself, I know there's no way she can hear all the way across the field.

'That was good,' Mum echoes, nodding at Merritt with satisfaction.

The triple of brushes is next, and while I can't say for sure, I think it takes Mason a heck of a lot longer to get to them than it did Otto, and it's certainly not because he isn't capable of the same speed.

'She's not moving enough again,' Merritt says. She could try yelling it at the top of her lungs, but even then I don't think Sophia would hear. We can't see her every move from here - how long her reins are, of if she's really using her leg - but we can see Mason's outline, and he doesn't look how a horse galloping across a cross country course should. I remember how Otto galloped to the combination, how he was full of running as he pulled me towards the first brush, and how he jumped like he had wings attached to his sides and springs in his feet. Mason can look like that, too. When he went to Junior Europeans with his former rider, when Sophia first got him, he was a force of nature. The kind of horse you stop and stare at because you can't help not to, can't walk past without the greatness blowing your way and pulling you in like a spell. Something everyone watches because, if only for a moment, you are witnessing something incredible, and life makes sense.

Mason is not an unhappy horse. He isn't worked enough, and when it falls to Sophia to look after him he spends more hours than usual in his stable, but be isn't miserable. He's fit and healthy, never goes without care or a meal, and still does whatever ridden job is asked of him. Nobody who were to pass him at an event would ever think there was anything wrong with him, and there isn't. He's in much better shape than most of the horses on the circuit, and he can still beat a lot of them.

But the spark is gone.

He's not a horse you'd stop and stare at, and it's not because his appearance has changed. Not physically, anyway. There are plenty of good horses out there, that go clear week after week and do their job. Horses people don't notice, don't stop at stare at.

And then there are those they do.

And they aren't always the best horses. Or riders.

It's the combinations that give their all. That work hard and work together. The horses that are so special, not because they're more talented than the others, but because they try harder. And you can *feel* it, even on the ground beside them or watching them on TV from the comfort of your sofa. There's always one horse that everyone notices, one horse everyone would kill for a ride on, one horse that makes everyone's heart skip a beat.

When Mason and the girl who produced him came into a ring, you noticed. You noticed the trust in the horse's eyes, the way he jumped every fence as though it was his last, the way the two of them gave everything they had.

That spark of a horse is not the one I see in front of me now.

As Sophia turns to the first brush, she still isn't moving with impulsion. Four strides out from the fence, her brain decides to kick into action, and she kicks in return, pushing the horse forward. But it's too late, too stupid, and Mason accelerates as she asks, but the interference has interrupted his rhythm, and what should have been four strides becomes a long three as he's pushed to the fence. Sophia kicks again and holds on tight, surely realising the mistake she's made, asking for an impossible stride, and Mason takes charge, chipping in the fourth stride and launching into the air, the jump awkward as he fights to miss the obstacle with his forelegs.

But Mason is special, and he looks after Sophia, landing them safely on the other side. Sophia has lost her balance, and there's another fence two strides away.

Mason carries on, Sophia doing little in the way of helping him, and locks on to the second element. The bad jump over the first fence has made the distance awkward, two of Mason's strides still leaving them far off the second fence, and be it because of her earlier mistake or because it's what she would have done anyway, Sophia sits tight to add another, but Mason knows better. He doesn't want another uncomfortable jump, and he takes off, jumping the brush on two strides as he's supposed to. Sophia gets caught behind the movement, catching the gelding in the mouth as she sits back far in the saddle, and Mason jerks his head in discomfort.

Merritt winces, Mum gasps, and I hug Troika tighter to my body protector as Sophia jolts on landing.

But there's still a third element.

Now Mason's confidence is definitely waning, and he doesn't accelerate to the next brush. I don't know what Sophia's thinking - if anything - except that she seems to be alternating ideas, because after firing (incorrectly) for the first fence, and holding (incorrectly) for the second, she decides that taking a flyer is the best way to go again. Her arms flap as she pushes Mason towards the last element, three strides away, and I realise with horror that she's about to take it in two.

Confidence is something you build up like credit. Every good jump pads the account, and a few bad ones in a row empty the reserve.

For what is probably the first time in his life, Mason says no. The stride Sophia is asking for is impossible, and he knows it.

His front feet skid into the base of the jump as he slams on the brakes, and he comes to a standstill in time to keep Sophia from flying over his neck.

Mum gasps again, while Merritt expresses her anger in the form of a four-letter swear word.

I'm silent.

It's not a surprise, and I've known for months that it was only a matter of time before Mason said no, but I didn't want it to happen. Sophia drives me crazy sometimes, but I don't want to see her fail. I want her to look after her horses and acknowledge when she does something wrong, not crash and burn.

And I also know that in a moment she'll re-present Mason to the fence, and they'll jump it this time, because he's not a stopper, he was just asked for an impossible stride.

Except it wasn't.

Except I know he *could* have jumped it, if he'd really wanted to.

Because the old Mason would have found an invisible fifth leg. He'd have overridden his rider and made sure to add another stride, or used all his might to make the fence on the long one. That's the difference between a good horse and a great one - making the impossible possible.

And Sophia still has a good horse.

But the foundation is cracked. The greatness is gone. The spark has fizzled. Luck has run out. The confidence account has emptied.

chapter 5

'More scrambled egg?' Mum asks.

I nod, putting my plate down beside her as she tips the saucepan to serve me another portion. 'Thanks.'

Mia gets up from the table to take my place beside Mum. 'Are there any more pancakes?'

'Not yet. Do you want another?'

Mia nods, returning to her seat at the kitchen table. 'Please,' she adds as an afterthought.

'Oh, nice save,' Mum says, grinning at Mia over her shoulder, and the two of them laugh.

'Weekend fry-ups are the best,' I say to Mum, forking scrambled egg onto a piece of toast.

'They are,' Mia agrees.

'Well,' Mum says, pouring pancake mixture into a frying pan, 'aren't you both lucky, then. Are you riding before your friends get here, India?' she goes on, turning around and resting her hands against the oven towel rail behind her.

'Lungeing,' I say. 'Freya and Sybil are coming at half-ten, and I've already mucked out, so I'll go back out at nine.'

'All right.' She lifts the edge of the pancake with a spatula and lowers it to the pan again. 'Remind me who Sybil is again.'

'You *have* met her,' I say for about the tenth time this week, ever since inviting her and Freya for the day. 'She's Freya's best friend, she lives down the road from her, and you've seen her at events - she has a grey and a bay. She's based at Rose Holloway's. *And* you saw her at Tatts.'

Mum frowns. 'Was she at team training last week?'

'No,' I say tiredly.

Ever since the cross country session, things have been somewhat mundane. Merritt got Sophia and Mason jumping again, and there have been no more disasters, but there's now the possibility of something going wrong evermore present in the air. For me, there were only two noteworthy occasions. The first was Siren scanning not in foal, much to everyone's disappointment. While not taking on first cover is not uncommon, the young mares usually take more easily, and Siren had been so uncomplicated, and had good pattern throughout her season, that we were surprised. We're now waiting for her to come back into season in order to cover her again.

The second event was the pony team training clinic, which was a bit uneventful in itself. After cross country schooling Otto, I took Fendi out with Merritt and the mare was just as good as her friend had been a few days before. And while neither misbehaved at the clinic, they certainly weren't as good as they had been - well, at least I didn't feel I rode them as well. Freya was at the clinic with Leo, and the two put me and my ponies to shame.

'Thank you,' Mia says as Mum slides a pancake onto her plate. She picks up the box of caster sugar and pours it steadily over her breakfast.

'Do you want some pancakes with that sugar?' I say.

'You have to put loads of sugar on,' Mia says matter-of-factly, setting the box down and licking sugar granules from her fingers. 'You can't only have lemon,' she adds, squeezing half a fruit over her layer of sugar. It's no wonder that aged twelve she's already had more cavities than me and Sophia combined.

'You both take after your dad,' Mum comments. She, like Sophia, rarely eats dessert, despite always making sure there's one on the table.

'What time is Saffron coming, again?' Mia asks with her mouth full. Mia and Sophia have both invited friends for the day, too, and their respective best friends just happen to be sisters, and the daughters of one of Mum's closest friends. If Darcy'd had a middle daughter, I'm sure we'd have been pushed on each other from birth.

'Darcy's dropping Lottie and Saffie off at lunchtime,' Mum says.

'Why doesn't Lottie drive them?' I ask.

'Darcy doesn't trust her to drive Saffron.' Mum sighs. 'Are you going to get your ponies exercised before then?' she asks Mia.

'Uh-huh.'

'Uh-huh,' Mum repeats, her tone more serious. 'You'd better.'

'*Yes,*' Mia snaps. 'What about Sophia? She hasn't even been outside yet.'

'I'll go lunge Otto and Fendi now,' I say quickly, standing up from the table. I can't take any more Sophia drama today.

I'm putting the pessoa back in its bag when I spot the car coming up the driveway, and I zip up the sack at full speed before throwing it into the tack room and breaking into a run, heading for the house.

'Hey,' I call, out of breath as I reach the gravel in front of the house.

Sybil and Freya turn at the sound of my voice and say hello back. I'm used to seeing them in riding gear, but today they're both dressed in jeans and jumpers.

'Hello, India,' Sybil's mum says, climbing out of the car. I'm not sure if I've ever officially met her, but when I've seen her at events I've always thought that she looks nice, and has a motherly feel about her. She's got to be a decade younger than Mum, but she doesn't come across any different. 'How are you?'

'Good, thank you.'

'How are your ponies? You riding a lot?'

I nod, focussing on Sybil's mum as I watch Freya and her look around from the corner of my eye. 'Yeah, they're in work. They're good, too. I just lunged them. They're going unaffiliated show jumping next week before the season starts.'

'Great! You're taking Ace show jumping next week, too, Sybil, aren't you?' she says. 'Are you going to the same place?'

We're discussing the coincidence that Sybil and I are both jumping at the same venue on the same afternoon when the front door opens behind us, followed by the sound of Mum's footsteps as she walks down the steps. The dogs come up alongside her and bark, rushing towards the guests with wagging tails. Mum scolds them quickly and the spaniels quit the noise, but they still run straight up to Sybil and Freya.

'Hello,' Mum says brightly, stepping towards us. 'Sorry about them,' she says about the dogs as Troika jumps up at Sybil. Mum says the dog's name and snaps her fingers, and Troi obligingly jumps down to sit.

'Oh, no problem,' Sybil's mum says. 'We've got two at home, and they're nowhere near as well-behaved as this.'

Mum smiles, clearly pleased with the compliment. 'I'm not sure if we've officially met?' She holds out a hand. 'Caddie.'

'Maya,' Sybil's mum says. 'And thank you so much for having the girls today. It's very kind of you.'

Mum waves her off. 'It's no bother, really.'

'This place is beautiful,' Maya says, looking around at the house and surrounding fields. 'And it's really not that far from us.'

'How long did it take you?'

'Twenty-five minutes from where we are.'

Mum nods. 'That's about right. We're twenty from Newmarket.' She looks back towards the house. 'Would you like to come in for a quick coffee?'

Maya starts to protest, but Mum insists, and she quickly gives in.

'Before I forget-' Maya turns back to the car and opens the passenger door, lifting a couple of white pastry boxes from the seat. 'I run a café,' she explains to Mum, 'so I just brought you a couple things for dessert or tea…'

Again, I see Mum is impressed by her manners. 'That's so kind of you! You shouldn't have…'

'Of course.'

Mum and Maya disappear inside, the dogs following them as they go through the door, and I turn to Sybil and Freya, glancing briefly at their feet to check they're wearing appropriate footwear to go trekking through the fields. 'Shall I give you a tour?'

'Wow,' Sybil says as we walk towards the first barn. 'This place is amazing. I can't believe you actually live here.'

'It's a bit messier than usual,' I say, unable to stop myself from noting every small job that needs doing. We're walking past paddocks, and I sigh as I spot a loose rail, eyeing the wood critically. 'We have as few people working over Christmas as possible, and even now we're still behind,' I explain. 'It's ridiculous.'

'How many people do you have working for you?' Freya asks.

'Uh.' I start counting on my fingers. 'We have the stud manager, four full-time grooms, someone in charge of all the maintenance, a couple of regular night men, and then Bree who's *our* groom.' My foot hits a flint, and I pick up the stone and toss it to the nearest fence post.

'And how many horses?' says Sybil.

'Broodmares? I think we have thirty at the moment, and we

71

probably have twenty yearlings we didn't send to the foal sales last year, and about ten foals already on the ground.'

'*Sixty* horses,' Sybil repeats, almost horrified at the thought.

'They're not all ours,' I say. 'Only twenty of the mares belong to us, and the others board.'

'Sixty horses between four grooms,' Sybil says, shaking her head. 'That makes looking after event horses seem easy.'

'Mares and foals make *all* other horses look easy, trust me.'

As we carry on to the barn, I answer more of my friends' questions, not even having to think as the words come out. *Three barns. Sixty stables, twenty in each of the barns, plus some yearling pens and a row of isolation boxes. All the horses get turned out in July and stay out until December, when the pregnant mares need to start settling into their boxes, and the barren ones come in to stay in the light all evening to bring on their cycles. The horses going to the sales start coming in six weeks before, with yearlings going on the walker and foals walked in hand to get fit, and the mares for no reason other than to keep their coats glossy before they go into the bidding ring.*

I take Freya and Sybil to see the barns, which are empty of horses and already mucked out, and then we head to the fields.

'This is Pearl,' I say as the bay mare comes up to the fence. 'She's one of my favourites. She's due in a few weeks.'

Pearl pushes her nose against Sybil and Freya in turn, and both of my friends smile at the mare's friendliness.

'Are they all this nice?' Sybil asks, scratching the mare's head.

I laugh. 'God, no. I wish. There's a reason Pearl's my favourite and it's because there aren't many like her. Just wait until you meet Medusa.'

True to form, Medusa threatens to attack us when we get near the nursery paddock, but that doesn't stop Sybil from letting out a delighted squeal when she spots her foal.

'Oh my god, he's so cute!'

'No,' I assure her, 'he isn't. He's a demon in a foal's body. He had both his front legs around one of the groom's necks the other day. No joke. And because Medusa won't let us near him, he's wild.'

'He still looks sweet,' Freya says with a shrug.

I tap her arm as I start walking along the row of boarded nursery paddocks. 'C'mon. I'll show you a foal that *is* sweet.'

As we reach the next paddock, Sybil lets out another cry.

I cluck to the bay mare. 'Bubs, c'mere.'

Because *she* isn't the devil's spawn, Bubble walks up to us as I call her, her little filly following on long, spindly legs.

'She's so cute,' Freya says.

'We can go in with these two,' I say, opening the gate. 'Bubble's fun, she'll let you do anything with her baby.'

The gorgeous mare stands still as the three of us creep into the field, and I gesture at Sybil and Freya to go on ahead while I close the gate behind us, making sure it's correctly latched.

'Bubble,' I tell the mare, turning back around, 'Freya and Sybil are here to cuddle you and your baby. Okay?'

Bubble stares at us a moment, her kind eyes the colour of dark amber, then steps forward to check each of our pockets for Polos, and it's with Freya that she strikes lucky.

'Can she have one?' Freya asks me, taking the packet out of her waistcoat pocket as the mare nudges her hand.

I nod. 'Yeah, she loves them. She'll start licking you like a dog as soon as you feed her, though.'

Freya slides a Polo from the packet and Bubble takes the mint greedily from her hand, eating it in a few loud crunches. She nudges Freya for another, which she gets, and then starts delicately licking her arm, leaving a trail of slobber across Freya's jumper sleeve.

'I warned you,' I say.

'It's all right,' Freya says, scratching Bubble's neck, while Sybil's attention is on the foal.

'You can go towards her,' I tell Sybil encouragingly. 'Seriously, she's super friendly. And Bubble doesn't mind, she'll just try to get you to give *her* attention instead.'

'I'll stay with her,' Freya says, looking just as happy to devote time to the mare as to the foal, which I smile at. When you're around the horses on the stud every day, it's usually the mares you develop a fondness for.

Sybil holds a hand out to the filly, who steps forward. 'What's her name?'

'She doesn't have one.'

'What?'

'You don't name them?' Freya says.

'Well, no,' I say, feeling defensive. 'I mean, sometimes we give them nicknames, but they're only going to be sold. And they go to the sales unnamed.'

'I can't believe you don't name them,' Freya says again.

'What am I supposed to call her, then?' says Sybil, her eyes melting as the filly rests her nose on her hand.

'We just call her Baby Bubble.'

'Well, then, hello Baby Bubble.' Sybil stays nervously still, and I walk past her to reach Baby Bubble.

'You can get close, they're not frightened.' I drape an arm over the filly's neck as proof, and Sybil comes closer. 'She likes giving kisses,' I add, as the filly delicately stretches her nose out towards Sybil.

'She's just too cute,' Sybil says.

Freya walks up to us, Bubble following her. 'She really is.' Bubble butts her shoulder, and Freya turns to smile at the mare. 'Don't worry,' she whispers, 'you're still my favourite.'

Baby Bubble laps up the attention, lifting her nose to each of my friend's faces, and I answer more questions about foal handling as we make a fuss of the Thoroughbreds, explaining how you lead a foal to the paddock, your left hand holding on to a foal slip and your right arm draped across their body to encourage them forward.

'I don't know how you get anything done with all this cuteness around,' Sybil says. 'Do you not get upset when you have to sell them?' she asks, and I think she's asked me this before, but I guess it's different when you're faced with the foals as they are now.

I shrug. 'I dunno. I mean, I worry more than I get upset, because what happens to half the horses after they finish racing is anyone's guess, and sometimes I'm upset to see them go, but it's all I know. I'm upset when they don't go for the right price.' I pause, watching as Baby Bubble chews Sybil's sleeve. 'Every now and then there's one I wish we could keep, and even though I know it'd never happen, I imagine that maybe we'll keep one, but it doesn't happen like that. I mean,' I go on, having to correct myself, 'we *do* occasionally keep some to race, but it's always with a business head, and not like keeping a pet or anything. But… yeah. It's harder with the colts,' I say, 'because as a rule, we don't really keep those.' *Other than Intrico,* I think, grateful what is now one of the world's best Thoroughbreds was once an unsaleable youngster.

'That must be hard,' Freya says.

'I think it's the first world problem of all first world problems,' I say, glancing at Sybil to lighten the mood, remembering saying these words to Alex some months ago. 'But, yeah. Like this one time there was a colt I absolutely loved, and I convinced myself for too long that maybe we'd be able to keep him, which of course we didn't, and that's what wakes me up at night. I wonder what happened to him, if he's even alive.'

'Was it one of hers?' Freya asks, nodding at Bubble.

I smile and shake my head. 'No, Pearl's. The first mare we saw in the field.'

Sybil runs a hand down Baby Bubble's neck. 'Is that why she's your favourite?'

'I think it's why *he* was my favourite,' I correct her. 'I've loved all her foals. That's why I can't wait to see this year's. She's even having a colt.'

'What, you already know?'

'Yeah,' I tell Sybil. 'We found out at the sixty-five day scan.'

'Wow. That's, like, twice as early as people, isn't it?'

'Madness,' I agree. 'Do you want to see Siren?'

Bidding goodbye to the two Bubbles, we leave the nursery paddocks and head towards the larger fields on the other side of the barn. The barren mares and the ones that are still a way off foaling are turned out together in a herd, with fifteen acres to themselves, and come in only at night during these short days. As foals never go in these fields, the fencing is older than most of the post-and-rail on the property, and doesn't consist of a run of Keepsafe. The rails are sturdy but they show their age, the creosote long gone and the wood covered in green, some of the rails marked by teeth.

'Have you guys ridden today?' I ask as we walk across the field, towards the mares that are grazing at its farthest end.

Sybil nods. 'We took the three ponies for a hack.'

I frown at her. 'Did you lead one of yours?'

Freya laughs. 'No, I think Ace would've thrown Sybil off in a heartbeat if she'd tried leading a pony off her.'

'She's not *that* bad,' Sybil says, though from what I've heard about the mare, I'm tempted to disagree. 'No,' she goes on, 'Rose's daughter Mackenzie hacked Jupi. She's completely in love with him, and he's safe as houses so I let her ride him sometimes.'

'You're both so lucky to live near enough each other to go riding together,' I say.

'You have your sisters,' Freya points out.

'Yeah, and you've met them. Riding with Sophia isn't exactly fun, if she can even be arsed to ride her horse, that is.'

'Sophia had Mason competing at Novice last year, right? How's he doing now?'

'Uh-' I hesitate, but then decide to go on, because why should

I cover for Sophia all the time? 'Nothing's gone wrong or anything,' I clarify, 'but - you remember when we ran into you cross country schooling?' Freya nods. 'Well, he stopped for the first time. And it wasn't his fault, Sophia just put him on a bad stride, but...'

'But he didn't try to jump out of it,' Freya finishes.

'Yeah,' I say. 'And she just does my head in. I mean, we have a full-time groom, and it's not like Soph has to look after him during the week or anything. She only has to feed and muck him out on weekends, and she can't even do that.'

'Who mucks out if she doesn't?' Sybil asks.

I sigh. 'Mum. It's weird, because she can actually be quite strict where horses aren't involved, but it's like she's just blind to anything Sophia does when it comes to Mason.'

'What about the ponies?' says Freya. 'You doing well with Otto and Fendi. What does Sophia think about that?'

'I don't know,' I tell her honestly.

'But what does she say about it?' Sybil pushes.

'Nothing,' I say. 'I swear,' I go on, taking in their disbelieving expressions, 'one day, the ponies were Sophia's, then she aged out of pony classes and got Mason, and the next day I started riding Otto and Fendi, and that was that. We've never said anything about it.'

'That's crazy,' Sybil says, slowing as we reach the herd of mares.

'Is it, though?' I say. 'I mean, how many ways could that conversation go? "Hey, you wrecked these two ponies, but I've fixed them! I can ride them and you can't!" Like, what else is there to say?'

'Fair point,' Freya says. One of the younger mares notices us and steps forward, away from the others, and Freya rubs her head as she gets nearer.

'I still don't know how you *don't*, though,' Sybil says. 'I mean, my brother doesn't ride, but I can't imagine either of us not saying something if the same thing happened.'

'Trust me, Sophia and I are quite good at not speaking to each other. That's a maiden,' I say to Freya, nodding at the mare she's stroking.

'What's a maiden?' says Sybil.

'A mare who hasn't had a foal before, who's having her first,' Freya explains before I can, reminding me that both her parents have jobs in Newmarket and that she's no stranger to Thoroughbred lingo.

'Your little sister seems really nice,' Sybil says. I'm sure she's said that before, but she wouldn't be the first person to tell me how much they like Mia more than once. I don't know if it's because Mia is a genuinely nice person, or because everyone expects her to be an obnoxious, spoiled prima donna and is so surprised to discover she isn't that she comes across as even nicer than she is.

'Mia's fine,' I say. 'I know I joke about her, but really she's great. She's nothing like Sophia. Or me, for that matter. She's just easy, and she's good with her ponies. There's Siren, there' - I point at the un-rugged mare and click my tongue. 'Ren-Ren, come on.'

The chestnut starts walking towards us, her coat glossy despite the time of year. I go to stroke her, but she just pushes me for treats, not one to enjoy being fussed over, and moves on to Sybil when she realises I haven't any.

'I still can't believe you bought her,' Sybil says.

'She's so nice,' Freya says. 'She reminds me of Leo.'

'She's like a bigger version,' I agree. 'Yeah, she's really sweet. Now we just need her to take next cover.'

'How old is she again?' Freya asks.

'She just turned four.'

'It seems so young to have a foal,' Sybil says.

I lift a shoulder. 'Not really. Some people cover them at three. And she'll be five by the time the foal's born.'

'But then that's all they do for the next fifteen years of their life,' Freya says. 'Isn't it? Have foals year after year?'

'I guess,' I say. 'I don't really think about it. I mean, we tend to think that the ones that end up as broodmares are the lucky ones.' It's an easy life, being a broodmare. Well, with the exception of being a living pincushion.

Freya scratches the mare's neck. 'Of course they're not unhappy. Just seems like a bit of a waste, is all.'

When we're out of the field, walking towards the house, I glance back over my shoulder, at the mares in the grass, at the one as red as a robin's chest, watching us leave, and wonder what else she could do.

chapter 6

'You busy tonight?' Dad says to me before I even cross the threshold. I've just walked in from putting Otto and Fendi to bed, having waved off Freya and Sybil an hour ago. Dad is sitting at the kitchen table, hunched over a sales catalogue. I've already read the book cover to cover and written out a list of every horse I like.

'Why?' I ask, stepping into the kitchen. I walk up behind Dad, glancing over his shoulder, and see that he has my list in front of him, all sixty-nine lots I fancy scrawled down on the back of an envelope. The catalogue is open to the page of a mare whose name I instantly recognise as one of my favourites on paper. 'I like her,' I say, stabbing the page with my finger.

Dad huffs in acknowledgement. 'Won't be cheap.'

'Won't be crazy,' I counter. 'Anyway, why did you ask if I'm busy?'

'You up for a round of foal watch tonight? Mike bailed.'

'Yep,' I say without hesitation.

Our table is rarely clear, but during breeding season it's even more of a mess than usual. Sales catalogues always cover the surface, but at the moment it's cluttered with stallion books and pages. I flip one of the catalogues open, and it falls on the page of the stallion we sent Siren to, and I stare at his muscular bay body, picturing what the foal may look like…

'I'll watch till twelve or one, then you're happy to take over, yeah?'

'Yep,' I say again, flipping the catalogue closed, the image of Siren's foal galloping from my mind. 'I don't mind.' I stand up from the table and stretch my arms overhead. 'I'd better make myself another coffee…'

The ringing of my alarm clock disorientates me, because my body clock knows it's way too soon to get up. I hit the top of the clock and squeeze my eyes closed in protest, pulling the duvet up around my neck, then my mind connects the dots. *Foal watch*. This early in the year, the thought of sitting up in the barn is still exciting, but there comes a point when I have to refrain from murdering my ringing alarm clock.

I swing out of bed, switch on the lamp, pick up the blanket covering my duvet, wrap it around myself, turn off the lamp, and walk through the dark to the doorway, where there's a sliver of light beneath the bottom of the door and the floor. Lights are left on every night throughout the house, and the landing is lit up like Versailles, the wooden floors gleaming and the persian carpets bright. The upstairs of the house consists of five half-floors, and this one I share with Mia. I used to be on the one below, with Sophia, but I swapped bedrooms a year ago, preferring the smaller - *cosier* - and more neutral space of the one I have now. The floor above mine and Mia's has two attic bedrooms, with low exposed beams and a newly-remodelled connecting bathroom, occupied by our cousins when they come to stay. Sophia has the bigger en-suite below Mia and me, with my old room having been redecorated as a master-suite for guests, and our parents' room covers the remaining half-floor, the biggest bedroom in the house, and adjoining not only a huge bathroom but a dressing room large enough to have a party in.

Framed paintings and photos hang on the walls of every landing, and I pause at the top of the steps to stare at one of the few family portraits we have. It was taken six years ago, one of the only photos I have ever allowed of myself in which I'm not on a horse. The photographs were shot for an article on the stud, promoting the "family heart" of the business.

The five of us are standing with Bubble and her foal of the year - a stunning bay colt with a white blaze - in one of the paddocks. Dad holds the three-month-old foal, standing beside him so the colt's front legs are level with his own. Sophia is on his other side, her head turned to look at the foal, a smile on her face. Mum holds a shiny Bubble's lead rope, her face tilted mid-laugh as she glances up at Mia sitting on the mare's back. I'm next to Bubble, standing in baggy jeans and a large jumper, my ponytail frizzier and blonder than it is now, and if you didn't know any better, you'd think I was looking up at Mia, but it's the mare I was watching. It wasn't the brightest of days, but that only makes us stand out more against the green and grey backdrop. Everything was so simple then, before the eventing bug took such a strong hold.

I love Otto and Fendi, would crawl through fire for them, love riding them, but sometimes, usually in the middle of the night when my thoughts are free to wander, I wonder what things would be like now if they'd never come along.

There's something weirdly relaxing about being free to stay up all night. After Dad heads for the house, released of his shift, I settle into the armchair in the viewing room, the door into the stable aisle closed lest heat from the electric radiator should escape. I've brought Troika with me for company, and the spaniel settles herself on the ground, between my feet and the heater. I walked out of the house with the blanket off my bed wrapped around me, tucking my pyjama bottoms into boots, without even grabbing a coat.

'Call me if you need to,' was all Dad said before staggering out of the viewing room. Tonight will be the first time this week he's even made it to his bed.

The night mode footage is black-and-white, and I stare at each stable's thumbnail, identifying which mare is which. It's hard to watch all the mares at once on a screen as small as an iPad, and I could also find myself trekking all the way to the barn for a false alarm - or not getting there quick enough - so it's easier to sit in here to watch when I'm on sole duty. None of the mares is dripping milk, and Dad doesn't think any will go tonight, but horses are nothing if not unpredictable, and we can never risk not having someone keeping watch.

Staying up all night when you know in your gut that a mare isn't going to foal is a special kind of torture.

'Six hours,' I say to Troika, checking the time on my phone. Six hours of sitting awake. How hard can it be?

The first hour and a half, also know as The First Film, is easy. When I first started foal watch shifts a couple of years ago, and found myself struggling to stay awake, I discovered the gory brilliance of horror movies. It was impossible to fall asleep after an hour of watching characters avoid axe-wielding madmen, so I watched another. And another. Before long I'd seen more horror movies than I could remember, more murdered bodies than I could count, but the problem was that the effect had worn off. Plots were unoriginal, and I soon failed to find anything that could keep me awake, let alone scare me into a state of being unable to sleep. I once drifted off without realising it, and was only woken by Mum's scream when she opened the viewing room door at six in the morning to see a woman being disembodied on the screen.

It's become a game now, to find a horror movie spooky enough to pique my interest. Nothing scares me so much as makes me laugh, but the latter still keeps me awake, and so the first hour and a half of foal watch is spent watching ridiculously stupid people try and fail to escape death.

'Don't go in there,' I say aloud, gripping a freshly-brewed cup of coffee as I stare at the screen. Troika lifts her head at the sound of my voice, and I glance down at her. 'They shouldn't go in there, Troi, should they? They're going to get their heads cut off.'

Troika stares at me, her brown eyes wide, and lowers her nose to her paws just as screams ring out from the TV as a few teenage girls get sawn to death.

'Told you,' I say. Troika lifts her head again, and I shrug. 'They shoulda listened, shouldn't they?'

It's not even two o'clock when the movie credits roll, and I stand up from the chair, stretching my arms out. *Now* I feel tired. Like with most things in life, the roller coaster effect applies to foal watch: there's the initial rush of adrenalin, but then you reach the middle and you never know how you'll reach the end, but then you reach another downhill point and you're flying.

Many hours of practice have prepared me for the middle moment, for the times when I don't think I can keep going. First I make another coffee, and when that doesn't work, I stand up and start doing jumping-jacks. I move around until I can bear to sit still without being consumed with the desire to fall asleep, then look for something spooky to watch. I'll try to make it through another film, which is always a challenge, but if I do - *once* I do - the end is easy. Lack of fatigue hits like a second wind, as does a boredom of watching TV, and I switch to another activity. I've mastered one-person chess and card games, both of which can keep me entertained for a while, played in front of the camera screens on the wall, which I glance at instinctively every sixty seconds, without having to remind myself to. Stallion books and catalogues fill the viewing room as well as the house, and sometimes I'll spend hours flipping through the pages, researching bloodlines and planning the stud's future offspring.

I pick up the nearest book, my eyes scanning pedigrees until I become completely absorbed. Lost in a daydream of kind, beautiful mares with amazing race records and pedigrees to die for, and the sales-toppers they'll breed, that'll go on to become listed winners, and they'll be announced as being bred by Tricklemoon Stud -

The viewing room door opens, making me jump, and I sit up straighter in my chair.

'Morning,' Dad says as he pokes his head around the side of the door. 'You all right?'

I nod, stifling a yawn as I pull my blanket up around myself. 'What time is it?'

'Just after five. I'll do the next hour if you want to go in for a bit.'

'I'm fine,' I say, stifling another yawn. The stallion book is open in my lap, and I tap the page I was looking at. 'Have you thought of putting Hallie to Stargaze Extreme?'

Dad walks over to me, his hair rumpled and his glasses slightly askew. 'I still like the idea of her going to Aggorat.'

'I know, but Stargaze Extreme has the same backbone as Effection, who obviously sired her-'

'Her Group 2 winner,' Dad finishes, nodding. 'I know. She's a good match with both. Stargaze Extreme is double the price, though,' he points out.

'Yeah, but he's a first season sire. And there's already a buzz, so you can practically guarantee a good foal sale.'

'If it's born with four legs.'

I grin at his lame joke. 'Yeah, if it's born with four legs.'

We talk for a little while more, even as Dad insists that I can go back to the house. I last until staff start arriving for the day of work ahead, by which point I feel wide awake but also know I would crash if my head hit a pillow.

Troika and I walk into the kitchen to find Mum making coffee and Mia eating ice cream straight out of the pot - because it's Sunday, and if you can't have ice cream for breakfast on a Sunday, when can you?

'Everything all right?' Mum says. 'Coffee?'

I nod, collapsing onto one of the kitchen chairs.

'What did you watch?' Mia asks, because she knows movies are a vital part of foal watch.

'A horror thing on Netflix,' I say. 'Can't remember what it was called.'

Mum places a cup of coffee down in front of me and presses a kiss to the side of my head. 'Good girl. Well done. You want to go nap for a bit?'

I swallow a mouthful of caffeine and shake my head. 'I'll do the horses first, or I won't be able to get back up.'

Mum picks up her coffee cup and wraps her hands around it, leaning back against the kitchen counter. 'You riding, Mia?'

'Timed canters,' Mia says through a mouthful of chocolate ice cream. 'In the field.'

Mum nods. 'Good.'

'I'm not riding,' I say, raising my hand. 'I'll just put that out there.'

'No, you're fine,' Mum says.

'I'll ride them for you,' Mia says.

I swallow another mouthful of coffee. 'Sure.'

'I can also lunge one if you like,' says Mum.

'I don't mind,' I say, rubbing sleep from my eyes. 'What time is it now?'

Mum shakes her wrist, her Rolex watch sliding out from beneath her jumper. 'Six-fifteen.' She raises her eyebrows. 'Six a.m. on a Sunday and we're all up.'

'And it's not even for a competition,' Mia says.

'Living the dream,' I say, and Mum laughs.

'Living the dream, all right.' Mum looks at the table, and stands up straighter. 'Are you hungry? Shall I cook us up a fry-up or something?'

'Oh, yes please,' I say. 'Do we have anything in? You did a fry-up yesterday.'

Mum opens the fridge door, bending to look through the shelves. 'We have some bacon that needs using. Are there any eggs?'

'Yeah.' I tilt my head to see the egg basket by the oven. 'Loads.'

'Can you make fried bread, too?' asks Mia.

'Also known as heart disease on a plate,' I say.

'I can make fried bread,' Mum says patiently, pushing up her cashmere sleeves, the V-neck jumper revealing a Tiffany diamond pendant.

'I'm starving,' I say, taking another swig from my coffee.

'That reminds me,' Mia says, dropping her spoon in the ice cream tub. 'Mummy, can we get a puppy?'

'What?' Mum spins around from the cupboard with a tin of bakes beans in her hand. 'No we can't get a puppy. We *have* two puppies.'

'How did you get "puppy" from "starving"?' I mutter, but Mia's focused on Mum.

'We have two *dogs,'* Mia says.

'Well, what do you think puppies become?'

'Can we get another dog, then?'

'No!' Mum cries. 'Where's this coming from?'

Mia has been going on about wanting a Cockapoo for ages, which Mum refuses on the grounds of thinking it absurd to spend a fortune on a crossbreed dog, so I don't exactly find this topic totally unexpected, but I don't anticipate Mia's response.

'Flora's dog's had puppies,' she says. 'You love Flora's cocker spaniel!'

If an expression can melt in a second, that's what Mum's does.

'Oh, I do love that dog. Has it really?'

Mia nods, jumping up from the table to pull her phone from the charger on one of the counters. 'They're four weeks old, and they're *so* cute.'

Mum steps away from the oven. 'Let me see, then.' She bends to look at the phone screen, and a small squeals escapes her lips. 'Oh, they are nice, aren't they? How many are left?'

'Just two,' Mia says expertly. 'The golden ones. And we always say we're missing a golden spaniel to have one of every colour.'

'Wait, let me see,' I say, spinning in my seat as Mia brings me the phone. The picture on the screen shows five cocker spaniel puppies sitting in a row - two black-and-tan, one black-and-white, and two golden. 'Oh my god,' I coo, pointing at the puppy on the end. 'I like that one.' It's the smallest of the two golden ones, and his expression is dopier, almost like he were a cartoon character in a Disney film.

'Me too,' Mia says.

'Which one?' Mum asks, turning around as she lets bacon fall into a pan with a loud sizzle. 'It has to be that one, hasn't it?' she says, only to then contradict herself by shaking her head. 'But no, we can't get one.'

Mia sticks out her lower lip. 'Why not?'

'Because we have two dogs already that aren't getting enough attention.'

'They get loads of attention!'

'Oh really?' Mum spins around with a spatula in her hand. 'When was the last time you took either of them for a walk?'

'They don't need to go for walks, we've got a hundred acres,' Mia says.

'When you start looking after the dogs we have,' Mum says, 'then maybe you can get another one. But until then…'

Now if anybody else heard this conversation, they'd take Mum's answer as a clear *no*, but I've had fourteen years' experience speaking Caddie Humphries, and not only do I know she is just as enamoured with the puppies as Mia is, but I'll eat my hat if there isn't one scurrying about our kitchen floor in a month's time.

Dad walks into the kitchen just as we're finishing up a second round of pancakes and bacon and other unhealthily-fried foods, the sight of which makes his eyes goggle.

'Want some?' Mum says.

We always joke that if Dad were a horse, he'd be one of those annoying, stressy maidens we can never put weight on regardless of how much food we pump into them. His cheeks are hollow, skin stretched tight across his jaw, body one straight stick with not an inch of fat to spare. And he certainly isn't skinny for lack of eating. If you ask him, he'll say it's the twenty-four-seven stress that comes with caring for horses that prevents him from being able to gain weight.

'Thank you, Cads,' Dad says as he pushes a final piece of fried bread and mushroom onto his fork. 'This is great.'

'What would you do without me?' Mum croons, clearing away his plate.

'He'd have died of starvation years ago,' I say. I've never seen my father so much as boil an egg.

Dad grins at me then turns to Mum. 'Why do you think I married you?' he quips, the way he glances at Mia and me enough to show that he's at least partly joking.

'I think I'll start charging you all. Five pounds a meal,' Mum says. 'What are you up to today?'

'Quiet enough, today,' Dad says, which is probably the closest thing to a day off he ever gets. 'I thought I might pop down to Newmarket a bit later to check on the horses.'

I straighten up in my seat. 'Can I come? When are you going?'

'Mid-morning?'

'I thought you were exhausted,' Mum says.

'Yeah,' I say, 'but I want to see Breck. I haven't seen her since before Christmas. I'll still feed and muck out first.'

Mum holds up her hands. 'Your choice.'

'What time are you leaving?' I ask Dad, because his idea of mid-morning could mean anything.

'Nine?'

I nod, then suppress a smile at our idea of mid-morning on a Sunday being nine o'clock, when most of the world is still wrapped up in a duvet. 'Okay.'

Horses are bred to be sold, that's the rule. We breed horses to send them to the sales, not to keep, that's what we always say, but every rule has its exception.

Never more than two or three at a time, but we always have some racehorses in training, though it's always with a business mind. Once a mare has a successful runner, both her and all her future offspring's value skyrockets. It's often the first foals we keep, so we can get a win out of them while we can still get another ten foals out of the mare, thus upping their sales price, or the fillies we really have a hunch will do well and become great broodmares. I've still never forgiven Dad for not keeping my favourite foal of Pearl's and racing him, even if he was a colt, but it wasn't viable at the time, and as Dad likes to remind me, clearly he was right not to, seeing as he failed so miserably.

Sundays are quiet in racing yards, and only a handful of lads are around, mucking out and putting horses on the walker. Dad and I nod to them as we pass, exchange a few words with the ones we know better, and carry on to the row of boxes where Breck is stabled.

'Hey, Brecky,' I say as I spot the familiar grey head looking out over the door. Breckan pricks her ears at the sound of my voice, and I hurry over to her, sliding the top bolt across. 'How're you doing? I miss you.'

Breck lowers her head to my waist as I walk onto the shavings, and I wrap my arms around her before taking a step backwards, admiring her. She's bulked up since the last time I saw her, muscle bulging through her shiny neck. Rugs cover her clipped body, her feet are coated in hoof oil, and there isn't a single tangle in her tail. Her dark grey coat is almost roan, but it's lightening every day, and based on how pale she already is for her age, I'm sure she'll be close to white in a few years' time.

'She looks good,' I say to Dad, and he nods in agreement.

'She does. Now we just need to see if she can actually run.'

One of the lads hurries over to whip Breck's rugs off, sliding on her halter and clipping her to the back wall, and as Dad admires the filly's improving shape, I think of the possibilities ahead. Breckan is the first foal out of our mare Scottish Escape, and it's still unknown whether she'll be able to match her dam's two wins. Scottish Escape's racing career was cut short by an injury, and while her page is nothing to frown at, it's nothing to sing home about, either, though we're certain she'd have been a force to be reckoned with if she hadn't been retired to the broodmare paddock so early. The mare has perfect conformation, and Dad is confident she could become an essential broodmare, but only Breckan can prove it. For the past twelve weeks, she's been doing fitness work, building up her muscles and tendons with weeks of walk and trot before even attempting a canter, and it's only now that she's been cantering up Warren Hill that she's fit enough to start *really* galloping, where we'll get more of an idea of her ability.

Both her parents were successful, but that doesn't mean anything in this game, even though it's the foundation on which our business is built.

'Exciting,' I say to Dad, drawing out each syllable as the lad steps back to let us look at the filly, holding the layers of rugs in his arms as we take in her bulging hindquarters and evenly-muscled neck. Her legs are straight, pasterns short, shoulder sloping. And she has the perfect temperament to match her conformation.

Racing has its flaws, plenty of them. But I have yet to discover a feeling that can top the adrenalin and euphoria of watching a foal we bred cross the finish line with his nose in front.

* * *

I slide my foot into the boot and bend my knees, turning to reach the zip at the heel. It does up easily, well-worn from many uses, and I slide the catch through the slip in the leather button strap to stop the zip from coming undone.

A dull, grey sky stretches out overhead, one that makes it impossible to tell the time, but last I checked it was close to three p.m. *At least it's not raining,* I think, recalling the wretched weather we've had this past week.

'Ready?' Mum calls.

'Just need my hat,' I say, jumping up the living compartment steps to grab my skull cap off the sofa.

When I jump back down, onto the wet turf, Mum stands holding Fendi's reins, a violent wind whipping her hair in all directions, and the chestnut mare is stock-still, her eyes alert. Sophia has already ridden Mason in the eighty and the ninety, pulling off clear rounds in both, and the brown gelding is in the back of the lorry, pulling at his haynet, while Soph is sitting on the ramp, huddled in a coat and staring down at her phone. They both should be jumping in higher classes than that, *have* jumped in much higher classes, but after a couple of dodgy sessions at home, Merritt advised Mum to stick to the lower heights for this first show jumping outing of the year, and then had to dissuade her from entering the metre after their clear rounds.

'Ready?' Mum says again, looking angsty.

'I'm not late,' I say, walking up to the pony. Her body may be still, as though she were one of Newmarket's horse statues, but the wind is blowing her flaxen mane and tail all over the place.

'You're not early, either.'

I let out a sigh of annoyance. 'Just chill. It's fine.'

'Don't tell me to chill,' she snaps, stepping away from Fendi as I take the reins. 'Do you want a leg-up?'

'Yes, please,' I say in an equally short tone, cocking my left knee. Mum hoists me into the saddle with ease, having had many years' experience giving leg-ups, and I pat Fendi's neck as my feet find the stirrups.

'All right?'

'*Yes.*' I grit my teeth, shivering as a cold gust of wind blows up my jacket. 'I'm fine, I've got plenty of time.'

'Not pl-'

I don't hear the rest of Mum's sentence, because I've already started riding away, towards the warm-up. As much as I've missed competing these past months, I certainly haven't missed my mum's helicopter parenting. For somebody who is so laid-back in other areas and rarely strict, you'd never expect her capable of being as uptight as she gets at events, and this is only unaffiliated show jumping. I can't figure out if she's competitive by nature, desperately wants her daughters to win every time out, or just wants us all to do our best and be happy, but she turns into an absolute show mum Nazi. It used to bother me, used to fluster and distract me, but I've learned to tune her out now, learned not to take anything she says at a competition to heart, to the point of barely noticing when she becomes obsessive. It must be the break that's making me more susceptible today, left me out of practice, because these small digs are nothing.

Today is a day I'm grateful to be jumping indoors, though I have a warm-up in the outdoor ring to get through first. A couple of puddles rest in the sand, rippling every time the wind picks up, and I thank my lucky stars that our arena at home never floods.

Six combinations are moving around the ring - the *small* ring, I daresay - and I walk Fendi on the inside track, avoiding the horses galloping around the perimeter of the school, and far enough away from the fences in the middle to avoid being a nuisance.

I rarely notice other horses at competitions, always focussed on my own and the job in hand, but I glance around while Fendi walks, absentmindedly checking out each steed. Of the six combinations, half are clearly amateurs - an underfed horse with ill-fitting tack; a skinny girl on an overweight, unfit cob that is blowing like a train; a black pony whose back is clearly shot, judging by the pained expression he wears and the way he joins his hind legs in canter every other stride. It almost makes me want to ride away. But then there are the other three combinations, the ones I feel I belong in the same category as, and seeing horses go well like that makes my heart sing. There's one guy I recognise as a local show jumping professional on a young horse, making everything look effortless; the other rider Merritt is coaching here today, a girl my age on a chunky grey Connemara I drool over every time I see; a spicy little bay mare - she's sweet, really sweet. In fact, she looks familiar…

'Hey, Sybil!' I call, moving Fendi towards the bay mare and pulling her to a halt.

Sybil smiles and halts Ace beside my pony, out of the way in a corner, dropping her reins. 'Hey!'

'Have you already ridden?' I ask, my eyes roaming over the bay mare. Although they stand at the same height, Ace is nothing like Otto or Fendi. My ponies are bigger builds, with cheeky pony expressions and laid-back attitudes. Ace is leaner, like she has something in her that isn't a pony breed, with a refined head and an eye that reminds me more of a young Thoroughbred than an event pony. She's in beautiful condition, with an evenly-muscled top line and rounded quarters, and while she doesn't really have any weight to spare, she isn't thin either. Her forelock covers a white star I know is heart-shaped, the reason her show name is *Ace of Hearts*. The mare isn't the sort of pony I'd ever want to ride myself - why people like flighty and sensitive horses is beyond me, because I don't think there's anything fun about worrying you're about to be thrown on the ground - but I love her to look at. I don't mind strong and brutish, like Harvey and occasionally Otto - lean towards those sorts of horses, even, I think as I remember the chestnut Thoroughbred mare at home I can't help but be drawn to - but unpredictable doesn't appeal to me at all.

'Not yet,' Sybil says, resting a gloved hand on Ace's neck. My eyes go to her jacket, which is smartly cut and navy blue, not the usual tweed one she wears. I wonder if it was a Christmas present... 'We're doing the hundred now, and then the one-five.'

'Me too!' I say.

'Have you got Otto too?'

I shake my head, twirling a strand of Fendi's flaxen mane around my index finger, and recall what I discovered when I brought him in from the paddock a few hours ago. 'He only went and pulled a shoe in the field this morning. I swear he knew he was supposed to come out today.' The light bay pony looked very proud of himself when I led him into the yard earlier, his right fore bare, and the shoe I then discovered in the muddy field was twisted so severely that I couldn't help but think Otto had stood on it intentionally to avoid working today.

'They're good at that,' Sybil says.

One corner of my mouth tugs into a smile. 'Yeah. Soph and Mason went clear in the eighty and the ninety, though,' I say.

Sybil forces her lips into a smile. 'That's cool.'

I nod. 'Yeah,' I say, but my voice doesn't sound very convincing. With the exception of people Sophia is actually friends with, speaking of her riding successes to anybody is always awkward. I may think she's not a great rider and only gets around thanks to Mason and the halo he wears, but it's different to have others think that. I'm allowed to complain about her and criticise her riding, but I get uncomfortable if anyone else does. Well, except Alex, I guess, because she is anything but tactful, but she does it in such an upfront way that I don't mind. Plus, as the person who produced Otto, I feel she's entitled to.

When I tell someone about Sophia doing well, I know that's all they're thinking. Even if they don't mean to. And even if I think the same thing, *Passenger on a pushbutton horse*, I don't like other people to.

'She seems nice.'

My mind had drifted off, my eyes losing focus of Fendi's mane, and I look up at Sybil's voice, trying to remember where we left off and what she's referring to.

'Sophia,' Sybil elaborates. 'She seems nice.'

I smile sadly and nod in agreement. 'She *is*. That's what makes things tricky.'

'Remember to sit up after fence five and steady her before the turn,' Merritt says to me, leaning against Fendi as I wait to go into the ring. The course is set up in the indoor arena, and we're huddled under its overhang, in the in-gate between rows of seats, trying to shelter ourselves from the storm.

'Yep,' I say, the word clear and confident. This is how Merritt and I work - she gives me clear and confident instructions, and I answer her in the same way. 'This is my friend,' I add, nodding at the combination trotting in the ring, awaiting the start bell, eager to hear what Merritt thinks of Sybil and Ace.

Half an hour ago, a few horses after Sybil's clear round I didn't get to watch, Fendi took the top rail of the last fence in the metre class to cost us a placing. We're not here *to* place, as Merritt reminded me - and an upset Mum - but to practise, to practise for the *real* competition. We're not here to go for the clock, but to notch up a tidy, confidence-giving round that will put us in good shape going into the new event season.

Still, I'd rather canter through the finish flags penalty-free.

'Nice pony,' Merritt says as the start bell rings and Sybil pushes Ace into a canter, circling around the metre-five fences.

'She's really tricky,' I tell Merritt quietly, noting Rose Holloway standing some ten yards away, watching the round intently with her arms crossed. 'She trains with Rose Holloway.'

Merritt nods as Sybil turns Ace to the first fence and hits it on a perfect stride. 'They've done a good job.'

The bay mare canters on to the second fence, her quarters engaged and her ears forward. She moves with impulsion, supple to the bit, the picture of health. Sybil's face is full of determination, her eyes only on the fence ahead. The two look like they're working as a team, communicating with each other. Sybil sits quietly in the saddle, her position not perfect but not interfering either.

I watch the mare rock back on her haunches and propel into the air.

Watch her take off.

Watch the mare tuck her knees and lift them around her chin, stretching so her front and hind cannon bones are almost level with one another when she's in mid-air.

Ears forward, head straight, eye on the job.

That's what we need to do, I think, scratching Fendi's withers as though this transmits the message to her.

Sybil and Ace jump clear, the doors open for Fendi and me to enter the ring, and I push her straight into an impulsive trot, shortening my reins and feeling the mare come alive beneath me. She's always been light in the contact - sometimes too light - and there's little weight in the reins as I push her forward, my legs firmly against her sides.

'Well done,' I say to Sybil as I trot past her and Ace, my friend's face taken over by a huge grin.

'I can't believe it,' she says, clearly in shock, and I catch sight of her leaning forward to embrace the mare before she has passed me, heading for the gate, out of sight.

Fendi flickers her ears back and forth, eyeing up the fences. The contact in the reins becomes even lighter, and she prances as though the sand surface were hot coals, shortening her outline and growing about two inches.

'Good girl,' I say, pushing her onto a circle, making her move. She'll settle once the bell rings, once she's away, because it's the anticipation that gets to her, and once her job begins, that's her focus. Although the contact in the reins is light most of the time, Fendi gets strong once she starts jumping, and she wears a gag at competitions, so I can bring her back between the fences without having to fight her, because if I *do* fight her, she tells me exactly where to go.

The chestnut mare flicks her toes, curving her neck into a contact, her back light beneath me. *Clear round*, I think. *Jump it like Ace just did.*

Which is what we do.

chapter 7

Mist is turning to rain, the small droplets clouding the air before drifting noiselessly to the ground. I pull gloves from my pockets and fasten my hat, frowning at the bad weather. The days have been warmer recently, but rain and mud are the price to pay. I had the good sense to dress for it at least, wearing my waterproof racing jodhpurs over a pair of leggings.

'Ready to get wet, Ottoman?' I say. The bay pony stands with his ears back and his eyes closed, as if to say, *No, India, I am not.* 'Well, get ready.' I tuck Otto's flash noseband into its keepers, and step back to inspect him critically. A year ago, the pony was lacking top line, but now muscle runs all along the top of his neck and his spine, right to his tail, the way it did when Alex had him. A strand of mane is lying on the left side of Otto's neck, and I flick it back to its correct position. 'Are you going to be good today?'

Horses are funny. Some days - some weeks, even - everything goes well. Exercises work and corrections are easy to apply and progress is steady. But then, without catalyst, things don't go so well. Be it because of the horse or the rider - usually the rider - sessions don't go as smoothly, nothing you do works, and you're left going in circles, both literally and metaphorically. This past week has fallen into the latter category.

Nothing extreme has happened since the show jumping outing, nothing has gone terribly wrong, but nothing has gone right. Otto's been rushing away from my leg and getting strong, but I haven't been able to correct him the way I have with Merritt. Fendi's been floaty in the contact, not really taking a hold, flicking her toes instead of engaging her hind end when I ask for more impulsion, and since our last lesson, a few days after the jumping rounds, I haven't felt like I've managed to correct it.

Bree pops her head around the stable door, rain dripping from her tied-up hair. Originally from California, Bree came to the UK to work in racing, but soon found that Newmarket life wasn't for her, and made the switch to sport horses. Her family is always sending her care packages of American sweets and chocolates, which she brings to the tack room for us all to share. Bree has introduced me to the delicacies that are Twinkies and Hershey's Kisses, while I have converted her to Flakes and Candy Kittens. She's nearing thirty but could pass for a teen, with bleached blond hair, and it's a shame she didn't like racing, because she's the perfect size for a jockey. She rents a semi-detached cottage a few minutes away, which she shares with a couple of roommates who also work with horses.

'Does he have his hay yet?'

I shake my head, and Bree comes into the stable to untie Otto's haynet. 'Do you know how much longer they'll be?' I ask. Sophia finished school earliest today, therefore getting the first slot with Merritt. More hours of daylight in a day mean that Sophia, Mia, and I have been able to resume after-school riding lessons. Mia always gets the last slot because Mum insists she does her homework before riding, because too many times she has neglected to do so and then had a meltdown because it isn't done. I don't think of Mia as academic per se, but she's a perfectionist when she wants to be, and horses and schoolwork aren't things she likes to do badly at.

'Not much longer, I don't think,' Bree says, pulling the haynet free from the ring. 'I saw Sophia standing with Mason on a long rein, so I think they're just finishing up.'

I nod. 'Thanks. I'll start walking him around, then.'

Otto looks as enthusiastic as I feel as I drag his lazy body out into the rain, and he shows his discontent by ducking his head against the oncoming wind and stomping his right fore loudly against the concrete.

'You're such a drama queen,' I say to him, and the pony pins his ears and shakes his head as if to accentuate my point. 'Otis,' I warn. 'This is probably why you lost a shoe.'

The farrier did both ponies the other week, and I swipe a brush over Otto's newly-shod hooves, coating them in oil. I love seeing tidy feet and clean shoes, and it lessens the memory of standing out in the cold for two hours making idle chitchat with the farrier and stopping the ponies from nibbling him.

Otto stamps his foot again, while I'm trying to run oil over the coronet band of his right fore, and I tap his shoulder. Most days I find the pony's character amusing, and could watch his antics for hours, but today isn't one of them.

'Trust me,' I tell him, chucking the paintbrush aside and straightening up, 'I don't want to be out in this weather any more than you do.'

'How's the pocket rocket been this week?' Merritt asks as I ride Otto into the school, passing a wet Mason and Sophia. The latter doesn't look like she wants to rip anybody's head off, so I take it the lesson went all right.

'Miserable,' I say. 'I was working on the same things we did last time,' I go on, 'but he just keeps fighting me and not wanting to know.'

Merritt frowns beneath the hood of her large waterproof coat.

'Oh, has he?'

'I didn't get to hack him this week,' I admit, 'which never helps' - Alex always kept the pony's mind occupied and took him out a lot when he was hers, giving him a change of scenery, and he always turns sour after a few days running in the school - 'but still. I'm sure I'm doing something wrong, too,' I add.

'Well, warm him up and we'll see,' Merritt says.

Of course with Merritt's help, the issues I've been having with Otto are fixed in no time. She tells me exactly when to add more leg, when to steady him with the outside rein, when to change exercise and occupy his mind with something else, to the point there is no possibly of him *not* going right.

'Guard the right shoulder,' Merritt says as I ask Otto for a shoulder-in down a long side. 'Keep him moving with your left leg. Right shoulder, don't let it get away! Too much bend. Good. And ride him straight. Good.'

I scratch Otto's withers as we ride out of the left shoulder-in, pleased I was able to control him. He can execute lateral movements perfectly, but he never does so unless he has to. I have yet to sit on a horse that goes more nicely than Otto does when he's working correctly, when he's between your hand and leg and every stride feels like a step of a dance, but it's not something he does on his own if he can help it. I can't say I blame him.

'Okay, give him a breather, then get him together again and trot him over the upright.'

The fence is tiny - fifty centimetres - and with a placing pole in front of it. Otto bounces back into a trot when I ask him to, getting strong again, and I circle him once before turning to the fence. When the pony sees the coloured poles his ears prick forward, his head comes up, and he rushes towards it, breaking into a canter.

'Go wide,' Merritt calls before I reach the fence, and I steer Otto farther right, missing the fence with strides to spare. 'Circle him around it until he settles.'

I do as Merritt says, passing near the obstacle until Otto stops anticipating going over it, and try again. The pony still gets excited, still pulls against the reins and tries to drag me in, but he stays in trot until the placing pole, clearing the fence easily.

'Circle near the jump again before turning back to it,' Merritt instructs me.

We spend five minutes going over the exercise, circling and jumping and changing rein, until Otto is both calm and bold, approaching the upright steadily but still jumping with power. Merritt sets up the second element, an eighty-centimetre upright two strides away, and we work on the same thing over the two jumps.

'You don't want to fight him, but you want to make sure he's always on the end of your rein,' Merritt says as Otto lands clear over the second jump, bounding forward exuberantly. 'Don't pull or hold him back, but make sure he's listening to you, that you *could* pull up if you needed to. Make sure you're always having a conversation, so that when you do ask him something he doesn't think you're shouting an order and then runs away. Strong arms and soft hands - not the other way around.' She walks to the third set of wings and sets an upright, this one at a metre. 'Again. Coming from the left.'

The sky is still grey, my clothes are soaked through, and water is dripping onto my face from the visor of my hat. Heat radiates from Otto, like my own personal radiator.

With Merritt's words in mind, I think about always communicating with Otto as we ride through the turn towards the grid, making sure he knows what's coming. The pony pricks his ears when we face the line of jumps, but I sit softly, keeping my hands low as he breaks into a canter stride over the placing pole, and ride the distances as they come.

'Good,' Merritt calls, walking towards the last fence. 'Much better. You didn't rush him or hold him back, you just went with him, and you were listening to each other. You didn't over-ride but you still kept riding. Good,' she says again, lifting a green-and-black pole from the ground and setting it on the obstacle's second pair of wings, making a parallel oxer. 'Over this once well and that'll do him.'

Otto chucks his head as I push him back into a trot, his strides choppy. I add more leg and ride him forward, focussing on maintaining a rhythm, and turn him straight to the line. He chucks his head again, but I ignore it. It's cold, and wet, and we can both go in as soon as we do this last line, and I'm not about to start circling a dozen times again.

The pony canters two strides before the placing pole, and I take a check on one rein, a reminder to get him listening, but Otto sets his jaw against me, and, instinctively, I pull. He keeps going towards the fence, though, and chips in a stride, awkwardly chucking his shoulder to avoid hitting the rail, and as we land, I click my tongue and start pushing to make the two strides. Otto responds to my demand, responds too much, and shoots forward to fly over the second element with way too much speed, and I can distantly hear Merritt telling me to sit up and collect him, but there's no hope. We land too far out on the other side, in the one-stride distance, and in a moment of stupidity, instead of holding Otto back to squeeze in the stride, I kick. *We can bounce it,* I think.

I'm wrong.

And Otto knows I'm wrong, because he flickers an ear, hesitant, but then sits back on his haunches to take off, and I prepare to go with him, except the pony knows better. Seeing the distance is impossible, and too close to the jump to fit in the one stride now that I've hurried him, Otto lowers his front feet back to the sand, slamming on the brakes, and because I'm already leaning forward, because I thought he was about to take off and going to jump, I go flying.

The reins are still in my hands as I fall into the spread, and Otto jumps back at the noise of my body hitting the rails, but I keep hold of him and jump to my feet as quickly as I can. Merritt leaps forward to take Otto, and I pass her the reins before leaning forward to rest my hands on my knees, focussing on my breathing.

'You all right?' Merritt asks, and I feel her put a hand on my back as I nod. 'Winded?' she says, and I nod again, unable to speak. I *knew* I shouldn't have turned to the grid, knew the trot wasn't good enough.

Air rushes back to my lungs, and I straighten up. My side hurts from hitting the poles, which are somehow still intact, and my legs don't feel so dry beneath my jodhpurs anymore.

Dusting wet sand off my waterproof trousers, I glance at the poles still in their cups, grit my teeth, and walk over to Merritt, taking Otto's reins from her hands and giving the pony a pat on the neck. 'I'm doing it again,' I say simply, raising my left foot to the stirrup and swinging straight up into the saddle.

Merritt grins. 'Attagirl.'

The phone answers on the fifth ring.

'…I swear to God, Waffles, if you try to bite me one more time, I am selling you to the meat man. Hello?'

I smile to myself and shake my head as I walk down the barn aisle, glancing into the stables. 'Alex? It's India.'

'Oh, hi,' she says, sounding happier with me than she does with Waffles, which is hardly surprising. I've only seen him a few times, but the grey gelding is something of a handful, and Alex, who has a seat of glue, seems to spend more time falling off him than she does riding him. I asked her once why she doesn't sell the horse, and she looked at me as though I'd suggested she sell a vital organ. 'Are you all right?'

'Uh, sort of, I-' I pull up my sleeve to check the time on my watch, frowning. 'What're you doing with Waffles? It's half-past eight and it's dark.'

'I'm pulling his mane. I've got Excel Talent training tomorrow, and I haven't had time to do it yet. And he's such a little *sod*' - she enunciates the last word loudly in such a way that makes me think she's speaking more to the horse than to me - 'that I can't trust him to be good tomorrow morning. If I left it till then, he'd probably let me do half or something before throwing his toys out the pram and then I'd have to go with him looking like I attacked his mane with a hatchet.'

I pause at the door of one of the stables and peer in at the sleeping mare. 'Don't you have someone who can pull manes for you?'

Alex scoffs. 'Some of us have to do those things ourselves, you know.' Before knowing her, a comment like that would have made me wish a black hole would open up beneath my feet and swallow me whole, but now that I do, it goes right over my head. I've learnt that nobody should take anything Alex says to heart. 'No, but seriously,' she goes on, 'no one else really likes handling him.' *Can't imagine why,* I think. 'And I like pulling their manes myself. Anyway, I'm guessing you didn't call to hear me talk about my brat of a horse.'

'No,' I admit.

'How's Otto?' she says before I can go on.

'He *has* been really good,' I say honestly. 'He's been to team training, and I took him cross country schooling a few weeks ago and he was absolutely ama-'

'India?' comes Mum's voice as she steps into the barn aisle. Like me, she wears a big coat over her nightclothes, plaid pyjama bottoms tucked into wellies. 'Who're you talking to?'

'Sybil,' I lie. 'Dad just asked me to watch this lot while he's in the yearling barn. Mike's watching from nine. I'll be in then.'

'What's he doing in the yearling barn?'

'One of them started to colic at feed time, and he thinks he's fine, but he's just checking. I'll be in in a sec.'

'Okay. I've done night check on the others, so I'll see you inside in a bit,' Mum says, not looking convinced, but she turns around and starts walking back towards the house nonetheless.

'You liar,' Alex says into my ear, and she sounds like she's grinning. 'I've trained you well. Can't think why your parents don't like me.'

'They think you're a bad influence,' I deadpan. 'Plus *you* think their precious daughter wrecked your pony.'

'Huh. Well, can't really argue with either of those.'

'Funny that.' I pull the phone away from my ear to check the battery, remembering how low it was when I started, and am annoyed to see only three per cent remaining. 'My battery's gonna die in a minute,' I say to Alex.

'Well, what did you call me for, then?' she snaps.

'I fell off Otto today,' I say.

'I've fallen off him more times than I can remember. What's your point?'

I sigh. 'He stopped at an oxer and I went flying.'

Alex grumbles something at Waffles before responding. 'Did you get a bad stride?'

'Sort of… we landed far out and I tried to bounce a one-stride,' I say sheepishly. 'Alex?'

I have to hold the phone away from my ear for the sound of her laughter.

'I'm sorry,' she finally says. 'Ha, that's a classic. Okay, sorry. Did you get back on?'

'Yes.'

'Did you jump the line again?'

'Yes.'

'Did you forget your brain again?'

'Ye- what? I didn't try to bounce it again, if that's what you mean.'

'Then why are you calling me? Not that I dislike your voice,' Alex says, her tone, as usual, both calm and serious, as though her conscience streams out of her mouth in a running commentary without filter, 'but I don't see what the problem is?'

'I dunno,' I admit.

Alex laughs again. 'Jones, I'm sure everything's fine. The best horse in the world will stop if the rider's stupid enough to bounce a one-stride.'

'He's looking good,' I say enthusiastically, thinking of how much muscle he's gained, how he looks more like he did with Alex.

'Good, I'm glad.'

I look down at my coat and fiddle with the zip, twisting the tassel around my finger. 'He hadn't stopped in ages,' I say. 'I thought I'd got him over that.'

'Jones,' Alex says again, a nickname she's very proud of herself for coming up with. 'It's done. Over. What happens in the ring, stays in the ring, and when you ride into it again tomorrow, everything resets. Okay? Don't carry mistakes with you. Drink some tea, eat some chocolate, and forget about it. All right?'

I nod. 'Yeah. Okay. Thanks. Sorry I rang, I just wanted to talk.'

'Anytime. And you're doing fine, remember that. Way better than your evil stepsister.' I've pointed out many a time that Sophia isn't my stepsister, but Alex insists that "evil sister" doesn't have the same ring to it.

I lean back against one of the barn walls, staring down the aisle at the night sky through the double doors, and voice the desire that is always fluttering in my chest. 'I want him to go as well for me as he did for you.'

Alex's answer is immediate. 'Whether or not he does is only up to you.' She pauses. 'How's Fendi going?'

'She's okay. She's not quite so hard to win over.'

'Yeah, well. She's carted so many people around.' I hear Alex let out a short breath. 'Otto will look after you, though. Once he thinks he has a reason to.'

I nod again, blinking away tears. 'Thanks. How-' I cut myself off, leaning up from the wall to follow a sound coming from one of the boxes. 'I'm sorry, I have to go. Thanks again. Good luck tomorrow.'

Alex snorts. 'Yeah, if this horse of mine would just stand still and stop being such a -' The last word is lost as my phone finally dies, and I shove it into my coat pocket, marching towards the sound of rustling straw.

The chestnut mare is rolling, straw sticking to her sweaty body. Baby's Brought Up, a Group 2 winner and one of our best broodmares.

'Hey, girl,' I say, watching over the door as she stands up, and I see a bag beneath her tail, two limbs already showing. 'It's okay, you've done this before.'

The mare paces around, and I grab the nearest foaling kit from the aisle. I take out a pair of gloves, pinch the top of the sleeves and stretch out the plastic to stop them falling down my arms, pull them on, and return to the stable door. The mare's still pacing, steam rising from her body, and I reach for my phone, to call Dad and tell him to get here, but when I touch the screen, an empty battery symbol pops up, and I remember that's it's dead.

'Dammit,' I snap. I hurry down the aisle, stepping out of the double doors, and call once. 'Dad!' I can see the lights on in the yearling barn, fields separating us, and the distant lights of the house. Has Mum already made it back to the house? 'Mum!'

Why does sound never travel when you want it to?

There's no answer, and at my raised voice, the other mares in the barn start pacing, with one letting out a whinny.

'I'm sorry,' I say to them, walking back down the aisle. Yelling is only going to cause more trouble. 'I'm sorry,' I say again, and I head back to Baby's Brought Up's stable.

The mare is lying down again, her sides heaving. It's not like I haven't done this a million times before, I remind myself. And most of the time it's clockwork. But still, I'd rather, at the very least, have the option of calling someone if something were to go wrong.

I ease the door open, whispering words of reassurance to the mare as she rests her head in the straw. She's always foaled easily, and this time is no exception. With little effort, the mare gives a final push and the foal - filly? I'm sure she was expecting a filly - comes out. I move towards the small body and immediately pull the bag over her head, down her ribcage, and my face breaks into a huge smile as the filly shakily lifts her head. She's bay, with an uneven white star, and a tiny snip on her nose.

'Clever girl,' I tell the dam as she turns to sniff her foal.

From the box by the stable door I grab a bottle of antiseptic, and I spray some on the filly's umbilical cord. 'It's all right, good girl. You're so brave. Good girl.' I continue to babble to the foal, while the mare lowers her head back to the straw. 'You looking at your baby, mama?'

For a few minutes, I watch from the stable door. Baby's Brought Up licks her foal again, once, then lowers her head to the straw, still not making much of an effort to move. When she lifts her head again, some five minutes later, I think she's finally going to start tending to the foal, but too late, I realise she's going to roll. 'No, careful!'

The mare swings back, legs going into the air and sending straw flying. Without thinking I leap forward, for the foal, and grab hold of the filly's legs to pull her towards me with all my might. In the next second, Baby's Brought Up rolls over, landing heavily in the spot where the filly was lying.

'It's okay, it's okay,' I say to the foal as she fights to move away from me. Weighing between one hundred and one hundred-and-fifty pounds at birth, newborn foals often outweigh me, their small bodies surprisingly strong, and this one is no exception. 'I'm trying to keep you safe,' I growl at the foal, keeping hold of her as the mare continues to thrash. 'Don't you colic on us,' I mutter, ducking as a hoof flies this way. I click my tongue. 'Come on, up you get. That's enough.'

Baby's Brought Up continues to roll, and with every full turn she does my worry increases. I drag the filly as far into the doorway as I can without her being on the concrete aisle. 'It's all right,' I say to her, scratching her neck. *Why, why,* why *is nobody here?*

You're here, I remind myself. *Do something.*

The filly wriggles in my arms, and I hold her down as the mare rolls this way again, hooves flying. She'll be fine, it's the mare I need to worry about.

I lean out of the stable, fingers searching for the cardboard edge of the foaling kit. I drag it nearer, keeping one arm draped over the foal, and search through the contents. Bute, I need bute. The mare is thrashing because she's in pain, and bute is a painkiller. What else can I do?

I grab a plastic tube of bute paste, set it at two doses, and pull off the cap. 'Stay here,' I say to the filly, releasing her to jump back into the stable.

'You're all right, mare,' I say, edging around the Thoroughbred's body to reach her head. 'You're going to be all right.' I grab hold of her leather halter and stick the tube into her mouth before she can realise what's going on. Bute paste won't kick in for a little while, but it makes me feel better to know I've done *something*, however minor. Now I just need to the mare her up.

I slide the tube into my coat pocket as the chestnut pulls faces at the horrible-tasting paste. 'Hey, come on.'

I scratch the mare's head, balancing on a straw bank to hold on to the side of the halter, and as she suddenly thrashes again, taking me by surprise, I lose my balance and slam into the back wall of the stable. My sides still hurt from hitting the deck earlier, despite bathing in Epsom salts and swallowing two Ibuprofen, and I know

I'll feel even worse once I have time to think about it, but for now, my attention is only on the mare, even as my hand stings fiercely from scraping against the concrete blocks, piercing the plastic glove across my knuckles. 'Come on, mare,' I snap.

Baby's Brought Up continues to move as I perch by her head, trying to both keep myself safe and keep the mare calm. With a final grunt, she rolls back down on her right side, stilling, and I move forward to kneel beside her neck. *Breathe, India, breathe.*

'Get up, mare,' I snap. My nerves start to frazzle, but as quickly as the worry settles, it disappears.

I think I'm a calmer decision maker in stressful situations than I am under normal circumstances. I develop a tunnel vision - all I can see is the problem in front of me, and every other thought vanishes from my head to allow me to focus solely on the task at hand.

'Come on, girl,' I say, scratching her neck.

The mare is still, catching her breath, and I make the most of the lack of flying hooves the glance at her tail, and see the afterbirth still attached. *Okay,* I think, *that's probably why she's in pain. Once she passes it, she'll be all right. But until then…*

After a few minutes, the mare stands, and I let out a long breath. Steam rises from her whole body, flanks white with sweat, but she's up. She spots the filly in the doorway, still safely out of the way, and starts moving towards her. I smile when she lowers her nose to the bay body and starts licking, and then slowly, waiting a minute to be sure the mare isn't about to roll again, I move the foal back into the straw bed.

When the sound of footsteps walking down the concrete aisle resonates behind me, I've just finished tying up the afterbirth with baling twine, which serves as an anchor and also prevents the mare from stepping on it, and am sliding a warm bran mash through the door.

'India?' Dad's voice.

'I'm here,' I call, stepping out of the stable.

Dad stops in his tracks, taking in the gloves on my arms, the foal box in the aisle, the open stable door. 'What-'

Before he can go on, I tell him everything that's happened. About the birth, the filly, the mare starting to colic because of the afterbirth pains, how I moved the foal out of the way, and gave the mare bute before she finally got up.

'I didn't know what to do. My phone's dead, and I tried yelling…'

Dad walks up to the stable and peers in, at the mare eating her bran mash, the healthy filly trying to figure out how her legs work. Then he looks at me, and a small smile tugs at the corner of his lips.

'What would I do without you?'

chapter 8

I grip the lead rope in my left hand, scratching the red mare's neck as I glance to the right, trying to glimpse the scanner screen. Siren fidgets in the stocks, looking none too pleased about having a vet's arm up her backside, and I scratch her neck again, reassuring her it's almost over. Her second cover was sixteen days ago, and I can't think of any reason she wouldn't have taken this time around. Saying that, there was no reason for her not taking the *first* time around, either…

'Well.' The vet retracts his arm and pulls a long, plastic glove off the scanner probe. 'Not in foal.'

'What was that?' Dad calls, stepping back over to us, having excused himself to answer a phone call.

'Not in foal,' the vet repeats, throwing the muck-covered glove onto the ground. 'And she doesn't look like she's coming back around yet, but I can PG her…'

As the two of them talk, I focus on Siren, running my fingers across her wide forehead as she stomps her right fore and nudges my pocket irritably, clearly fed up with this whole ordeal. Could she be an event horse? No reason why not. Freya's words, about the mare being wasted in the broodmare paddock, come back to me, and I wonder whether her not being in foal is really such a bad thing…

* * *

When the event season ends, the next one always seems ages away. The days get shorter, the nights longer, and mornings of plaiting and loading up the lorry can't come soon enough, until they do, as though no time has passed at all.

The new season officially begins the first week of March, but Merritt has told Mum to withdraw Sophia and me, since we both had some small hiccups these past weeks and have missed out on a few do-over jumping sessions due to heavy snowfall. I try not to let my disappointment show, because I have only myself to blame, and I also know, at the end of the day, that Merritt is right. It's better to start a week or two later and be prepared than go out and compete for the sake of it and have all your hard work unraveled. Mia is competing Harvey and Doris today, and I'm going along as groom, not only because I never say no to a horse-related day out, but because I'm suffering from event withdrawal symptoms, and being in that atmosphere, even on foot, is intoxicating.

'I've got Harv's travel boots on, Mia,' I call to my sister, stepping out of the dun pony's stable. It's the perfectly reasonable morning time of half-past seven, and Mia's dressage test isn't until eleven. Bree is working, mucking out and keeping an eye on the horses left behind, while Mum and I are Mia's gofers. Sophia didn't want to come, because getting up at seven on a weekend to go stand in the freezing cold at an event she's not riding at didn't appeal to her, and I'm sure she'll be in bed till noon, especially since she has Bree looking after Mason now the season has restarted.

'You ready, M?' Mum asks. 'You sure we've got everything? All four saddles-'

'Yes, yes, I'm sure,' Mia says impatiently, pulling off Doris's heavyweight rug and swinging a show sheet onto the grey mare's back. 'Of course I have everything.'

And we believe her. She's immature at times, easily distracted, and more excitable than a puppy, but Mia is always on the ball when it comes to her ponies and being ready for an event, not only taking responsibly for packing all of her belongings, but never forgetting anything.

'It's not exactly far,' I say to Mum. 'If ever we've forgotten something, we can just call Sophia and make her bring it.'

'Oh how I love the first event of the season!'

The voice is unmistakable, and even without turning around in the hot drinks line I know who I will find behind me.

I shake my head to disagree. 'It's too cold.'

Alex grins and steps nearer, making the woman behind me in the queue shoot daggers at us with her eyes. 'It's perfect,' Alex says, clad in white jodhpurs, a navy jacket, a hat and hairnet, and carrying a short whip in one hand. 'You don't feel the cold once you're riding,' she points out.

'Fair enough.'

She holds up a finger dramatically. 'But that isn't the only reason I love the first event of the season.'

'Uh-huh.'

'No, no,' Alex says, shaking her head. 'The first event of the season is a *hoot*. I mean, at no other event do you see so many falls in an Intro' - I've noticed Alex almost always calls BE90 *Intro,* the way she also calls BE100 *Pre-Novice* - 'and it is just the most hysterical thing ever. No one gets hurt or anything,' she clarifies as the woman behind us clears her throat in a disapproving manner, hitching a spotted Cath Kidston bag up her shoulder, 'but it's just all the amateurs who fall, because they've probably not even taken their horses out since the last event. And then they get back on and fall *again*. Except that's not allowed anymore with the new rule change, is it? Anyway, it's still just so funny. And then all these twelve-year-old kids are crying. I love it.'

'That's the spirit,' I say drily. 'Do you want a coffee?'

'No I don't want a coffee,' she says, sounding appalled. 'You can get me a hot chocolate, though.' She pauses while I order, then goes on. 'I mean, if you're just going to come to an event to get eliminated and cry, then stick to Pony Club, I mean, seriously. This is the professional eventing circuit, why do you need to ruin it for the rest of us?'

'They're providing you with entertainment,' I say. 'Plus, it's all their entry fees that are funding eventing for everyone else.'

'Oh, yeah, that's true.' The woman in the queue shoots us evil looks again, and I wonder if she's a nightmare Pony Club mum. 'Anyway. You're not riding?'

I shake my head as our drinks are put down, handing the man behind the counter a five pound note. 'Next week,' I say, not wanting to explain I'm not riding because I haven't ridden well enough recently to. 'Mia's riding today.'

'Who's Mia?'

'My little sister.'

'Oh, yeah, there's a third one of you.' Alex takes a sip of her hot chocolate, leaning forward to avoid spilling it on her clean clothes. 'I forget that. How's she doing?'

'All right,' I say. 'Don't have Doris's score yet, but Harvey got a 29 dressage and went clear show jumping.'

'Is Harvey the dun?' Alex asks, and I nod. 'I love that pony. 29? Huh, not bad.'

'So when's your next ride?'

'Uh, now?' She looks around. 'Supposed to be, anyway. I'd better get to the warm-up ring, actually.' Alex starts walking towards where horses are working in for show jumping, and as she seems to be assuming I'm going to follow, I do.

'A groom's bringing him to you?' I ask, jogging a couple of steps to catch up.

Alex laughs, covering her mouth to stop hot chocolate from coming out. 'I wouldn't leave a groom to get a horse ready unless I'm on one already,' she says derisively. 'No, it's not my horse. I'm just riding him today. You know Leni? Her black one.'

'Lochmere?' I say. 'How come Leni's not riding him?'

'She broke her wrist last month falling off one she was breaking for Amanda.' Amanda Walton is a retired eventer, and while she's a successful trainer, she's not known as a nice one. Sophia tried one lesson with her, and one lesson only, which I think is a record. Suffice to say Amanda did not humour Mum's demand that Sophia not be criticised one bit. 'Anyway,' Alex goes on, 'Leni's got him entered for Gatcombe at the end of the month, so he needs a run before then.'

'Have you competed him before?'

She shakes her head. 'Never even sat on him. He'll be fine, though,' she adds. 'Oh, there she is.' Alex drains the last of her hot chocolate and hands me the empty paper cup before striding towards the approaching black horse. He's not overly tall, probably sixteen hands, with lovely conformation and an alert look, his coat just clipped. Leni leads the Thoroughbred confidently, dark blond curls contained beneath a woolly hat, and a cast poking out from beneath the waterproof coat that covers a pair of jeans. 'How's my steed?' Alex calls.

'Bit full of himself,' Leni says, pulling the gelding to a halt beside Alex, who starts running down the stirrups. Up close, Lochmere looks less relaxed than he did from afar, his eyes out on stalks and fixed on something in the distance. *Typical Thoroughbred*, I think. 'You ride that nutty thing of yours for fun, though,' Leni goes on, 'so I'm not overly worried.' Her eyes move to me, and she smiles politely. 'Hi.'

'Hi,' I say back, wondering how somebody as polite as Leni

and someone as different as Alex can be such good friends. 'I saw Leo the other day,' I tell Leni, wanting to say something other than *hi*. 'He's looking really good.'

Her smile grows. 'Good, I'm glad. He seems to go really well for Freya. As does Otto for you,' she adds.

'What can I say,' Alex says, tightening Lochmere's girth. 'You and I produced some pretty good ponies.'

'They still have to be ridden well,' Leni says, winking at me.

Alex cocks her left knee. 'Leg me up, Len.'

I go to move forward, putting the paper cups down at my feet to help, but with only one arm, Leni hoists Alex into the saddle before I can.

'Give me a shout if you need a fence set,' Leni says.

Alex pats the horse on the neck. 'Anything I need to know?'

'Nah, you're fine. He's perfectly schooled,' she adds smugly, which Alex sneers at.

As the black gelding walks away, his rider looking as though she's always ridden him, I'm left not really knowing what to say to Leni, but luckily she saves us from standing in silence.

'Oh, there's Georgia,' she says, waving at somebody who's walking this way from the trailer park. 'Do you know Georgia?'

I shake my head. 'Um, I don't think so, but I'd better be going, anyway. I'd just come to get a drink, and my sister's going cross country in a minute.'

'Okay. Well, good luck, I hope she goes well.'

'Thanks,' I say, before hurrying back to the lorry, bracing myself against the freezing wind.

Doris and Harvey both go double clear, and both place in the top ten, leaving Mia delighted. Snow starts to fall just as Doris sets out of the start box, and by the time the grey mare crosses the finish line I can barely see for the large flakes, but not even ten minutes later has the sky cleared again.

We drive slowly on the way home, snowflakes falling once more, the mood in the cab joyous, Mia sitting with photographs and rosettes on her lap while she demolishes a bag of Mini Creme Eggs.

Bree has finished all the evening stable chores when we pull into the yard. Snow has stopped falling, and the thin layer that had settled on the ground during the past hour is already melting. Mason, Otto, and Fendi are groomed and rugged up for the night, standing on thick beds of shavings and pulling at overflowing nets of steamed hay.

While Doris and Harvey are unloaded, I let myself into Otto's stable, checking the pony over, even though I know Bree won't have missed anything. He nudges my arm, lowering his head, and I scratch the top of his neck, where there's space between his cover and his ears. 'You'll be competing soon, Otis,' I reassure him. 'Your other mummy says hi,' I add quietly.

Fendi is also busy stuffing her face, but she stops when I open her stable door, turning to nudge my pockets for treats. The mare's thick forelock falls right above her eyes in a blunt line, and I straighten it to the centre of the her head.

In no time at all, Doris and Harvey are in their stables, overnight rugs on and legs wrapped. Bree's already prepared feeds, and we all hang around to watch the horses eat, during which time Mia shows Bree her photos and rosettes, before heading to the house.

'We're back,' Mia yells as she kicks off her boots and runs to the kitchen, her arms full with the day's haul.

I slam my heel into the bootjack and pull my foot from the wellie, my eyes on the walls of the mudroom. The wall space above the dog beds serves as a Hall of Fame, framed photographs the first thing you see when you walk in. There are the early ones of me and Sophia showing, on little ponies that are still parading around rings with even littler riders today. Doris, her coat lightening over the years as her rider changes, from Sophia to me to Mia. Harvey, ageless in all of the pictures, the different coloured and patterned hat silks giving away the change of jockey. There are some photographs of Sophia on Otto and Fendi, but not many. There are quite a few of them with me, including some from the last event of the season, where they both went double clear to pick up placings. My favourite is one of Fendi going over a skinny table designed to look like a chariot, her knees around her chin and her ears pricked forward, me going with her. There's also a show jumping picture of Otto I love, captured with the big country house the venue is famous for as the backdrop. Mason features in a few photographs, and in every one Sophia is behind the movement, her hands not allowing, her lower leg forward, and her bodyweight back.

I wonder how long it will be before Mum hangs up today's photos.

Mia is peering in the slow cooker when Mum and I walk into the kitchen, at the meal Mum prepared early this morning, and Dad strolls in through the other door, from the sitting room.

'How did it go?' he asks.

'Great!' Mia bounds towards him and shoves the pictures and rosettes into his arms. 'Look!'

Dad holds the rosettes away from him and squints. 'Now, who won these?'

Mia giggles. 'Who do you think?'

He pretends to ponder. 'Harvey and Doris?'

'Yes, but who was on them?'

Dad frowns. 'Troika?'

Mia laughs again. 'No!'

'Are you sure?'

'Yes!'

'Alice?'

'No!'

'Huh.' Dad hands the rosettes back to Mia. 'I don't know, then.'

Mia rolls her eyes. 'Daaaaad.'

'Miiiiiia,' Mum says, walking up to her and placing her hands on her shoulders. 'Why don't you go shower and change into your pyjamas before dinner.'

'O-kay,' she sighs, putting her belongings down on the table.

'Hey, Mia,' Dad says as she walks past him, and my younger sister stops to look at him. 'Well done.'

'Uh-huh,' Mia mumbles, trying to stop from smiling as she hurries out of the room.

Dad turns to Mum, putting an arm around her shoulders. 'All all right?'

Mum sighs. 'Yeah. Just tired. Everything okay here?'

'Yeah. Mike's on night watch tonight, but none of the mares looks like she's gonna go.'

'Huh, we might actually get a full night's sleep,' says Mum. Though Dad is the only one who gets up for foaling, it's his ringing phone that alerts him, thus waking them both. 'Where's Soph?'

'She - she wasn't with you?'

'No.'

'Oh.' Dad frowns. 'She must be in her room, then. I haven't seen her today.'

Typical, I think.

'You've got to be kidding me…' Mum marches out of the room, her cheeks blown out, and starts calling, 'Sophia!' as she heads for the stairs.

Dad shakes his head as he takes a seat at the table. 'You wanna get plates out?' he suggests.

'Sure.' I open the nearby cupboard and start stacking china. 'Did Siren get scanned today?'

'No, Monday.' He shakes his head again as I place the plates on the table. 'I think we'll have to PG her,' he says, referring to an injection of prostaglandin that brings mares back into season early. Most mares don't suffer any side effects, but others have horrible reactions to the jab and can sweat profusely for hours among other things, which isn't nice to watch.

The thought of Siren being in discomfort makes me squirm.

I open the cutlery drawer, keeping my back to him. 'Do you think maybe she shouldn't be a broodmare?'

'Huh?'

I turn back around and shrug, still not meeting Dad's gaze. 'I just thought maybe it's not worth it. She's only four, maybe she could be retrained to event or something.'

Dad scoffs. 'A waste of good bloodlines, riding a mare like that.'

A waste. The same words Freya used when told the mare would be a broodmare. I guess what qualifies as a waste depends on which side you're standing.

I think of saying more, but Mum comes storming back into the room, looking no less angry. 'She's been in her room all blooming day,' she says, lifting the lid off the slow cooker. 'Lazy brat. That's two days running now she hasn't worked Mason.'

'Sell him,' I deadpan, though I mean it.

'If I could, I would,' Mum says, and her response baffles me so much that I stay silent. *You can!* I think. *He's your horse! They're* all *your horses,* as she so often likes to remind us. 'I need a drink.' She walks out of the kitchen, and I hear the lock of the wine cellar door turn, followed by the sound of Mum's shoes padding down the stone steps.

'Are you still going to the Ocala Breeders' Sale this month?' I ask Dad.

He starts to shake his head, then nods, then shrugs. I laugh to myself, because those three consecutive gestures describe my father better than I could ever put into words. 'I'm gonna *try.* We have two mares due that week alone, though, so we'll see.'

'Can you open this, Art?' Mum asks Dad as she walks back into the room with a bottle of red, handing it to him as she returns to her meal.

'DONE!' Mia yells, her pyjama-clad body running into the room. 'Is dinner ready yet?'

'Almost,' Mum says tiredly, stirring the contents of the pan.

Mia looks over Mum's shoulder. 'You put mushrooms in? You know I hate mushrooms.'

'Then don't eat them.' Mum glances up. 'Can someone get plates?'

'I already put them on the table,' I say. 'You want them?'

'Yeah, I'll serve up here. Thanks,' she says as I place them down beside the slow cooker. 'Can you give Sophia a shout? I *did* tell her it was ready…'

'SOPH!' I yell. 'DINNER!'

'Well I could've done that,' Mum says.

'You said shout,' I point out.

'And since when do you ever do exactly as I ask?'

'I think the words you're looking for are *Thank you, India*,' I say, carrying the plate Mum offers me to the table. '*Thank you, India, my most favourite daughter.*'

'Hey, I'm her favourite,' says Mia.

'Neither of you is my favourite,' Mum says, heaping another portion onto a plate. 'Alice is my favourite.'

Mia takes the bait and launches into an argument about how the dogs don't count, while I argue that Mum's answer isn't fair on Troika, and Mia's still talking about it when Sophia pads into the room, wearing tracksuit bottoms and a sparkly jumper, her long hair tied up.

'What're you going on about?' she asks, sitting down in her usual spot.

'Mum says Alice is her favourite daughter,' Mia responds.

'That's not fair,' Sophia says, turning on Mum. 'What about

Troi?'

'Exactly!' I cry. 'That's what I said!'

'Yeah!' Sophia's bright blue eyes meet mine before going back to Mum. 'How could you even say that? Poor Troi. You've never liked Troi.'

'I don't dislike Troi,' Mum says levelly. 'She's just more in your face. Troi's needy, and Alice stays out of the way. Besides, Alice was here first. Loyalties.'

'Uh-huh,' Sophia mutters, looking at me again, and I match her expression as she smiles to contain a laugh.

I don't hate my sister. Not even close. I hate how she can be lazy, how that laziness affects her horses, but that's not the same thing. We're different in many ways, but Sophia isn't a horrid person. And sometimes we get along so well I can't imagine two sisters ever having a better relationship. That's what makes this situation hard. It would be so easy to hate her, to never speak, to rub my results with Otto and Fendi in her face, but I couldn't actually do that to her. Even though Mia and I are closer in age, there were times when Sophia and I were inseparable. And while that's not the case anymore, the feeling resurfaces from time to time. I'll have just come in from the stables, wound up with her for something she's done - or *not* done, more to the point - furious Mason's been ignored all day, and Sophia will be in the sitting room, watching TV, and she'll speak before I can say anything.

'*Matilda* is on TV,' she'll say, and before I can put into words my anger, she'll add, 'Remember when we set up boxes of Cheerios on the kitchen table and tried to make them move with our eyes?' And my anger will fade away as I remember our younger selves searching for an inner telekinetic ability, and how we stared at boxes of cereal for over an hour, until I moved Sophia's without her noticing, and she did the same with mine, and we convinced ourselves we'd succeeded with our minds. I knew Sophia had discreetly nudged my box of cereal, though, even though I was happy to convince myself I'd done it telekinetically, just as she must have known I'd done the same to hers, but it didn't matter.

That Sophia, the one that was my best friend, still shines through the one she is now, even if it isn't very often, but it's enough to keep in place the thin thread that holds us together.

'Have you seen my pictures?' Mia asks Sophia, her dinner untouched as she reaches across the table for the photographs.

'They look great, M,' Sophia says, looking through the photos with great attention. She holds up one of Doris jumping a trakehner, snowflakes clouding the grey pony's body, Mia's mouth open as they fly through the air, the two of them looking determined. 'I like this one.'

'Me too,' I say, then to Mia I add, 'You saw a real flyer at that one.'

Mum presses a hand against her chest. 'My heart was *pounding*,' she says, over-enunciating each word.

'It wasn't *that* bad,' Mia says self-deprecatingly.

'You did well,' I say.

'You really did,' Mum agrees, spearing a piece of chicken with her fork.

'This is great, darling,' Dad says, nodding at the food.

'It is,' I supply, the warm stew heaven after a day of running around in a freezing wind.

'It's nothing, I just threw it together this morning.'

'It's great,' Sophia says, swallowing a mouthful and putting her fork down in a way that suggests she's about to go on. Beside her, Mia is prodding every aliment with apprehension. 'So, Mum, you know how it's the Easter holidays in three weeks?'

'Yes, I do know that,' Mum says, her voice cautious.

'Okay,' Sophia says chirpily, and I wonder if what's coming next is the only reason for her nice mood this evening, and I feel a pang. 'So, I was thinking, maybe we could go skiing the first week? The season isn't over until the middle of April, and you said before that maybe we could go at Easter.'

Mum swallows a mouthful of wine. 'I don't know, Soph.'

'But you said we could!' my sister insists, and I suspect her patience is going to wear thin quickly if she doesn't get her way. 'We haven't been in so long.'

'You know we can't just up and leave!'

'A few days off won't kill anyone,' Sophia says. 'We've got two events before we go, and Bree can lunge and hack out the horses while we're away. Besides, I think it would do us all some good. We can have a break, and then get back and focus on the season.'

'I want to go skiing!' Mia says.

'Eat your dinner,' Mum snaps, not even glancing at Mia's untouched plate of stew as she speaks, watching only Sophia. 'It's not just your horses,' she goes on, stretching the *your* to me and Mia. 'It's breeding season, you know that.'

'It's not like we're ever helping,' Sophia says.

'I am,' I point out.

'Well, you don't have to come.'

And there goes the trace of the sister I used to have.

'If anyone's going skiing, we're all going,' Mum says, though when she says *all*, it's a given that she doesn't mean Dad, because he never goes anywhere during the stud's busiest six months, with the exception of the sales.

'I don't want to miss Pearl foaling,' I say quickly. 'If she goes two weeks over, she's due on the seventh.'

'We'd be back by then,' Mum says, then her face turns more serious. 'You're all riding at Weston Park that weekend' - she looks at me - 'it's India's first Pony Trial. We can't just leave.'

'Bree can keep the horses fit,' Sophia says. 'They're fit enough as it is, they only need to be hacked. There's no point drilling them a week before a big event.'

'Well, that's true,' Mum concedes.

'We could leave on the Saturday and come back on the

Wednesday, so there'd still be two full days to get ready. It's easy to fly there.'

'No, I don't want the hassle of flying,' Mum says. 'I'd rather drive straight there.'

Sophia perks up. 'So we can go?'

'I don't know.' Mum picks up her wine glass again. 'It's been a long day. We don't need to discuss this now, there's still time.'

'But we need to let people know! I was talking to Lottie and Rosie about it.'

'You've already invited Lottie and Rosie?'

'I only said we *might* be going,' Sophia says. 'And then Darcy can come, too, and bring Saffron to stay with Mia!'

'Oh please, Mummy,' Mia says, playing exactly the role Sophia wants her to.

'Soph, not now.' Mum stifles a yawn. 'And what about India? You can't just invite all your friends.'

Sophia lifts one shoulder. 'Well, she can invite a friend, too,' she says as though I weren't sitting right here.

Mum looks at me. 'Who would you invite? How about Ottiline?'

'No, not Ottiline,' I say quickly. I've known Ottiline for years, and while I like her fine, I'd sooner bang my head against a wall than spend a week in the mountains with her.

'Well,' Mum says, 'who, then?'

I shrug. It's not that I don't have friends at school - I do - but I've never been good at making friendships go any further, because I'd rather spend my free time with the broodmares than socialising, and I make no effort to hide that whenever I'm invited somewhere. 'Um, I don't know. Freya and Sybil?'

'You don't know them that well,' Mum says.

'I know them enough,' I say.

'Why don't you just invite one?' she asks, and I can't believe how quickly this "suggestion" of Sophia's has turned into a sure thing.

'I can't invite one and not the other! Sophia's inviting two friends. Besides, you like Freya and Sybil,' I add, remembering how happy Mum was when they both jumped up to help clear the table when they stayed for lunch last month, suddenly grateful they had that initiative. There's nothing Mum hates more than rude house guests.

'They were very polite,' Mum admits. She looks at Sophia. 'So, us four, Darcy, Lottie, Saffron, Rosie, Sybil, and Freya. How many's that?'

'Ten,' I say.

'Well, if Darcy's happy to drive, I guess we could go in two cars.'

'So we can go?' Sophia says excitedly.

'I'll talk to Darcy about it tomorrow,' Mum says calmly. 'India,' she says in a more frantic voice, 'you'd better contact Freya and Sybil and see if they really can come.'

'Okay,' I say. And then, because Mum doesn't stop staring at me as I try to finish my dinner, I say, 'Now?'

'Yes, now.'

'Um, all right.'

I get up from the table and head for the mud room. My coat is still cold from being outside all day, and I pull the phone from the pocket and open up a new message to Freya and Sybil.

Hey, don't suppose you both want to spend Easter in the Alps?

chapter 9

In the two weeks leading up to the holiday, we go to that many events. Mum drives Mason, Otto, and Fendi in the lorry, and we scrounge one of the Tricklemoon horseboxes for Harvey and Doris, Bree at the wheel.

I'm excited at the thought of finally being back in the saddle at an event, of putting on my cream breeches and navy jacket and riding into a warm-up, tannoys crackling, immaculately turned out horses around me, while I'm focussed only on my own. All the off-season months come down to this, and when I step out of the lorry in the early morning hours, onto a grassy field, surrounded by other horseboxes, neighs resonating in the vehicles, it's like I never left.

My first event of the season is both successful and anticlimactic. Otto and Fendi are in the 100, and are unsurprisingly fresh for their maiden event of the year. Their dressage tests are passable but not good enough to place in the first few, both excited to be out, tenser than usual and not making the movements look effortless as they are capable of. Fendi is so hot in the show jumping that I have little choice but to sit back and steer her to get around the metre-high track, which is exactly what I do, and we go clear. Otto is less confident than he has been, trotting into the ring unsurely, ears pricked and nostrils flared as he tucks his nose to his chest, dropping off the bit, and snorts at the coloured poles and fillers no different from the many he's seen before. I had to sit steady on Fendi and let her get on with the task at hand, but with Otto *I* am the one who has to get us over the jumps, which we do, but with one down when he decides to back off the second combination and I only just manage to get him over the two elements, clipping the top rail of the first.

The speakers announce my four penalties as I trot out of the ring, and I feel slightly disappointed, but Merritt greets me with Mum, and she is anything but crestfallen.

'Bloody well ridden, girl,' she says, slapping my leg. 'Ride like that and you can ride round any track you like.'

It's the beginning of the season, the ground not the best, and going for time is the last thing on my mind. I just focus on the jump ahead of me, on each pony having a confidence-giving round, and they both go clear, though neither places.

The next weekend is my first Novice, Otto and Fendi both entered in the U18 division. I don't sleep the night before, tossing and turning, watching the foaling cameras on my iPad, my eyes focussing on Pearl, her sleeping body curled up in the straw, as my mind wanders to her colt. I wonder where he is, maybe standing in a shelterless field, ribs protruding from his body, if he's even still alive. Maybe he got bought by a foreigner and is racing in Spain or Saudi. These thoughts run laps around my mind, and I swear I've only closed my eyes for a second when my alarm clock rings, and I sit up to silence it, blinking as my eyes adjust to the light of the iPad screen, focussing on Pearl again, and I realise I've been asleep longer than I think, because the mare is standing and munching on her hay.

At five a.m., beneath the stable lights, I brush clean shavings out of the ponies' tails as they eat their feeds. Fendi turns her head to look at me between mouthfuls, plaited forelock revealing her large stripe and Roman nose some would call ugly but I think is beautiful. Green flecks of alfalfa dust her lips, and she regards me thoughtfully, large ears pricked forward.

'You all right, Fen?' I say, stretching out my left arm to reach her nose, tickling her upper lip with my fingers. 'I know the tracks you've been doing for the past couple of years probably seem ridiculous to you, but don't worry. Today you're going around a real course.'

The venue is packed, the jumps are huge, and Mum is either going to have a hernia or make one of *us* have one.

'Why are you so anxious, Mummy?' Mia scoffs, hunched over as she screws studs into Doris's shoes, Mum pacing the length of the lorry beside her. 'It's just an event.'

'And hell is just a sauna,' I mutter under my breath.

With five rides between us, there isn't much time to think or breathe. Throughout the season, we often try to compete no more than three horses at a time to alleviate stress, so if an event is running over multiple days, we'll have Mia compete on one day and Sophia and me the next, or each of us a different day if the event is near and running classes long enough. When we're all riding together like this, Mum's anxiety levels shoot through the roof and she drives us all crazy - or, crazier than usual.

By the time I'm riding Otto into the show jumping ring, Sophia and Mia have finished riding for the day. Mason and Doris both finished fifth in their respective divisions, while Harvey behaved like a prat in the show jumping, dragging Mia into both combinations and rattling the first rail of each, and then picked up a 20 cross country for taking off between a numbered element and making Mia cross her tracks to regain control.

The show jumping course is intimidating, but I don't think about it as a whole, just assess each jump as it comes, and the treble, which I was most worried about, jumps best of all.

The disadvantage of having two rides in a day is also the biggest advantage: little time to think in between rounds. There's no time for doubt or second-guessing yourself. I just have to suck up whatever worry is on my mind, take a deep breath, and get a move on.

It's ridiculous, when you think about it. All the hours spent in the saddle - and, some days, in the arena sand - all the time in the yard, all the fences jumped, all the hours of grooming and mucking out, all the half-halts and shoulder-ins practised, all the grids jumped… every little thing, every chore you perform on a day-to-day basis, is working towards five minutes of your life. All the literal blood, sweat, and tears, of which there have been plenty. All for this one moment, to be galloping a near half-ton animal towards a big solid fence with the best possible chance at making it to the other side. And there's no thinking about all this while it's happening, because when you're on course, all you can see is the fence framed between your pony's ears, and making it to the other side takes up all the room in your brain. There's a fence, and a horse beneath you whose every breath you hear, the wind rushing past your ears, and there's your own heart, thudding loudly in your chest.

It's terrifying and amazing all at once.

And when both ponies come home clear, my first ever Novice rounds, their first successful Novice rounds in years, I feel as elated as I always imagined I'd feel.

* * *

'I'm so excited,' Mia says, holding Harvey's reins at the buckle. 'Aren't you excited?'

I lift one shoulder. 'I guess. I mean, it's not like we haven't been before.' Fendi steps to the left to avoid a puddle, and I duck to miss a branch as she sends me into a bramble bush. 'You're an event pony,' I remind the mare.

'*I'm* excited,' Mia says again.

'Good for you.' I lean forward to rest my head against Fendi's mane, eyes closed, and her short, silky mane bobs with her stride, tickling my face and filling my nose with the scent of pine shavings.

'What's up with you? Are you turning into a moody teen like Sophia?'

'I'm not moody,' I snap, sitting up. 'You think Sophia's a moody teen?' I ask, thinking the words don't sound like ones my younger sister would come up with.

Mis shrugs in the saddle. 'That's what Mummy says.'

Aha. 'Well, I'm not. Are you sure you aren't? You're thirteen later this year.'

'I'll *never* be a moody teen,' Mia says, horrified by the thought. 'Never, ever.'

'If you say so.'

We've been on half-term for precisely seventy minutes, and unsurprisingly Sophia wasn't in the mood to ride when we got home from school, mumbling excuses about having not packed, but Mia and I are dreading a break from riding, and changed out of our uniforms at top speed before hurrying out to the stables and tacking up our ponies. Bree will be keeping them in work while we're away, but still, it doesn't feel right to leave them. Though now the holiday is so close, and I know my friends are going, I'm also really excited. They've both competed this month, and I was just as excited for their successes as I was for my own.

Sybil and Jupiter came sixth in their maiden BE90 of the year, and Freya came second in her first U18N with Leo, then only went on to win the Aldon Pony Trial the next weekend.

Sybil's response to my message was immediate and accompanied by a million exclamation marks, while Freya's took longer to come in, and expressed worries about leaving Leo so close to Weston Park. She did eventually say yes, though, after their Aldon win, saying her mum has promised to keep Leo lunged and a quieter few days would do him no harm. Sybil said something similar about Jupiter, that he'd been working hard to meet the first few events and that he'd benefit from a quieter week, and her mind was made up when Rose's daughter Mackenzie offered to ride him while she's away, keeping the pony fit for his event a few days after we get back. And to convince Sybil further, she's at a standstill with Ace at the moment because the mare picked up a non-serious injury earlier this month, but one that's sidelined her for a couple of weeks and means she isn't ready to compete yet. When a horse is off for a week with an injury, you actually lose double that because of the time it takes to work them back up to where they were when they left off, so I feel for Sybil. The unpredictability of horses is almost reason enough not to work with them. It *is* reason enough for most people, but as Dad likes to say, you're not sane if you choose to spend your life around them, in which case I'm very happy to be insane.

Sybil, Freya, and I were all concerned about leaving our ponies, but the three of us came to the same conclusion: the ponies are at peak fitness, a few days off would do us some good, and there are still seven months of the event season left, so what's five days?

'Wanna trot down here?' Mia asks as we come to a wide, uphill track in the woods.

'Sure.' I squeeze Fendi's sides, and the pony glides effortlessly into a smooth trot, her neck flexed, mouth quiet, hind legs active. Even on a hack like this, I focus on keeping my back straight, my shoulders square, my weight in my heels, my hands still. In our last lesson, Merritt pointed out that I was collapsing my back when I rose the trot, slouching each time I sat in the saddle, and I make a conscious effort not to.

Beside me, Mia doesn't look like she's focussed on anything related to her own riding as she trots Harvey along the trail, yet everything she's doing is correct. The dun pony is slightly more open than he would be in a dressage test, but he's trotting into the bridle, his neck always breaking at the right place, a solid muscle that can't *not* go in the correct shape due to years and years of schooling. At fifteen years of age, the pony is still fighting fit, coat and mane shining with good health, expression alert and not sour. Some ponies genuinely love to work, love to have a job, love to be ridden and fussed over, light up when they see a fence, and Harvey is one of them. It's customary for event horses to get the winter off, to come home from the last competition of the season and have their shoes pulled and be turned out. Our ponies get turned out in October, but Harvey only ever lasts a month at best before he starts getting restless, and if he isn't brought back into work by that time, he takes matters into his own hands - hooves? - and jumps the fence to come and find us, sometimes making it all the way to the house. We've tried bringing him in every night, sticking to his usual routine, but even that isn't enough stimulation for the mischievous pony. I'll be making breakfast, minding my own business, then I'll hear one of the dogs bark and turn around to see Harvey's pink nose staring at me through the kitchen window, as if to say, *Hey, guys, what's taking so long? Get out here, I'm bored.*

It's something that's happened many times over the years, and we now all know that as soon as Harvey starts pacing the fence line, we have a few hours to bring him in and chuck a saddle on his back before he decides to exercise himself.

'It's cold,' Mia says when we bring the ponies back to a walk at the end of the bridleway, before it comes out of the woods and leads onto a lane that takes us back to the stud. She shivers dramatically beneath her coat. 'Do you think it will be cold in France?'

'I bloody hope so,' I mutter. 'We're going to ski.' Though it's often not cold at all when we're on the slopes - the opposite, even, because the reflection of the sun off the snow means we tend to come back from the Alps with legendary sunburns.

Fendi trots a few strides to catch up with Harvey, shod hooves making a sound as satisfying as popping bubble wrap as they hit the tarmac, and I stay sitting in the saddle to bring her back to walk, frowning up at the grey sky. 'Do you think it's going to rain?'

Mia shrugs. 'Dunno.'

We turn left off the country road, into our driveway. Wrought iron gates hang between stone pillars, a sign reading *Tricklemoon Stud* on the right pillar. The gates are on a timer, and in the day, they open automatically. I ride Fendi up to the censor, and the gates rattle before slowly starting to swing open. Above me, grey clouds are moving furiously, and as we wait to access the driveway, lightning flashes overhead.

'Did you see that?' I say. 'I'm sure there's supposed to be a storm this evening.'

'Dunno.'

'Didn't Dad say something about it last night?' I ask, recalling a conversation I wasn't really paying attention to. 'About getting everyone in because there was going to be a big storm?' Most of the horses are in every night, anyway, but getting the yearlings in will take a little while, and certainly delay the usual afternoon schedule.

'Dunno,' Mia says again.

But he did. By the time Mia and I have put away our ponies, rain is tipping down, accompanied by a bitter wind that knocks you sideways. Bree has already tied haynets and is now making feeds, so I leg it for the nearest broodmare barn, where I find one of our most loyal grooms, Donna, sopping wet as she puts a horse away and hurries off for another. I'm about to follow her, but then Dad comes out of another box.

He stops when he sees me standing in the aisle. 'Everything all right?'

I nod. 'I just came to see if you needed any help,' I say, shaking water off my hood.

'If you want. The rain keeps turning to hail, and there's supposed to be thunder and lightning all night, so we're bringing everyone in.'

I nod again. 'Siren?' Because really that's who was on my mind when I came over here. She finally went for her third cover this week, after first failing to come into season, being PGd, and then not producing a follicle big enough to warrant a cover. Now we wait, but I don't think Dad's holding his breath. 'Has she been brought in yet?'

'That bloody red mare out there,' comes Earl's voice as he comes into the barn, responding to my query. He's leading a grey broodmare, whose coat is black from the rain, the two of them dripping water with every step.

'You want me to bring her in?' I ask loudly, as the rain turns to hail and starts to drum against the tin roof of the barn so loudly I can barely hear myself think.

Earl scoffs. 'You can try.'

The mare is standing in the farthest corner of the field, tail clamped and quarters turned to the wind.

'Siren!' I call. 'Ren-Ren!'

The Thoroughbred refuses to acknowledge me as she stands by the post-and-rail fencing. All the other mares from this field have already been brought in, and Siren is the last one, alone, which doesn't seem to bother her.

'Don't be stubborn,' I yell, rain drowning my words. 'Siren!'

I know she can hear me, but Siren isn't moving.

'Hey, come on.' I edge closer, expecting Siren to run away, but she doesn't. 'Why couldn't Earl catch you?' I step up to the mare and clip a lead rope to her leather halter. 'There. What's the problem?'

Hail pounds against my coat, and I scratch Siren's neck in

reassurance, thanking my lucky stars that she's let me catch her. 'Good girl.' I apply pressure to the rope and turn towards the barn. But the mare doesn't move.

'Come on, Ren-Ren.' I pull on the rope again, trying to lead Siren, but she won't budge. A sharp tug gets her to turn a step, but as she comes face-to-face with the strong wind, she shakes her head and turns back, her body a deadweight.

So this is what Earl meant.

'I'm trying to get you *out* of this bad weather, you stupid horse,' I mutter.

For five minutes, I keep trying. Pulling on the rope, pushing Siren on a circle, using my voice. But the mare won't budge, won't turn her head into the violent wind.

Thunder rolls so loudly I feel it in the ground, and lightning flashes overhead, momentarily lighting up the dark sky, and my legs quiver.

'Siren. Come *on*. You can't stay out in this. The sooner you move, the sooner you can get inside and be dry. And eat.' *Eat!* I unzip my pockets, and almost cry with relief as my fingers wrap around a half-packet of Polos. 'Hey, Ren, you like Polos?'

I tear back the foil and pull out a mint, which sticks to my wet fingers. The mare still doesn't pay me any attention, but I hold the Polo right under her nose, and then she notices it and lips the mint up eagerly. 'You like those, don't you?' More than like, judging by how she's now happy to try *not* looking like a depressed horse in an RSPCA advert. 'Come on.' I pull another Polo out of the packet and hold it away from Siren as I coax her to turn towards the barn. She greedily stretches her nose out for the treat, but soon decides it's not worth turning her face into the wind for, and spins back around.

'For goodness' sake, Siren,' I cry, feeling desperate now. Maybe I should've grabbed a chifney? Though I can't see a bit in her mouth making much difference at this point. 'Come on. You're gonna get us struck by lightning or something.'

But she *is* greedy. As much as she doesn't want to face the wind, Siren wants the treat, and I continue to move the mint towards her nose before pulling it away, trying to get the horse to move with it, too.

'Come on, Ren-Ren. You can do it.'

It feels like ages, and it might well be, but after some time, even though the weather is still not easing up, I get Siren to turn and take a step. Then another. And another, all the while coaxing her with treats. A crash of thunder rolls overhead, making me wince, and the mare just stands stock-still, body shivering in the cold, offering me quiet reassurance.

'Who'd have thought you'd be so relaxed,' I say, the words like a whisper to me but more like a shout over the sound of the rain.

Dad and Earl are at the gate when we reach it, clearly on their way to look for me.

'You all right?' Dad calls as he slides back the bolt.

I nod. 'I couldn't get her to move,' I shout.

'I'd have left her there,' Earl says bitterly, his grey hair flattened by the rain.

'She'd have frozen,' I say.

'Would've served her right.'

I lead Siren to the barn, and she walks at my shoulder the whole time, surprisingly polite. We both relax when we reach cover, and I move down the aisle ahead of the mare, her unshod hooves leaving water marks on the concrete. The stable is bedded down with straw, a pile of hay in one corner, and Siren is only too happy to hurry inside, dragging me to the forage.

The mare starts stuffing her face, and I unclip the rope from her halter and grab fistfuls of straw from the bed, bunching it up to rub over her coat, wiping off the excess water. More thunder rumbles, echoing beneath the roof, and even as some of the mares next to her spook and spin at the noise, Siren doesn't so much as twitch.

'Good girl,' I say to her, feeding the chestnut mare another Polo.

Siren turns from the hay to look at me, water dripping down her head, and I look back, *really* look at her. I forget she's only four, what with her pushy nature and big build, but really she's just a baby. One of the horses that slips through the racing industry's cracks - too slow to race, not fashionable enough to breed from, and not a type people retrain for anything else. The words *chestnut* and *mare* in the same sentence send people running, especially when you throw *Thoroughbred* into the mix, but I know better - after all, Fendi speaks for herself. A chestnut mare is either your worst nightmare or your greatest ally, depending on how you treat her. Siren isn't the most gentle, but who can blame her? She's never been taught to be. She was taught to be brave, to run, to be fast and bullish, so that's all she knows. It's not her fault she wasn't any good at it.

'Do you want to be a broodmare?' I ask the Thoroughbred. Does she really want to spend the better part of two decades having babies, when she's still a baby herself and has never had a chance to do anything else? After all, what differentiates her from any other young event prospect? A pulled mane, a body clip, and thirty kilograms?

I squint at the mare and try to imagine her that way. Sopping wet like this, her coat is sleek, accentuating her nice shape and making her look less like a fluffy pony. She almost resembles a sport horse, with her normally-unruly mane plastered down like that. And if she didn't have a hay belly...

The idea of Siren being a ridden horse seemed ridiculous some time ago, but looking at her now, in her stable, a horse like any other, I think, *Why not?*

chapter 10

It's still raining when I carry the last bag to the car at six a.m. the next morning. Water covers the gravel, and I walk on the tips of my shoes, trying to dodge the worst of the puddles. I've already been up for almost two hours, packing - because I neglected to do so yesterday, despite reassuring my mother to the contrary - and seeing to the horses. Bree doesn't start work until seven, so I fed and hayed the eventers early, gave Otto and Fendi plenty of extra affection to make up for my upcoming absence, and made a dash to the stud barns, which, in contrast, were full of life, to check on Siren and Pearl. The chestnut mare was happy to be inside the barn as the storm raged on, and I treated her to some Polos before quickly giving Pearl a kiss and reminding her to wait for me to get back before foaling.

'Is that all your stuff?' Mum says as she marches out of the house, her handbag over her arm. She got up not much later than me this morning, if the sound of the hairdryer coming through her bedroom door is any indication. I'm not sure why she bothered making herself look nice, because with a twelve-hour trip ahead of us, I'm sure we'll all come out the other side looking much less than stellar.

I nod as I swing the boot closed. 'Yep. And there's plenty of room for Sybil's and Freya's.'

'Okay. Soph and Rosie can put their bags in Darcy's car, anyway. Speaking of…'

I turn my head as Mum's words drift off, listening to the engine coming up the drive, and see Darcy's shiny Range Rover come into view, the same model as ours.

Mum lets out a squeal more appropriate for someone my age as Darcy climbs out of the car, and the two hug and let out more excited sounds. If I didn't know any better, I'd think they hadn't seen each other in years, and didn't live a mere ten miles from each other.

'Oh my god, I'm so excited!' Mum says.

'It's going to be so much fun!' Darcy agrees, pushing her dark hair behind her ears as her eyes go to me. She's taller and skinnier than Mum, the latter due to being a workout-addict, and is dressed for a yoga session or a long run. 'Hey, India!' she squeals, and I'm treated to a hug myself, which I return. Mum and Darcy were at boarding school together from the age of twelve, and have been best friends ever since. I've known Darcy since I was born, and she's as good as family. To my knowledge, she's never had a job, has been a stay-at-home wife since she got married right after university, but Darcy is razor-sharp, with a general knowledge that could trump most people, and a generous nature you wouldn't necessarily expect from someone who had her privileged upbringing.

If only the same qualities had reached her eldest daughter.

'Lottie,' Darcy calls. 'You going to come say hello?' Then to Mum, 'Where's Soph?'

'Still getting ready,' Mum says. 'You're okay with her and Rosie riding with you, yeah?'

'Yes, of course.' Darcy looks towards the car again, where I can see Lottie sitting in the front seat. Lottie is slightly older than

Sophia, and currently on a gap year. She's been riding and eventing for as long as I can remember, always on schoolmasters bought by her parents for a small fortune. While objectively I'd have to say she's a much better rider than Sophia, I'm still not sure she'd do so well if she weren't on such good horses. Then again, I'm sure everyone says the same about me. Lottie is a passenger, not a rider, but she gets away with it because she has nerves of steel and never doubts herself. But she is also precious and arrogant, and as nice as her mum and sister are, I hate having her around. She's supposed to be off to uni at the end of the year, but I'll believe it when I see it. To my knowledge, her sole ambition in life is to marry a Philippaerts twin.

'Where's Saffie?' says Mum.

Darcy laughs, crinkles appearing at the corners of her eyes. 'Fast asleep on the back seat. She'll probably sleep all the way to France.' Luckily Saffron takes after her mum, and she and Mia are far more enjoyable to be around than Sophia and Lottie. 'Who've you invited, Indi?'

'Sybil and Freya,' I say, though I'm not sure if she knows who they are.

'Oh, Freya who rides Leni's old pony?' Darcy asks, proving me wrong. 'That's great. And Sybil?'

'Sybil rides too,' I explain. 'She's based with Rose Holloway, down the road from Freya.'

Darcy looks at Mum, her face naively alight. 'This is brilliant, all you girls are going to be able to get along, then. Perfect.'

'I think I hear a car,' Mum says, looking towards the drive, and sure enough the sound increases, until a car I recognise as Maya's comes into view.

'DARCY!' Mia yells before the car has made it to the gravel in front of the house, appearing on the doorstep as she breaks into a sprint, running to embrace her godmother. 'Is Saffie here?'

'She's asleep,' Darcy says, smoothing back Mia's hair as the twelve-year-old wraps her arms around her waist.

'Don't go wake her,' Mum warns, which is probably exactly what my little sister was planning on doing. 'Can you go see if Sophia and Rosie are ready yet?'

'Why me?'

'Just go,' Mum says, and Mia turns back towards the house, calling Sophia's name as she runs, and Mum sighs at her impertinence.

'She's such a sweetie,' Darcy says adoringly.

'That's not the word I'd use,' I mumble, and Darcy responds by laughing.

Mum taps me on the arm. 'Make yourself useful and go help your friends with their bags.'

Water flies into the air as Maya's car rolls slowly across the gravel, and I start walking towards the vehicle, tightening my scarf around my neck. Maybe instead of the Alps we should just keep driving south to Spain and spend a week reclining on the beach, I think. I reckon we could reach the Gibraltar in twenty hours…

Nell is in the passenger seat, and both she and Maya are out of the car before their daughters.

'Morning, hon,' Maya says warmly, shouldering her bag. 'Not too much trouble getting up?'

'You kidding?' I say. 'Around here, we count ourselves lucky if we even get a chance to *go* to bed.'

Maya's eyes widen with interest. 'Really?'

I nod, watching as one of the car's back doors opens. 'My dad goes weeks without sleeping sometimes. I mean, he'll nap an hour here and there on the sofa, but that's it.'

'That's breeding season,' Mum says loudly, walking into the conversation with a smile on her face.

'I'll stick to the office side of racing,' Nell says, stepping closer. It's the first time I've ever seen her outside of a horse-related occasion, and she's dressed in smart work clothes very different from what she usually wears. 'Thank you so much for this, Caddie,' she goes on. 'Are you really sure this is okay?'

'Yes,' Maya chimes in, 'this is very kind of you.'

Mum waves them off. 'Of course. They're more than welcome. I'm sure I won't even see them.'

Maya starts unzipping her bag. 'And please let me cover all Sybil's expenses, and I can give you one of my cards in case of emergency -'

'No, no,' Mum says - to my relief, because I'm not sure either of Sybil and Freya's families can really afford mine's idea of a getaway. 'Absolutely not,' she goes on, 'they're guests. We invited them, it's all on us.' Her obsession with manners extends to herself, too.

'You're already doing enough,' Nell tells her, but Mum is adamant.

'No, Indiana has invited them.' I frown at the use of my full name, something she only does in front of other people. 'This is on us,' she repeats.

The three of them bounce the ball back and forth a few more times, but Mum won't so much as entertain the idea. Darcy comes up to us and introduces herself, which changes the topic, and as Sybil and Freya start climbing out of the car, I go to help them with their bags.

'We're all in the back of our car,' I tell them as we carry the bags to the boot. Both of their bags are small, much smaller than mine, Mum's, and Mia's, and there's plenty of space to spare. 'Sophia and Rosie are riding with Darcy, and Mia's in the passenger seat.'

'I'm so excited,' Sybil says as I swing the boot closed.

'Have you ever been skiing before?' I ask.

She nods. 'Once, but it was a while ago.'

I look at Freya. 'Have you?'

'Yeah, a few times with my cousins. I'm not sure how good I

am, though,' she says, though knowing Freya, I suspect that she'll be more than good.

'Sybil,' Maya calls. 'Did you get the pastries.'

Sybil doesn't reply, but instead sighs and walks back towards her car and opens the back door, grabbing a few paper bags from the middle seat.

'I figured nobody will have had any breakfast,' Maya says as Sybil approaches her and the other mums.

'Oh, you shouldn't have,' Mum says.

'THEY'RE COMING!' comes Mia's voice as she emerges from the house, a rucksack on her back.

Mum frowns at her. 'What are they doing?'

Mia comes to a standstill a few feet away, her face set in a look of feigned ignorance she is starting to master. 'How do I know?'

Maya, Nell, and Darcy chuckle, which was Mia's intention, and my little sister smiles triumphantly, while Mum looks less impressed.

'Can you put one of these bags in each car,' Mum says to Mia, gesturing at Sybil.

Mia starts walking again. 'What is it?'

Mum sighs through her nose. 'Sybil's mum has very kindly brought everyone breakfast.'

Mia's expression changes. 'Oh, yay!' And she takes the bags happily and peeks at the contents as she heads towards the two Range Rovers.

'I do try to feed her, I swear,' Mum jokes. 'She's got a sweet tooth. Such a fussy eater.'

'That reminds me,' says Nell, 'please don't worry about Freya. She's slightly picky, too, and she doesn't eat meat, but she'll sort herself out. Don't worry if she doesn't eat much, that's normal for her.'

'No problem,' Mum says. 'We tend to eat out in the day and not even bother cooking at the chalet, anyway, so you'll fit right in.'

'This is the best blueberry muffin I've ever had,' Mia announces seriously, walking back towards us with the pastry in one hand.

'Mia!' Mum scolds. 'Those were for the car!'

Mia shrugs. 'I'll have another one in the car, too. There are dozens.'

'Oh my god.' Mum shakes her head and turns to Maya. 'I'm so sorry.'

'Don't be silly, they're here to be eaten! And there *are* dozens,' she adds, glancing at Mia, who grins.

The front door slams as Sophia and Rosie appear on the doorstep, laden with suitcases.

'Finally,' Mum mutters.

Unlike Lottie, Rosie is really nice, and while she events a little, it's only a weekend hobby, and this past year she's been much more focussed on her A-levels. She's tall and freckly, with long, strawberry blond hair, and a permanent kind expression.

'Hello,' Sophia says, her smile wide and her voice polite, as though she weren't even capable of being the pain she is most of the time.

More greetings are exchanged, and Sophia and Rosie head to Darcy's car, where Lottie climbs out to greet them.

'Right,' Mum says. 'We'd better get this show on the road.'

Darcy walks over to her car, while Mia bounces along to ours, and Sybil and Freya say goodbye to their mums. Despite Mum's insistence earlier, I still notice Maya press a credit card into Sybil's hand, which she slides into her coat pocket.

'Are you sure you'll remember to take Leo and Izzy's rugs off?' Freya asks Nell, face serious, and I think, *Izzy?* Did Freya get a new horse I don't know about?

'I'll go back and do it before going to work,' her mum assures her.

'And give them another slice of hay each. They got two this

morning, but they'll need more.'

'Yes.'

'And you'll lunge him this evening?'

'As soon as I get back from work.'

'And remember Leo's only on half a scoop of feed now this week, so he's getting extra chaff.'

Nell gently pushes Freya towards me and Sybil. 'I know how to look after him. Go.'

Freya still looks apprehensive, but she walks away, towards our Range Rover.

'I'll make sure they touch base with you when we arrive,' I hear Mum tell Maya and Nell as I open the Range Rover's right back door. 'And text on the other side of the Tunnel. We have Wi-Fi in the chalet if you want to Skype…'

Sybil climbs into the back seat from the other side, sliding into the middle seat as Freya follows and pulls the door closed. I kick my rucksack to my feet, making room for Sybil's too, while Freya keeps hers on her lap.

'Who's Izzy?' I say.

'Have I not told you?' Freya says, and she goes on to tell me the story of her father bringing an old schoolmistress pony back from an auction because she was going to sell to the meat man, and I think I'd like her dad if ever I met him.

'Do any of you get carsick?' Mia asks, turning in the passenger seat to face us when Freya has finished talking, and my friends both shake their heads. 'Me neither,' she says proudly. 'Unlike Sophia.'

'Funny how Sophia's never carsick when she has a text to type,' I say. Somehow I suspect she won't be feeling carsick with Darcy, either. The bouts always seem to come on when she's in a bad mood and convinced Mum's taken a longer road just to annoy her.

'I've got my iPad,' Mia goes on, holding up the tablet as proof, pink earphones dangling from it. The case is turquoise with a big

Apple sticker stuck to the back of it. 'I've downloaded movies to watch on the way. What are you doing?'

'We don't need to *do* anything,' I mutter, pulling my seatbelt over my shoulder.

'Um, I've got a book,' Sybil responds to my sister.

'Me too,' Freya says.

Mia pulls a face. 'I don't really read.'

'Maybe you should,' I say, 'you'd be smarter.'

'You don't read, either!'

Which is true. Other than books for school, the last thing I read was the Racing Post. Dad doesn't have time to read, Mum only owns books by Jilly Cooper or Jane Austen, and the sole bookworm of the family is Sophia, who has shelves full of those sentimental teen romances where you can guarantee one of the main characters dies.

'I'm already smart enough,' I retort, and Mia pulls a face at me before turning back in her seat as Mum opens the door to the driver's side.

'All sorted?'

'Yep,' all four of us mutter.

Mum settles in her seat and secures her seatbelt before looking back at us all in turn. 'All right. Let's go.'

It takes two hours to drive to the Tunnel. She might have downloaded movies for the journey, but Mia sure doesn't watch any of them.

'How old are you? Are you fourteen like India? I'm twelve, but I'll be thirteen this year. Did you know my middle name is Isabella? What's yours?'

'You can ignore her, you know,' I say, resting my head against the window.

'Eloise,' Sybil says unsurely.

'Oh, my sister's called Eloise,' Mum comments.

I straighten in time to see Mia fix her gaze on Freya. 'And you?'

'Mia,' Mum says, 'Sybil and Freya might like to sleep.'

'Um, I have two,' Freya answers Mia. 'Aoife Elizabeth.'

'Sophia's middle name is Elizabeth, too!' Mia says. 'And Mum's.'

'And Lottie's,' I say.

'And Rosie's,' Mum adds. 'Darcy is Darcy Elizabeth, too.'

'Does every girl in England just get Elizabeth as a middle name?' I say.

'Well, it's often a family name,' Mum says reasonably. 'I think most families have had an Elizabeth at some point.' She looks at Freya in the rear-view mirror. 'Are you named after a family member?'

Freya nods. 'I have grandmothers called Aoife and Elizabeth.'

Mum holds a hand out towards Mia, keeping her eyes on the road. 'There you go.'

'My mum's middle name's Elizabeth,' Sybil says. 'It's Rose's middle name, too.' She pauses. 'And Mackenzie's. You're right, almost everyone has it as a middle name.'

'It's a very nice name,' Mum says.

'Hey, it's-' I stop myself just in time, and luckily no one seems to notice. I was going to say, *It's Alex's middle name, too,* but I've learned not to bring Alex up, even though Sophia isn't here. Knowing the middle name of my sister's enemy-of-sorts would just lead to questions.

'Didn't you breed a horse called Mia Isabella?' Freya says.

'Yeah, one of Bubble's,' I say. 'We had horses named after each of us, but Sophia Elizabeth and Indiana May were both useless.'

'Uh, no.' Mum meets my eyes in the rear-view mirror and smirks. 'Tell the truth.'

'That *is* the truth.'

'The *whole* truth.' Mum shakes her head, taking the story into her own hands. 'Sophia Elizabeth was useless, granted, but the trainer we sent Indiana May to said she was, I quote, the most stubborn creature he'd ever had in his yard.'

'She was perfectly fine with us,' I grumble.

'Uh-huh,' Mum singsongs.

'While we're on the subject of names,' I say, swiftly changing the subject as I glare at Mum in the front seat, 'I'm not really sure what the point of calling me India*na* and not just India was.'

'It's a lovely name,' Mum says defensively. 'It's only natural to shorten it to India. And India is getting so common now. When I was in the hospital with you, two other people on the same floor called their daughters India the day you were born alone.'

'Uh-huh,' I mutter. 'And it's also because my great-grandmother was called Diana, and you liked the name India anyway.'

'Well, you know what they say - two birds, one stone.' Mum's stomach chooses this moment to growl loudly, and she utters an apology. 'I forgot to eat this morning,' she comments. 'I'll get something at the Tunnel.'

'There are loads of pastries left if you'd like one,' Sybil speaks up, grabbing the paper bag from her feet.

'Oh, no, that's okay,' Mum starts to say, but Mia interrupts.

'They're *so* good. You have to have one.'

'I don't have the greatest sweet tooth...'

'You love almonds,' Mia says, taking the bag from Sybil, and pulling out an almond croissant. 'You don't have to eat it all.'

Mum glances quickly at Mia, keeping her hands on the steering wheel. 'Well, maybe a bite or two.'

She eats two croissants before we reach Folkestone.

The crossing takes half an hour, during which Sybil and Freya look green at the thought of being in a train under the sea, but it isn't long until we're driving off the container in Calais, on the other side of the Channel.

'Woo-hoo, we're in France,' Mia sings.

Mum and Darcy have been following each other, and after driving for a couple of hours on the other side, we stop at a petrol station near Saint-Quentin to buy sandwiches and stretch our legs. We don't stop for long, and soon we're driving again, and we keep going all the way to Lyon before another pit stop. The earlier excitement is wearing off, and we've been driving in silence now, Mia falling asleep with her iPad in her lap, me with my head against the window, and every time I've looked up, both Freya and Sybil have been reading - Freya a book with a horse on the cover, and Sybil a thick fantasy volume I would only ever own to use as a doorstop.

It's some hours into the trip that I realise I've forgotten my iPad, which has software installed on it to watch the foal cameras, and when I say this to Mum, my voice panicked at the thought of missing Pearl foal, should she do so while I'm away, she's immediately dismissive.

'You're on holiday with your friends. You're not spending the whole time staring at video footage of horses. The whole point of this trip is to get *away* from horses.'

I stay awake after the pit stop in Lyon, eyes out the window. It's getting dark, and I barely see the mountains as we drive up them, the road ascending and twisty, which is probably a good thing because there's something awfully disconcerting about a possible plummet to an untimely death. It's only been a year or two since our last visit, but I can't remember the way. In fact I'm convinced there's a jinx on the place, something that prevents visitors from knowing the layout without being in it, because I never get lost once we arrive, but can never picture it when I'm away.

'Finally,' Mum says with a sigh, turning off the village road and into a driveway. Behind us, Darcy's headlights follow.

Mia looks at her iPad. 'Is it seven or eight o'clock here?'

'Half-eight, I think,' Mum says, opening her door. 'Delphine should be here, so I'll go see what's going on.' She looks at me. 'Look after your guests, India.'

I roll my eyes and mutter, 'Obviously,' as Mum climbs out of the car, Mia running behind her. I turn to Freya and Sybil as I unfasten my seatbelt. 'Right, so, this it it.'

We climb out of the Range Rover, stepping into the dark, snow-covered world. Freya or Sybil - maybe both? - gasps beside me, and I try to stare at the house with a fresh eye, try to take it in as though it were the first time I'm seeing it.

It's a three-storey building, set back from the road. The chalet is a quintessential chalet - wooden, with balconies, and decorative fretwork fascia. All the lights are on, and I can make out furniture through the glass doors on the top floor. As Mum said, Delphine, who maintains the chalet year-round, will be here.

Only the lower floor of the building is built of blocks, not being part of the house. It's where all the skiing equipment is kept, and also boasts a gym and sauna.

'This is your house?' Sybil says in disbelief.

'It's the family's,' I say defensively. 'It *was* my grandparents', but they gave it to Mum and her sister because they don't travel much anymore.' I turn back to the car, towards the boot. 'Shall we put our stuff in our room, then I'll show you around?'

We lift all our bags from the boot, as everyone in Darcy's car starts doing the same, but Freya, Sybil, and I make it to the house first, through the door on the lower floor that opens into a foyer.

'Mum'll be upstairs,' I say, stepping towards the back wall and pressing a button, and I turn around when I sense neither of my friends moving. 'What?'

'You have an elevator?' Freya says. Unlike Sybil, who seems excited by the scale of the chalet, Freya looks threatened by it, and tugs awkwardly at one of her sleeves.

I turn back to the wall, facing the metal elevator door and the button beside it. 'The kitchen's on the top floor,' I explain, feeling defensive again. There's a ding, and the door opens into the elevator. 'You coming? Before we have to share.'

Carrying their bags, Sybil and Freya follow me into the elevator, and I hit the button *1,* which takes us to the bedroom floor.

'Have you ever seen the film *Chalet Girl?*' Sybil asks me as we wait to reach the next storey.

I nod and grin, thinking of the extravagant family and chalet in the movie. 'What, you think this is like that? We don't have any Picasso paintings hanging on the walls, mind.'

'Oh, no,' Sybil says as the elevator door opens up on the first floor landing, where lush rugs cover a waxed wooden floor, and every bedroom door has heart-shaped carvings in the panels. 'This is *way* better.'

chapter 11

I wake up with a smile on my face, remembering where I am. I sit up slowly and glance across the room, at Freya and Sybil still asleep in the other bunk beds. The beds are built into the walls, with delicately-carved wooden fronts painted light blue, and each mattress is decked with a patchwork quilt.

Before sitting up, I reach for my phone on the ledge behind my pillow, checking for messages. Nothing. I let out a breath. I told Dad to let me know if ever Pearl foals while I'm away, and no news means the mare is listening to my instructions and holding on until I get back.

It's still dark out, the window panes fogged with condensation, and even though it's impossible, I swear I can smell the snow that lies beyond.

'These beds are so comfortable,' Sybil says when I come out of the bathroom ten minutes later. She's leaning back against the wall of her bed, while Freya is pulling jeans from her suitcase.

'Everyone says that,' I say to Sybil as Freya carries her clothes into the bathroom. 'Mum's a bit obsessed when it comes to bedding, and she spends a fortune on it. Seems ridiculous when we're only here one week of the year,' I add, wondering if my earlier comment was insensitive.

Sybil smiles, clearly not fazed. 'Trust me, it's worth it.'

I wait for Sybil and Freya to change before heading upstairs, in case they worry about using the elevator, which has happened with other guests in the past, to my bemusement. My cousins on Mum's side came here loads when we were younger, and you could always guarantee that whoever was youngest that year would get stranded on the bedroom floor at least once, and someone would find them sobbing in front of the elevator doors.

We're the first up, and I waste no time in raiding the cupboards for breakfast.

'We get first dibs on everything,' I say happily, carrying cereal and croissants to the table. The top floor is all open-plan, with the elevator coming out into the kitchen, an area with wide counters in the corner of the room, modern appliances, and windows that look out onto the village backdropped by snow-covered mountains. There's a dining table on the other side of the elevator door, complete with designer chairs with legs made to look like the Eiffel tower, and paintings on the walls. The sitting area takes up the whole other half of the floor, at the front of the house, with sofas arranged around a flat-screen TV in one corner, and a separate snug in another, around a coffee table we usually reserve for puzzles and games. Windows run along the front of the house, with double doors that open out onto the balcony.

In conditions like this, when the outside world is covered in snow, and you come inside with icy toes, often soaked through, there's something ridiculously satisfying about living on the top floor of a building, with no connection to the outside world. Like living in a bubble inside a snow globe.

'Morning, girls,' Mum says, coming out of the elevator ten minutes after we sit down. I'm moving on to a second bowl of cereal, and Sybil a croissant, while Freya is still eating her first slice of toast. 'Sleep well?'

'Really well, thanks,' Freya says, putting down her slice of Marmite toast - Delphine is convinced that all Brits live on Marmite, and always fills the cupboards with jars of the stuff when we come to visit. Though despite her polite voice, I can't help but think Freya looks slightly uncomfortable, glancing around the pristine floor as though elements of it could shatter if she made a wrong movement, and I hope I can make her feel more at ease before the trip ends.

'That's the most comfortable bed I've ever slept in,' Sybil says.

Mum perks up immediately. 'Isn't it? Arthur thinks I'm silly, but I got all the bedding shipped over from this place in London, and it is just *divine.*' She eyes up the items on the table. 'Have you found enough to eat? Delphine said she'd shopped with all of you in mind.'

'There's loads,' I assure her, pulling up my sleeve to check the time. 'Can we go off on our own?'

Mum walks to the kitchen, the heels of her ankle boots tapping against the floor, and switches on the coffee machine. 'Lifts don't open for an hour yet.'

'I know, but we still need to get stuff together. Can the three of us go off on our own?' I repeat.

'If you stick together,' Mum says. 'The older girls will probably want to go off, too, and Mia and Saffie are going with Christophe,' she adds, referring to the private ski instructor who taught all three of us to ski. This is the first year I'm not being made to remain under his watchful eye, and I'm way too excited about it. 'I don't know what we've got downstairs anymore, but I think we should have enough skis and boots, but you'll obviously have to go get helmets from the rental place.'

'Okay.'

'And we'll all meet at *Chalet de Pierres* at twelve.'

After breakfast, I take Freya and Sybil down to the ground floor, where we go into the garage. Skis hang on the walls, boots lined up below, and the cupboards are overflowing with snowsuits. Sizing is generous both ways, and it isn't hard to find things that fit each of us reasonably well, and we manage to get out the chalet before anyone else turns up.

'So how long does it take to get to the lifts?' Sybil asks as we walk through the village.

I shake my head. 'Not long. Five minutes to walk there, maybe.' I point behind me, the opposite direction to where we're heading. 'It's down there, just keep walking. The rental place is in the village, though.'

The ski rental shop is just opening when we get there, and finding helmets that fit is a quick process, due mainly to the three of us being more than familiar with hat sizing thanks to riding, and while my French is limited, I understand the person working in the shop when he expresses his amazement at all of us knowing our exact hat size, as though it were a special skill we should boast about on resumés in future.

'Don't we need to pay?' Freya asks as I start walking out of the shop, and I spin around to see her and Sybil unzipping their snowsuits to get to the pockets underneath.

'No, I've done it. I gave them the chalet name,' I explain. 'That's what you do in shops. You tell them which chalet is yours and they add it to the tab.'

It's ten to nine when we get to the lifts, and there are already people queuing, as eager as we are to get going. Shetland ponies line the mountain foothills, tacked up for rides, and we fuss over them while we wait for the resort to come to life, my eyes searching for the loyal skewbald I always rode when I was little. For years I'd choose to go on pony rides over skiing, before I got my own pony to ride, after which I stopped being so stubborn and decided I could at least *consider* skiing, which feels like a lifetime ago now. The skewbald Shetland was still here the last time we visited, but I can't see him as I search the row of tied-up ponies.

'Shall we start on the carpet lift on the beginners' slope?' I say to my friends, turning away from the horses. 'We can practise there and then if you're comfortable we can take a ski lift and go higher.'

Skiing is like riding a bike, because even if you go a year without seeing the slopes, you pick it up again in an instant. The carpet lift is a bit like one you get in an airport, except this one moves uphill. I knew before coming here, even without Mum warning me, that Freya and Sybil wouldn't be up to the same skiing level as my sisters and me, and that I'd be sticking to easier runs this week, but after three descents from the carpet, I'm less sure.

As I suspected, Freya is more than good. I can't say she skis as well as she rides, because she rides pretty damn well, but she certainly *could* if she spent as much time in the mountains as she does in the saddle. Sybil's skied before too, more times than Freya, and it's not even ten a.m. when we head to queue for the lifts.

The rush of skiing down a mountain, of gliding across the snow, the fresh air in your face, is almost as thrilling as riding a cross country course. Same adrenalin, same exhilaration, same steady balance and undivided focus. And I think that, for once, Sophia had a point in insisting we come here for the holidays.

Following Mum's instructions, we ski to *Le Chalet de Pierres* at lunchtime, where she, Darcy, Mia, and Saffron are already seated outside, basking in the sun. *Le Chalet de Pierres* is known for its desserts and pastries, and we all take great joy in browsing the huge buffet outside and selecting delicacies, which we wash down with hot beverages before setting off for another round of skiing. Lifts close around four, and that's when we start walking home, carrying skis and helmets through the village. All equipment is dumped in the garage, snowsuits wet from the snow hung up to dry, and we go up into the warm house, with the wooden walls and the soft furnishings, and life is good.

Over the next few days, we settle into a routine. Every day is the same in the best possible way - get up, eat, breakfast, ski. It's as simple as that. Though every day we go higher in the mountains, venturing down more difficult runs. We stay up late in the evening, rarely in bed before midnight, demolishing snacks while we play a game of poker.

At the beginning of the trip, even though I considered Sybil and Freya friends, I couldn't have said I really knew that much about them outside of horses, but that's no longer the case. I know Sybil's parents are divorced and that who she calls her dad isn't really her dad; I know that not only does she love fantasy novels, but her neighbour is a reclusive bestselling author and that she and her brother frequently pay him visits; I know that she only considers riding a hobby, and while she'd love to ride in a one-star, she doesn't see herself going any higher. Freya starts off even shier and quieter than usually, like she's uncomfortable and overwhelmed by the grandeur of the chalet, but after a couple of days she's a different person from the one that arrived. She's actually got a sharp tongue, quick to reply and catch on to things, and stronger-willed than I thought; she's far more concerned about the horses at home than either me or Sybil is; and to my surprise, she's got a big sense of humour, which I discovered when we were all watching a movie in which Freya noted an inaccuracy, and she had us all in stitches as she pointed out everything that didn't make sense, and mimicked the characters.

Tuesday morning we all go skiing as usual, and my friends and I tackle our first red piste of the week, which leaves us all exhilarated. We set off for England early tomorrow morning, and it was suggested at breakfast this morning, by Mum and Darcy, that we all head back to the chalet after lunch today to have a quiet afternoon and rest before the long drive tomorrow. Skiing isn't quite as exciting as cross country, but it's just as exhausting, especially after a rush of adrenalin wears off, and we are all happy to head inside after our red run, and spend the afternoon on the sofa, watching movies.

'India,' Mum says to me that evening. The sun has not yet set but the sky is grey, and the warmth inside the chalet has steamed up the windows. 'Come here a sec.'

Mia and Saffron have been watching movies with us, and I leave Freya and Sybil with them as I excuse myself to meet Mum on the other side of the room. 'Yeah?'

She stands with one hand on a kitchen counter, wearing a polo neck sweater despite the heat inside. Directly under a spot, her pearl earrings reflect the light as though they were illuminated as she looks at me, and I think of Pearl at home, relieved we've made it to the end of the week without her foaling. 'Darcy and I wanted to pop into town,' she says. 'Our last night, we were going to go have a drink of red and a fondue.'

I nod, glancing quickly at the sofa to check that neither of my friends overhead that. I'm sure more middle class sentences exist, but I can't think of one right now. 'O-kay…'

'Are you all right to keep an eye on Mia and Saffie?'

'Where's Soph going?'

'She's here, too,' Mum clarifies, 'but she's busy with her friends.'

And what am I? I think, but I don't say it. I can't even pretend to mind keeping an eye on Mia and Saffron, because it's such a small thing that it isn't worth arguing on principle. 'They don't exactly need babysitting.'

'No, I know, but I was just checking that was okay.'

'Of course.'

Mum smiles, and kisses the side of my head - this must be some drink she and Darcy are going to get. Then again, the cheese is pretty fantastic, too. 'Thank you. There's plenty of food, and it all needs eating.'

'Okay.'

'You can cook some pasta or something.'

'Yes, I'm sure we'll manage not to burn the place down,' I say drily.

Mum frowns. 'Huh?'

'Nothing,' I say. 'We'll be fine.'

'I'm so full,' Mia complains, rolling off the sofa and onto the carpet, flopping onto her stomach with a thud louder than you'd think her small body capable of making.

'I think what you mean to say is, *Thank you, India, for making us all dinner,*' I say.

Mia pushes herself up with her hands. 'It's not like you had to do anything! You just opened a packet.'

'And boiled the water,' Freya points out from her spot on one of the Eames lounge chairs, but I can hear her voice is laced with sarcasm.

'She also had to put the empty pasta packets in the recycling bin,' Sybil says to Mia, glancing at Freya, and they all snicker.

'See, now you're just mocking me. You know what?' I say, holding up my hands. 'I'm never cooking you all dinner ever again, so there.'

'Thank God for that,' Mia says, relishing in causing my friends to laugh.

'I thought it was good!'

'Thank you, Saffie,' I say to my little sister's friend, carefully enunciating each word. I shuffle up to the dark-haired girl on the sofa and wrap an arm around her shoulders. 'See? *Someone* knows how to show some appreciation.'

Freya smiles. 'I'm kidding, it was nice.'

'It was a bit chewy,' Mia mutters.

'That's how it's supposed to be,' I snap. Admittedly I didn't check the cooking time on the ravioli packaging until *after* it had already been simmering in the boiling water for four minutes, and found that it was only supposed to be cooked for two. Coated in olive oil and Parmesan, it was still perfectly edible. 'And you still ate it all.'

'I know,' Mia groans, holding her side. 'Are you sure we shouldn't have left some for the others?'

'Sophia's perfectly capable of cooking pasta,' I say. 'There's two packets in the fridge if they want some.'

Sybil glances towards the elevator. 'What do you think they're doing?'

I shrug. 'Don't know, don't care.'

With *Chalet Girl* on the TV - for the second time since we've been here - we chatter among ourselves, all going silent only whenever one of the funniest lines comes up.

'*I want to be a profiterole,*' Mia recites. 'I really want a profiterole now. Do we have any?'

'No,' I say.

'Aw.'

I look over my shoulder, at the kitchen cupboards, and stand up. 'Hey, what about Oreos?'

Delphine obviously remembered how much my sisters and I like Oreos, because there were half a dozen packets in the cupboard, and the five of us now have finished a second packet between us all when the elevator door opens and Sophia, Lottie, and Rosie step out.

'You're watching that film *again?*' Sophia says derisively.

Mia turns in her seat, hands clutched around a half-empty glass of milk with Oreo crumbs stuck to the inside. 'Because it's the best.'

Sophia raises her eyebrows and heads towards the kitchen. 'Uh-huh.'

'It's a good film,' Rosie says, walking up to us, and I shuffle closer to Saffron to make room for her on the sofa.

'What were you guys doing?' I ask her.

'Just hanging out,' Rosie says, eyes on the TV. 'I did some

revising, and Lottie and Soph were just chilling.'

Knowing Lottie and Sophia, I can easily imagine them sitting in a room for hours without looking up from their phones, either checking social media accounts or reading up on celebrity gossip, and the thought of doing so myself bores me stiff. Not that I could be in this Alpine snow globe and focus on schoolwork, either. How Rosie is such good friends with my sister and Lottie baffles me.

'We were tired from working out,' Lottie says, and I wonder if exercising, repeating movements in a room again and again, is even more boring than doing nothing at all. 'Where're Mum and Cads?' she asks.

'They went out,' Saffron tells her sister.

'They said they'd be back by ten,' I add.

Sophia opens and closes the fridge before walking to the kitchen counter nearest the sitting area. 'What're we supposed to have for dinner?'

'Well *we* have already eaten,' I say irritatedly, 'but there's plenty of food in if *you* want something to eat.'

'Why didn't you make dinner for us?'

'Why *should* I?' I snap back.

'Quit being such a baby,' Sophia mutters, turning back to the fridge. Responses bubble up inside me, but I force myself to keep a lid on them, not to start an argument. She glances to her right to look at Lottie. 'What do you want to eat?'

Lottie walks farther into the kitchen, newly-blond hair poker straight. 'Who needs food?'

Sophia laughs like it's the funniest thing she's ever heard, and I groan internally.

Lottie stands on her tiptoes to open an overhead cupboard, letting out a small sound of triumph as she finds what she has in mind. 'Bingo.'

Sophia giggles. 'Yes!'

I watch Lottie put the full bottle of liqueur down on the counter, and Sophia opens the mug cupboard. 'Rosie? Want some?'

Rosie looks over her shoulder, expression changing as she sees what Sophia and Lottie are up to. 'Um, no, I'm all right, thanks.'

Something in Rosie's voice must make Mia suspicious, because she stands up from her spot on the carpet to see what our sister is doing. 'Are you allowed that?'

'Of course,' Lottie says easily.

'But don't you dare tell Mum,' Sophia adds. Neither of our parents would think twice about any of us having a glass of wine or champagne in their presence, be it at Christmas or with a Sunday roast, but I'm not sure Mum would approve of Sophia raiding her liqueur cabinet in front of her friends while she's away, if only because it makes her look bad. Or more to the point, I don't think Darcy would approve of Lottie doing so.

'Mum doesn't allow that,' Saffron says, watching her sister.

'Mum's not here,' Lottie snaps. 'And I'm eighteen, it's not like I'm not allowed. Caddie won't mind.'

'Don't say anything,' Sophia warns Mia and Saffron again.

'Don't make them lie for you,' I say, anger rising.

Sophia glares at me with a look I can only imagine is disgust at the thought of us being related. 'Don't be such a telltale. Besides, it's not like Mum would care.'

'Darcy would,' I counter. 'And if it's fine with them,' I say levelly, 'then why do you need us all to cover for you?'

Sophia blows out a breath and smiles faintly as Lottie pours the spirit into mugs. I can imagine Mum and Darcy walking in in a few minutes and seeing their daughters clutching mugs without thinking they were full with anything but tea, and understand the cup choice. 'Tell you what,' she says, ignoring me and moving over to the sitting area with a mug in one hand, her eyes on Mia and Saffron. 'I'll give you each five quid if you don't mention this.'

'Done!' Mia says triumphantly.

Sophia smiles again. 'Great.' Her eyes drift to me, and the smile fades.

'All right,' Lottie says happily, putting the bottle back where she found it and coming over to us to settle on a spare chair. She and Sophia might be jolly, but the mood has turned sour for the rest of us. 'This is more like it. We should play a game!'

'We were actually watching a movie,' I point out.

Sophia scoffs, and hits the mute button on the remote. 'You've seen it a million times, I think you know how it ends.' She looks at Lottie. 'What shall we play?'

'We could play Pictionary!' Mia chimes in, and I almost throttle my older sister and her friend for the laughters that follow.

'Not *that* kind of game,' Lottie says.

Sophia lifts a shoulder. 'Poker?'

'Nah, I haven't got any cash.' I glance quickly at my two friends, thinking we were more than happy to play the game all week with nothing at stake, then stare down at my lap while Lottie looks at Rosie. 'Any ideas?'

Rosie shakes her head and says, 'No,' but it's obvious she hasn't put any thought into the question.

'We could just do a Truth or Dare,' Lottie says, stretching out the sentence so that it reaches everyone around the coffee table, and I realise none of us is getting out of this.

Sophia takes a swig from her mug before speaking. 'Who wants to start?'

'I will,' says Lottie. 'Someone dare me to do something.'

My friends and I keep quiet while those around us proceed to set and take on dares. Truth or Dare is such a harmless game in theory, because surely neither option can amount to anything dire under normal circumstances. So far, the dares are harmless. Stand barefoot on the balcony for sixty seconds, prank call a random number from the French phone book. And as people start picking Truths, these are no more dangerous, either. Celebrity crushes, embarrassing memories, greatest unfulfilled wish.

'I want to give someone a dare or a question,' Mia says, biting into an Oreo, face alight as she falls deeper into the excitement of the game.

'India hasn't gone yet,' says Lottie, eyes falling on me. Her slender fingers are wrapped around the mug of liqueur, and I focus on the turquoise of her nails as they tap against the white china, the nail polish the same colour as her FitBit.

Mia looks at me. 'India. Truth or Dare?'

I sigh, still not really wanting to play this game, but I'm sitting here, and even Freya and Sybil look like they're enjoying themselves now. 'Truth?'

From the look on her face, Mia was hoping I'd ask for a dare, but she comes up with a question in little time. 'Who's the best rider in the room?'

Sophia and Lottie groan at the question, clearly hoping for something juicier, but my answer is immediate. 'Freya.'

Lottie swivels in her seat, her eyes darting to Freya in the armchair across from her, as though only just noticing her. 'What level do you compete at?'

'Just Novice,' Freya says, looking away as she speaks quietly, sounding shy, the way she was the first few days she was here.

'Oh,' Lottie says, looking reassured. I wondered for a second if my saying Freya was inconsiderate to Sybil, but in fairness she's only going around 90 tracks, and I'm sure that had she been asked the same question, she would have answered *Freya,* too. I didn't expect Lottie to take offence, because I forgot about her inflated ego. 'Well, that's a good start, I guess.' She looks around the room. 'Am I the only one here who's gone round an Intermediate?' she asks naively.

'The level you ride at doesn't necessarily dictate who's the best rider,' I say icily.

Lottie frowns. 'Oh, I'm sorry, I thought that was the point of a competition?'

'Stop being such a brat,' Sophia snaps at me, voice even meaner than usual.

'You ride Leni's old pony, right?' Lottie goes on, speaking to Freya. She really mustn't have looked at either of my friends twice before now to only just be making the connection.

Freya nods, lips pressed together.

'I know Leni, you know, because she works for Amanda, who I have lessons with. Leni had already sold Leo to Olivia when she started working for her, though. Amanda Walton,' Lottie adds, as though there could be any question as to which Amanda she's referring to.

'She's a piece of work,' says Sophia. 'Amanda,' she adds, shooting Freya an apologetic glance, as though insulting somebody who has ridden her pony would be an insult to her, too. 'Not Leni, I don't know Leni. Though she's Alex's best friend, so I can imagine exactly what she's like...'

'Well, you're wrong,' I say loudly, standing up. Already I have a sense of foreboding, a premonition that these past years of frustration, of bottling my words and never confronting Sophia, are about to come to fruition, but I hope I'm wrong. 'You've never met her, so don't judge.'

Sophia holds her hands up. 'Geez, chill. I just said I don't know her, didn't I? Last I checked, neither do you.'

'Wait,' says Lottie, 'India knows Leni, don't you?' Her eyes find mine, and I will her to shut up, but she doesn't, and she smiles her too-white smile. 'I saw you chatting to her at an event a few weeks ago. With Alex.'

I lift a shoulder noncommittally and start pacing the room, on the other side of the sofas, looking for something to do that isn't obvious. Why is this place so tidy? I can't even clean in desperation. If it weren't for my friends sitting here, I'd walk away. 'I've met her a couple times.'

Lottie doesn't stop. 'You and Alex looked very chummy, I must say. I was a bit surprised, really, seeing as I thought she hated you all.'

'Since when are you friends with Alex Evans?' Sophia asks with disgust, and I'm surprised this is the first she's heard of it. I'd have expected Lottie to blab anything she considered to be good gossip immediately, if she really did see me that day.

Don't pick a fight, I remind myself. There's still time to pull the plug on this before it becomes an issue. 'I'm not *friends* with her,' I say cautiously. 'She's, like, seven years older than me. It's called being nice, you should try it.'

Sophia glares at me, and opens her mouth to respond, but Rosie cuts in before she can.

'Hey, guys, come on, let's not turn our last night here into a fight.'

'No one's fighting,' Lottie replies, looking very at ease, and I wonder if she thrives off causing trouble. 'We're just playing Truth.'

'I thought we were playing Truth or Dare,' says Saffron.

'We *were,*' Lottie says, 'but I think we should just stick to Truths. There are only so many dares you can do, anyway. Who wants to-'

'Since when are you friendly with Alex Evans?' Sophia interrupts, voice loud and strained, and I know, even more surely, that this conversation is not going to go unresolved tonight.

'I don't know,' I lie, still pacing. At this rate, I'm going to wear a track in the carpet. 'We're not friendly, we just say hello to each other at events.' Another lie.

'She's such a bitchy cow,' Sophia mutters. 'I can't stand her.'

The next sentence comes out before I can stop it. 'Trust me, the feeling's mutual.'

Sophia slams her mug down on a side table with lightning speed. 'What is *that* supposed to mean?'

'Nothing,' I mutter, as Rosie makes another attempt to shut down the argument, and Freya squirms in her seat, but Sophia keeps going.

'What, do you both bitch about me or something?'

'Don't be stupid.'

'Oh, so now I'm stupid?'

'What you're *saying* is stupid.'

'Hey, guys, come on-'

'All Alex did was blame me for Otto not going well-'

'BECAUSE IT WAS ALL YOUR FAULT!' I pause, both speaking and my pacing, surprised by how loud my voice came out, and keep going before I lose the nerve. 'It's your fault Otto started stopping, just as it's your fault Fendi started stopping, and now the same thing's happening with Mason, too! It's *your* fault all these horses go wrong, nobody else's! And you know why? Because you can't ride to save your own life, and you never will be able to because you won't take criticism. Everyone - me, Mum, Merritt - steps on eggshells around you to protect your precious ego, and you know what? I'm done. All you do is sit around, you never look after your horses, and then you get on and expect to know everything, expect everything to work like clockwork without having to lift a finger. You can't ride, and you won't *learn* to, and nobody dares say that because then you'll just go and have a meltdown. So, yes, to answer your earlier question, Alex and I are somewhat friends, because I spoke to her at the beginning of last season and asked for help, because, unlike you, *she* could ride Otto very well, and she had a right to be pissed that you wrecked him. Mum and Dad have spent hundreds of thousands on horsepower for you, and it's still not enough. And you have no one to blame but yourself.'

I blow out a breath, heart racing.

There.

I said it. Finally.

And I don't feel relieved, don't feel like a weight has been lifted.

I feel just as awful as I always knew I would.

Sophia grits her teeth. Her eyes never left mine while I spoke, and they're still open wide, irises glassed over with tears, and I feel like a load of poison has just been dumped in my head.

'Well, then,' Sophia says levelly, standing up. 'I hope you're happy.' And she walks away, towards the elevator, Lottie and Rosie jumping up to follow her.

I stare down at the floor, at my sock-clad feet standing on the plush carpet, and try to release a breath, but it catches in my throat.

Nothing good ever comes from playing Truth or Dare.

chapter 12

I don't see Sophia again that evening, and the next morning we each climb into our separate rides without so much as glancing at each other. Luckily Mum doesn't seem to have noticed anything being up, though she looks a little preoccupied, which I put down to the late night. I'm just grateful, and hope Mia has the common sense to keep her mouth shut during the twelve-hour trip.

Like all drives, the journey doesn't feel so long on the way back as it did the way here. My body is heavy with guilt, never giving my head room to think, and I don't let myself believe I'll succeed in dozing off, so I'm surprised when I open my eyes to see signs for the Eurotunnel out of the window, when we were hours away last time I checked.

The car is stationary in a queue, and beside me, Freya and Sybil are both asleep, as is Mia in the passenger seat. I straighten up, my neck aching from being at a ninety degree angle since Lyon. The weight of guilt is still inside me, and I wish I could take the words back, but I can't. Maybe it's for the best, to finally have it in the open. After all, Sophia isn't stupid, she must have known full well what everyone thought - thinks, even. What I said isn't exactly a revelation, and now we can stop tiptoeing around each other.

'You okay?' Mum asks quietly, and I look up to meet her eyes in the rear-view mirror.

I nod.

'You know,' she goes on, voice soft, 'I didn't think about it on the drive down, but I just realised the Jungle's gone.'

I snap my head to look out the window, which is stupid because I know we've passed the location anyway, but I'm still surprised to not see it.

The Calais Jungle.

Like everyone, I'd seen and heard about it on the news, yet it had never occurred to me we'd pass it when we drove through Calais ourselves on our last skiing holiday. It was just words and pictures before that, seen in newspapers passed through the letter box, the sort of horror story always so prominent in the news that, as awful as it is to say, I'd stopped paying attention, as though it were something happening in another world and didn't require thinking about. Except it wasn't, because there it was, in front of me. And it was awful. A couple of times before, we'd stopped in the centre of Calais for a drink or a bite to eat, and the town alone freaked me out. It's not unordinary, arguably a town like any other, with large industrial ports, but there is something eerie about it. A feeling that everyone who comes is passing through, that it's only temporary, except that's where things get creepy, because it isn't. People live there year-round, people call it home. But to me, it's a ghost town, the kind of place you could set a horror movie.

And then I saw the Jungle. I'd only heard it spoken about with displeasure, refugees causing trouble by staying there, but as soon as I saw it I realised, for the first time, that nobody would have been there unless it was their last hope.

We only drove past. I might have only seen the wide layout of plastic tents behind fencing for ten seconds, but it was enough to make me feel ill all the way to Courchevel, where we stayed in luxurious accommodation - our *second* luxury accommodation -

when these other people would have probably given anything for a single room.

'I forgot, too,' I say, staring out the window at the cars around us, all queuing to get to the Tunnel.

And while the thought of what I said to Sophia still hangs in my chest, and I still wish I could take it back, I feel more at peace. Escaping war and living in a refugee camp is a real problem; a wounded ego is not.

Sybil and Freya text their mums when we're half an hour from home, and when our car rolls up to the house, Darcy following, Maya and Nell are already here. It's not night-time, but it's almost dark, the sky turning cobalt blue.

There are hugs and too many thank-yous to count, and if it were earlier, I'm sure Maya and Nell would stay a while, listening to stories of the trip, but as it is we're all tired, and my friends are on their way home in little time, as are Darcy, Lottie, and Saffron. Rosie's being picked up tonight, too, but clearly her parents are less punctual. I'm quite happy to have her around, because so long as she's here, she's with Sophia, and the two of us can avoid another bust-up.

'I'm going to run see the horses,' I say as soon as Darcy's car pulls out of its parking space.

'No,' Mum says as she walks up the steps to the front door, 'come inside for a bit.' I frown at her, because she doesn't usually forbid me from doing anything, but she insists. 'At least carry your bag in and have a bite to eat.'

Other than the ponies in the ski resort, I haven't been around horses in a week and I'm suffering from withdrawal symptoms, desperate to be around their scent, to be in a tidy stable aisle, but the mention of food makes my stomach growl, and I obligingly follow my family into the house.

Alice and Troika rush to the door, barking and spinning with excitement, and I fall to my knees to greet them, more than happy to be licked and jumped on.

'Did you miss me?' I say to the roan spaniel, scratching her tummy. 'Did you?' I ask in the sort of voice one uses to talk to babies. 'I missed you, too.'

When we drove off the shuttle in Folkestone, I heard Mum call Dad to ask him to take portions of shepherd's pie out of the freezer, and I can smell it cooking in the oven when I walk into the kitchen.

'Ah, home,' Mum says, voice full of both fatigue and nostalgia. 'We spend our whole lives pining for holidays, but the comfort of coming home is always the best part.'

'Speak for yourself,' Sophia mutters, walking past us and heading straight for the stairs, Rosie trailing behind her.

Mum frowns at their receding figures. 'Is something up with her?'

'No idea,' I say quickly, shooting Mia a warning glance, which she interprets correctly by clamping her mouth shut and taking a seat at the table.

'Probably tired,' Mum says, opening the oven door to inspect the foil cases of shepherd's pie. 'Do you want to get changed before we eat? Get your pyjamas on?'

I pull a glass from a cupboard and walk to the fridge, holding it beneath the water dispenser. 'No, because I'm going out to see the horses after,' I say, downing the whole glass.

'It's late,' Mum comments, closing the oven door and moving to the sink, switching on the tap. 'Why don't you wait till the morning.' She shakes excess water off her hands before grabbing a tea towel.

'No, I'll go see them after dinner,' I say irritably. 'You said I could a moment ago.'

'All right.' Mum speaks quickly, turning back to the oven. 'Will you girls get plates and cutlery, please?'

Rosie's mum arrives just before dinner is taken out of the oven, and luckily for my growling stomach, she doesn't stay long. Sophia still hasn't looked me in the eye since last night, but we're all too hungry and too tired to make conversation, so the silence is far from suspicious.

'Oh, that's better,' Mum says, pushing her plate away as she puts her cutlery down on it. She hasn't even left a bite of her meal for once.

'Where's Dad?' I say.

'He said on the phone that he's keeping watch till nine.'

Mia rubs her eyes. 'Can I go watch TV and clear up afterwards?'

'Of course,' Mum says, sounding as tired as Mia looks.

'Do you want to watch *Dawson's Creek*, M?' Sophia asks, jumping up and following our younger sister to the sitting room. Sophia is always getting Mia addicted to teen dramas, and Mia loves them, though I'm not sure she actually understands half of what goes on. Even if I wanted to join them, I know I'm anything but welcome, and I wait for them to be out of the room before standing up.

'I'm going to make a coffee and go see the horses,' I tell Mum, switching on the Nespresso machine and taking a mug from the cupboard. It's a personalised mug, given to me as a Christmas present last year, printed with a photograph of me and Fendi flying over an open brush fence. We have quite a collection of photo mugs, with each event horse and dog having at least one dedicated to them. Bubble also stars on a few because, well, she's Bubble.

'It's late, India,' Mum says again. 'Do you not want to wait until the morning?'

'No, I don't,' I snap. Last night's argument has worn my patience thin, and I can't help the harsh tone that comes out. 'Someone has to do night check, anyway.'

To my surprise, Mum doesn't tell me off for talking back, or even try to dissuade me again. 'Fine. I'll go with you, then.'

I make myself a big cup of coffee with plenty of milk, before pulling on boots and a coat, and heading outside. Mum zips up her own waterproof coat as we walk, jeans tucked into her Hunter wellies, and we move in silence, but unlike the one at the dinner table, this silence is suspicious.

'You all right?' I ask as we near our yard.

'I'm fine,' Mum replies smoothly, her voice just that little bit too chipper, too forced.

I almost expect something to be wrong when we reach the row of stables, but five heads look out at me over the half doors, only just visible in the dusk, and I scold myself. Of course everything's fine - why wouldn't it be?

There are whickers from every horse, and I greet them each in turn. This is what feels like coming home to me - not stepping into a warm, familiar house, but being in an organised yard, with the horses that are family. It could be wishful thinking, but Otto and Fendi seem genuinely happy to see me, expressions eager as they nudge my arms and blow warm breath across my face, and I feel hopeful. Earning their trust has taken a long time, and I'm still not completely there yet, but I will be. Someday. And maybe someday won't be too far away.

'I missed you,' I whisper to Fendi, putting my coffee cup down on her grooming box to stroke her Roman nose.

'You ready to go in now?' Mum asks, sliding her hands into her pockets and pressing her arms against her sides. 'It's cold.'

'You can, if you want,' I say, planting a goodbye kiss on Fendi's forehead. 'I'm going to see the mares.'

'You can do that tomorrow.'

'I know I *can*, but I want to see them now.' I blow out a sigh. 'You don't have to come. Go get warm.'

'I really don't think you should disturb them now, India.'

I almost laugh. 'There's someone around twenty-four seven,

and the lights are on till ten. It's not like they're left to sleep all night.'

'No, India, please,' Mum says firmly as I start walking away. 'As your mother, I am telling you it's late, and I want you inside and in bed.'

'*As my mother,*' I scoff. 'It's, like, eight o'clock.' I throw my hands up and look towards the barn in the distance, its lights the brightest thing in the dark. 'Whatever, I'm going.'

'India.' There's something in Mum's voice - not anger, but almost desperation - that strikes a nerve, makes me waver, and I stop in my tracks. Her eyes are on me, and the expression on her face, even in the dark, makes my blood run cold, makes me feel the same way the guilt I've been carrying since last night does. 'I need to tell you something, and you're not going to like it.'

'What?' I say, slightly breathless. But even though I ask, I'm certain I don't want to know.

Mum looses a breath and steps closer. 'I've got some bad news, but I don't want you to get upset.'

'What's making me upset is you acting like an idiot,' I snap viciously, fear making me rude, and the fact that Mum doesn't respond makes me worry even more. If me speaking like that goes, then whatever she has to say must be bad.

'Dad called while Darcy and I were out last night,' she says slowly. She pauses before going on. 'Pearl foaled last night.'

'Wha-' I stop, stop asking about the foal, because I know, I already know. Know why Mum's been acting weird, understand her choice of words. He hasn't made it. 'The foal died?' I say, voice cracking.

Mum looks down sadly, all the answer I need.

I clear my throat, coughing past the lump that is stopping my words. Losing a foal is awful. Not only for the foal, and for us, but for the dam. Some mares get frantic, can't understand where their baby has gone, and the panic often makes them colic. 'Is Pearl okay?' I ask. 'Have they found a foster foal or-'

'*India.*' Mum's voice breaks. 'I'm sorry,' she sniffles. 'Pearl didn't make it, either.'

My ears start ringing, my mind goes blank, and I think I'm about to be sick. 'What? What - last night? *Yesterday?* Why didn't you tell me?'

'I didn't want to ruin your last evening,' Mum says, tears running down her face.

'What, because this is so much better?' I'm yelling now, but I don't care.

'India, please. This is hard for everyone.'

'NO IT'S NOT! None of you cares about the mares, you just care about making money.'

'Don't say that,' Mum says. 'You know that's not true. God knows nobody works with horses for the money.'

'They're still business investments,' I snap, marching towards the distant barn. 'None of you *really* spends time with the mares.' I break into a run as Mum tries to reach my side. 'You don't even know them!' I yell, running away, towards the distant lights, before she can stop me.

My chest aches from breathing in the cold air when I sprint into the barn aisle, and I stop a moment, leaning forward to rest my hands on my knees, the nearest mares spinning in their straw beds, alarmed by my dramatic entrance, before straightening up and walking down the row of stables, towards Pearl's. My feet move slowly, putting off the inevitable, as though, if I take long enough, the universe could set everything right, fix what has to be a mistake, and the outcome could be different, but it isn't. There's no bay mare standing in the box, no crooked white blaze looking over the door, no foal, not even a straw bed. The box has already been emptied and disinfected, concrete floor damp with Jeyes Fluid, the smell strong when I step into the stable, and it hits me like an epiphany that I'll never be able to stand the scent again. I hold on to the top of the door as my breath comes out in gasps, squeezing my eyes shut. I think of Pearl, of how gentle she was, how beautiful, and how she would have given her whole heart to anyone happy to receive it. I see her, with my eyes closed. The way she always looks happy to see you. The way she whickers and licks her lips when you approach her. The way she can make me feel like the only person in the world, looking at me over the post-and-rail fencing as though she lives her whole life for me, and how I can go up to her after a crappy day and she'll make me forget about everything else. *Could.* Past tense now.

You don't grow up on a Thoroughbred stud without seeing plenty of horses covered in tarpaulins and loaded into the back of a van. As the saying goes, where you have livestock you also have dead stock. And Dad always points out that Thoroughbreds are the most useless creatures on the planet, that they wouldn't survive two weeks in the wild.

But Pearl.

I wanted her to matter. I've always known something could happen, the way it always does, but I wanted her to serve a purpose, to leave behind a legacy, and not just be another broodmare, forgotten about before her body even reaches the end of the driveway.

'India?'

I hear Dad's voice, coming out of the viewing room, and I turn around to see him standing in the doorway. His phone is in his hand, which makes me think Mum has just given him a heads-up, just warned him I was coming here. There are thick bags under his eyes, and I doubt he's slept in the past forty-eight hours. Pearl must have foaled early evening yesterday, to coincide with Mum and Darcy being out, and I'm sure he'll have been up since then, won't have slept since the night before.

I try to speak, but my face crumples, and Dad walks forward to pull me into a hug, and I cry into his woollen jumper, because there's nothing else to do.

'What happened?' I ask finally, stepping back and wiping my eyes with my sleeves.

Dad opens his mouth to speak, then hesitates, and I can tell he's wondering whether to be honest or whether to be brief, and he picks both. 'The birth was difficult, and she then started spitting out her guts. We called the vets right away, to put her out of her misery. There was nothing anyone could have done.'

I clench my jaw. I can only imagine last night's scene, picturing something worthy of screen time in a slasher movie, the sort I enjoy so much, and step nearer the stable again, grabbing on to the top of the door. 'Her body-' I start to say through tears.

'I've told them we want the ashes,' Dad answers, saving me from finishing the sentence. 'We'll find a nice spot for her. We can plant a tree or something, yeah?'

I nod, more tears falling down my cheeks despite the small comfort that thought offers. We don't always ask to retrieve the ashes of a lost mare, but there's no question that we should do so for Pearl. 'And the foal?' I ask, pressing for more details and gritting my teeth in an attempt to block out the smell of Jeyes Fluid.

'Never took a breath.'

I look down at my hands, pink and ice cold. 'What did he look like?' I ask. 'The colt.'

Dad smiles sadly. 'Handsome as anything. Big, really big. Chestnut with a white face, and socks right up to his knees.'

'Of course he was,' I say, keeping my eyes down. Just like his Group 1-winning sire. Would it have been better to hear the foal was ugly and weak-looking? Maybe. I don't know.

Dad steps closer to me and wraps an arm around my shoulders.

'She was a good mare,' I say meekly. It's pathetic, but it's all I can think to say. A naked truth.

'Yes,' Dad agrees. 'She was a good mare.'

chapter 13

Fog hangs low, inches from the ground as I walk to the stables. I didn't go to bed until late last night, too many thoughts spiralling in my head for me to settle down, but when I finally did, I crashed as soon as I hit the mattress. I must have slept six hours straight, but I woke up this morning feeling as though I hadn't slept at all.

'Hey, kids,' I greet the horses. Some of them are bleary-eyed as they stick their heads over the half doors, their body clocks telling them I'm early, the sky darker than it usually is at breakfast time - especially as the clocks only changed a week ago - but they recover quickly, and Otto kicks his door as though I were late to feed, and not an hour ahead of schedule. 'Hold your event horses,' I say.

Individual neighs ring through the air when I carry the buckets out of the feed room, all five piled up in my arms in the correct order to go down the stable row - low-calorie feed for Otto, high-energy for Fendi, low-energy for Harvey, and conditioning for the other two. I empty each bucket into a manger, finding comfort in the methodical, everyday act, and just wishing that, if nothing else, I could give Pearl a feed one more time.

Instead of going straight to her feed, Doris turns her head to look at me as I empty the mix into her manger, dark eyes standing out against her near-white coat, and I wrap my arms around her neck, realising I don't remember the last time I *did*. After all, she isn't mine anymore, and there are plenty of other horses around here that need my attention more, but you never know when a morning feed will be a horse's last, and it's so easy to forget that a few seconds of your time could mean the world to them.

'You were the best teacher a girl could ask for,' I tell the little mare, scratching her neck. 'I'll never forget that.'

There's a full bale of hay in the steamer, and I put two damp slices into each haynet while the horses are finishing up their breakfast. Bree is working today, so I don't need to muck out, which leaves me with nothing more to do. I look around the yard, almost hoping for a mess to materialise, something I can fix, but, unsurprisingly, it's spotless.

In the tack room, I make myself a cup of coffee, and find a packet of milk chocolate digestives in a cupboard. I eat four, then feel sick. Still restless. All I want to do is ride, but the horses have only just been fed, and I'm in lumpy walking boots that won't fit in stirrups. I showered earlier, so I can't even waste time by going to do that.

I glance at the tack around me, at the bridles hanging from the wall, and shrug, an idea forming. *What's one ride?*

'Sorry, Otto,' I say to the bay pony as I let myself into his stable. He's pulling at his haynet, always a greedy guts, but it'll still be there when he comes back. 'I know you've just had your feed, but you'll live. Just this once.'

I pick out Otto's feet, brush shavings out of his tail, put on his boots, grab my hat, fasten his bridle, and remove his rug. Something catches my eye as I lead him out of the stable, balanced on Fendi's grooming box - the cup of coffee I carried out last night, barely drunk and now covered in a layer of dust. I swallow hard, remembering how I'd made the drink to come out and see Pearl, never expecting to find out what I did.

Otto nudges my shoulder, and I shake my head as I turn towards him, straightening his black forelock. 'Let's not think about that now.'

In the courtyard, I swing onto Otto's back from the ground, his sides warm against my legs, and click my tongue, heading for the school. I can't remember the last time I rode bareback. I used to play around with Harvey and Doris when they were mine, and I'll sometimes ride Otto and Fendi to and from the field when they're turned out farther away in summer, but that's it.

The air is crisp when I reach the school, and I lean forward to unlatch the gate, straightening up as Otto pushes it with his nose, swinging it open. I close my eyes as we step onto the sand, as the rising sun hits my face. It feels right to be on a horse. Early in the morning is the best time to ride. The day hasn't yet been ruined, most of the world is still asleep. There are no distractions, and I'm aware of nothing but the horse beneath me, as though the sand school were the only place in the whole world. I can see Otto's breaths in the air, drifting up above his dark ears, and can feel his heart beat through his body.

He's had a light few days and has only just eaten, so I'm not planning on doing much with the gelding, but as soon as I start, I find I can't stop. He's trotting with impulsion, carrying himself correctly, and I find my own balance easily. Temptation gets the better of me, and once he's warmed up, I ask him for a canter, touching him with my outside leg. Otto leaps into the gait with exuberance, and I smile, riding away from the worries, away from sadness about Pearl and guilt about Sophia. Riding cures all.

I'm always careful when I ride, making sure not to do too much, not to push my ponies or myself, never to do anything that could go wrong. Always erring on the side of caution, as we've been taught to, and careful not to do anything that could interfere with the horses' training programme. Mia and I finally managed to convince Mum to let us play around and have a puissance last year, though it ended with a broken arm, which didn't exactly help make her see the advantages of careless riding. But right now, I'm not sure if careful is always right. Maybe if Sophia had been reckless every now and then, had taken risks and been brave enough to face failing and falling, she would have succeeded. Had learned to make mistakes on her own, and everything hadn't always been so serious. If she hadn't always ridden in controlled environments, supervised to prevent anything going wrong.

Of course, the irony is that she failed anyway.

There's a course of fences set up, from when Mia had her last lesson before we went on holiday. A couple of the jumps are only eighty centimetres high, but most are set at a metre. Before I can change my mind, I sit up straighter, keeping my leg on, and widen the twenty-metre circle I'm on to direct Otto towards the lowest vertical. The pony slows his stride on approach, checking that this is what I'm asking for, making sure I mean it, and I respond by squeezing my legs against his sides, and we pop over the blue-and-white jump with ease, and I'm not the least bit unseated, so I carry on. Over the next jump, and the next, until we're flying over the metre-high oxer, Otto's knees tucked as I lean forward to go with him, fingers in his mane.

I bury my head in my pony's neck as we land, uttering words of praise and closing my eyes to breathe in his scent, his mane tickling my face. Otto slows to a halt and lowers his head to rub his nose on his knee, and I wrap my right arm around his neck, putting all my weight on him.

'Well that was pretty bloody stupid.'

I jump so hard I almost slide over Otto's head and fall onto the sand at the sound of the voice, which in turn makes him shy, but I right myself just in time, grabbing on to some mane for balance, and look up to see Mum standing at the edge of the school. She's dressed, with a coat pulled on over jeans and a jumper, but she doesn't look like she's been up for long, her face bare, her hair unbrushed, and yet to put her contact lenses in, a pair of black-framed glasses perched on her nose. How much did she see? Everything, I guess. Or at least me and Otto clearing that last oxer, if the look on her face is anything to go by.

'I know,' I say, deciding admission is my best option as I push Otto towards her. 'Really, really stupid, I know. I couldn't help it. The jumps were just *there*... I couldn't stop myself.' I pause, looking at her shivering figure on the other side of the post-and-rail fence. 'How did you know I was riding?'

'I spotted you from my bedroom window.' Mum's breath is visible in the air as she speaks, and she crosses her arms against her waist, hugging herself for warmth. 'Pretty bloody stupid,' she says again, but then her face morphs into a smile, and she steps forward, through the open arena gate, and lays a hand on my knee, which she squeezes. 'But also pretty bloody brilliant.'

In all the drama of last night, I forgot to check on Siren, and I walk along the bottom side of the property an hour after my ride on Otto, taking the longer route to her field. There's a paddock far away from the pregnant mares and youngstock that Dad uses to turn out horses we get from the sales, an isolation paddock and stable block we keep them in for fear of the abortion virus among others. Siren stayed there for a few weeks after she arrived, but we weren't too concerned about her, seeing as she came from a small yard up north and wasn't at the sales very long, lowering her risk of coming into contact with any disease. Since February, I haven't really been to see the four three and four-year-old fillies Dad bought at Tattersalls, but today I feel myself drawn to them, feet moving towards the field of their own accord.

Four mares pick at piles of hay along the fence line, barely glancing up at me. Each is fluffy and muddy despite it supposedly being spring, with a tangled mane and tail. You'd never guess each was sparkly clean and parade ring-ready two months ago, but they've certainly embraced natural field life. They've all been covered already, though I can't remember which mare went to which stallion.

'Hey, girls,' I say, leaning my arms against the top railing.

I run through their registered names in my mind, trying to put a name to each horse, which isn't so easy now they're all turned out together like this, especially since they're all bay.

'That one's sweet,' I say to myself, watching the smallest of the four fillies munch on her hay. She reminds me of Pearl - the angles of her head, the fine blaze, the chunky build. Faint Breath, I think that's her name. She was my favourite at the sales. Maybe she'll end up being as special as Pearl, too. Maybe I'll fall for her, and *she* will breed the winner. Maybe -

My thoughts are interrupted by Faint Breath suddenly spinning on her hocks, hay still hanging from her mouth, and launching herself at the mare to her left, ears pinned and teeth bared, for no reason I can see.

Maybe not.

The now evil-looking mare returns to her pile of hay, and I expect that to be that, for her to resume eating happily, but she doesn't. The other mare, the one that just got chased, is standing far away, not daring to return to her own forage, but that isn't enough for Faint Breath. She turns around, ears pinned again, and charges the other mare, looking even more vicious than she did a moment ago.

'Hey,' I shout, jumping through the railings.

The bigger bay mare isn't even trying to defend herself, only trying to get away, but still Faint Breath persists. She chases her with venom, ears pinned, and I do the only thing I can think to do: I run. And not away from the teeth and hooves.

'Get away from her!' I scream, tears suddenly running down my face as I jump between the mares. 'Get *away!*'

Due to a combination of my shouting and now being bored

of this game, the bully mare returns to the other two, totally unfazed, and I mutter some insults at her before turning my attention to the other filly. She's the only one whose name I can't remember, due mainly to it being completely unpronounceable.

'Hey, little one,' I say for lack of another greeting, because the filly is anything but little. She must be nearing sixteen-three, and I remember that, at a glance, she was my least favourite of the four fillies when I saw them at Tattersalls. She's won a race, though, and Dad liked her breeding…

The filly stands a few feet away from me, warily eyeing the other mares. Her nostrils are wide, head low, and I can see her sides heaving beneath her muddy winter coat.

'It's all right,' I say, and I might as well be speaking to myself, because I'm the one crying like a baby. 'They're not going to get you. They'd have to get through me first.'

I step forward, slowly approaching the filly, but the fear she has of the other mares she doesn't hold against me. I wasn't keen on her when I saw her in the parade ring at the sales because she isn't exactly the prettiest Thoroughbred out there, and she was also quite anxious. Her ears are too big, body angular, her dull bay coat absent of any white, generally just plain. But as Dad pointed out when I said this to him, she doesn't actually have a conformation flaw, and will look a lot better when she's not racing fit.

'They're mean, aren't they?' I hold out my hand, and the dark bay mare lowers her nose. Her breath on my palm makes the hairs on the back of my neck stand up, and I step closer. There isn't a mean bone in her body, I know it right away, just as Faint Breath must know to persecute her so mercilessly. When you've been around as many horses for as many years as I have, always looking at and acquiring new ones, you learn to sort the good eggs from the bad. You know, just from seeing them in the box and walking around the parade ring at the sales, what their natures will be like. Sometimes you're wrong about some things, but generally it isn't hard to tell a horse's character.

And I know for certain that there isn't an ounce of meanness in this mare. She was jigging at Tattersalls, but she must have just been worried. We try to go for the calmest mares, not only for our own sake as handlers, but because an anxious mare is more likely to abort, though occasionally the horse that is the calmest in the ring is the one that freaks out the most when they get home, because they'd switched off in the stressful environment, and only showed their true colours afterwards. Just as every now and then you get a mare like this one, who was worked up in the high atmosphere, and has settled outside of it to be the calmest of the lot.

'It's all right,' I say again, scratching the mare's fluffy neck, and right then, I feel it. A spark, a gut feeling.

Pearl is gone, and that pain makes me wonder why we all do this, getting up day after day to look after these animals that break your heart. But there are more horses out there, more stories to be written, more legends to be made. And other mares, like this one, who deserve a chance at doing something great.

'You need a name,' I say, wiping my eyes. 'Don't you?'

Her racing name contains more Gs and Qs than any word should, and I want this filly to have a real name, one that is really hers, and not just something typed on a piece of paper. Something that fits her, maybe an homage to Pearl…

'Gem,' I say aloud, testing it out. 'You seem like a Gem. What do you think?'

I scratch the big mare's neck again, and she rests her head against my shoulder.

When I finally make it to Siren's field, she's grazing happily in the distance, alongside a few other mares. I don't expect her to notice me, much less show me any interest, but she lifts her head as soon as she hears my footsteps along the grass, and starts walking away from the rest of the herd, towards where I'm standing at the railings, until breaking into an uncoordinated trot.

'Hello,' I say, smiling as the mare unceremoniously nudges me with her head. 'You're a bit of a bull, you know that?'

'You can say that again,' Dad says, stepping up behind me with a foal slip in his hand.

I smile, and he comes up beside me, leaning his arms on the top rail of the fence. Siren turns her head towards him, ears back as she wears a goofy expression, then turns her attention back to me and starts nudging me with her nose, wanting treats.

'She's not, you know,' Dad says after a while.

'Not what? A bull?' Siren pushes me so hard I lose my balance, and I stumble a step before coming back to centre. I grab hold of her head collar over the fence and run a hand down her fluffy red neck. 'I kinda think she is,' I say, letting her go again

Dad smiles and shakes his head. 'No, I didn't mean that. She's a bison.' The mare stretches out her nose innocently, only to pin her ears and bunt me when I lean towards her. I grin at her thuggish attitude, and Dad clears his throat before going on. 'I meant she's not in foal.'

'Oh.' I'd completely forgotten about the third cover, that Siren was due to be scanned this week. 'She didn't take?' I say, stating the obvious.

'Nope. And that's the three covers used, so I guess we'll put her to something different now.'

'Oh, yeah.' Most studs work on a three-go basis, a contract that ties you to the stallion for three attempts, meaning a mare must return to him twice if she doesn't take first time. You can still go back to them again after that, but it's generally assumed that the pairing isn't a match, and with a short window to get mares in foal, it's rarely risked. 'Who were you thinking of?'

Dad shrugs, watching as Siren grabs hold of the hem of my sleeve with her teeth and pulls. I grab hold of the top rail in time to stop myself from flying into it, and reclaim my arm, only for her to grab hold of it again. 'Not sure yet. The thing is, I'm not sure it's worth it.'

Of course it's not. He probably wants to stick her in the July sale, even though she'll probably make a thousand quid if we're lucky, and be rid of her.

'I mean,' he goes on, 'look at it!' He nods at Siren, playing tug of war with my coat. 'She's still a baby herself. She's gonna be a useless broodmare.'

'You don't know that for sure.' Though we have often found that the bullish, playful, confident mares surprisingly don't make the best mothers. It's often the tricky, more nervous ones, the ones that give us hell, who are the most maternal. 'She could be all right. She's easy to handle.'

Dad pulls a face. 'Nah, don't think it's worth it. And I've already spent enough in vet fees.' He pauses, and I turn to face him, ready to argue, ready to insist that he needs to keep Siren, that he can't just put a barren mare with no race record in a sale now, but then he grins. 'I guess you'll just have to have her, then.'

It takes me a moment to comprehend what the wriggling blur of fluff at my feet is when I step into the kitchen at lunchtime.

'What–'

'It's one of Flora's puppies!' Mia shrieks, jumping up from her chair.

'What?' I say again.

'We just picked him up,' Mum says, switching on the kettle.

'O-kay,' I say slowly.

The puppy jumps up at my leg, his front paws barely reaching my knee. I look down at his spaniel face, at his wide brown eyes and floppy ears, his coat golden and silky, and my heart melts.

'Isn't he the cutest?' says Mia.

I collapse to my knees, and the puppy wastes no time in jumping into my lap. He climbs up my chest and licks my face before I can stop him, and I laugh, falling onto the floor with him. 'What's he doing here?' I ask once the puppy gives me space to breathe.

'He's ours!' Mia says.

'Huh? Since when?'

'He'd been reserved,' Mum says, 'but the home fell through.' She shrugs. 'I thought we could all use a distraction.

'So you got a puppy?' I say.

Mum holds up her hands and smiles. 'Hey, what's a better distraction than a puppy? Actually, there is one other thing that will keep us occupied now.'

I frown sceptically. 'What's that?'

'We all have to agree on a name.'

I groan. 'Then the poor thing's never gonna get named.'

'I like Teddy,' Mia suggests.

'No,' Mum and I reply in unison.

'How are Alice and Troi?' I ask, looking around.

'They're locked in the other room for now,' Mum says. 'Troi looked a little too eager to play with him.'

I laugh. 'Of course she did.'

The cocker spaniel puppy rolls onto his back, between my legs, and I waggle my fingers above his nose, laughing as he tries to catch them. Mia sits down opposite us, and we're both leaning over the golden puppy when we hear the back door open, and look up in time to catch Mum's expression of feigned innocence before Dad's voice resonates behind us.

'Please tell me that dog isn't ours?'

* * *

'You coming?'

Siren turns her head, looking back towards the barn. She doesn't understand why we're going this way, convinced I'm confused. It's like she's saying, *Um, India, what's wrong with you? The building with all the food and all my friends is over there.*

'You'll be back soon,' I tell the Thoroughbred. 'But if you're not going to be a broodmare, then you'll have to earn your keep another way.'

Siren is still not convinced, standing with all four feet planted, but she's too curious to be stubborn for long, and eventually I manage to coax her forward, towards the distant sand school.

'You must have been a pretty useless racehorse to have not even *been* raced, seeing as you don't seem to have any injuries,' I say. Her handler at Tattersalls said she was untried because she matured late, which will be partly true, but they can't exactly have thought much of her. 'Maybe schooling will be more up your alley.' *And jumping, and cross country,* I think. After all, everyone knows that a slow racehorse is a fast event horse.

For twenty minutes, I lead Siren around the school. Well, to start with, *she* is the one leading *me,* dragging me in circles and never going where I want her to go. That is after she gets over the initial terror of seeing herself in the arena mirrors, which she spends a good few minutes snorting at, convinced there's another horse staring at her. It's only by walking into the glass head first that she realises the creature is her own reflection, except she then becomes enamoured with it, refusing to leave the mirror, until I drag her away with sheer force.

Like every racehorse I know, Siren doesn't like turning right, a bad habit that comes from everything always being done on the left in racing yards and having not been correctly broken at the beginning, just the standard three-day racing break. But despite her tough attitude, Siren isn't mareish, because she's too intrigued by everything and too fond of attention to be a stubborn mule, and she learns quickly.

I click my tongue, walking towards a pole on the ground. 'Come on, Ren-Ren.'

The mare baulks when she comes within an inch of the painted rail, snorting as she jumps into the air like a cat, leaping backwards, and I laugh. 'Don't be daft. Come on.'

I jump over the pole, holding on to the end of the lead rope, and stand on the other side. Siren watches me, ears back the way they always are - resting mare face, Dad calls it. Earl has another name for it. 'Come on,' I say again.

Siren lowers her nose to the pole, suspicious, then raises her head to look at me, and I move to the side just in time to avoid being knocked over as she leaps over the terrifying item. Her legs seem to fly every which way, but she gets over the pole without touching it. She comes to a standstill as soon as she lands, lips moving, and turns her head to butt it against me, which is her way of asking for Polos.

'You utter doughnut,' I say, laughing. Siren nudges me with her head again, and I do as I'm told, pulling a packet of mints from my pocket. 'Only because you *did* go over it. I'm not sure you reacting like that to a pole on the ground is very promising, though, if you're supposed to be a cross country horse. You need to be braver than that if you're going to event, Siren Sounding.' *Indiana Humphries and Siren Sounding.* I imagine my name announced in conjunction with Siren's, crackling through speakers on a cross country course, and my stomach tingles.

The sun is low in the sky, above the house, and a cloud shifts to send the light shining right into my face, and Siren shakes her head, red mane glowing gold.

She may becomes the world's greatest event horse, just as she may never jump anything other than cross poles without falling flat on her face. But standing here, beside this Thoroughbred mare I've grown to care about more than I ever thought I would, I don't mind what happens next.

I lead the mare over the pole again, and again she leaps over it like it's the most terrifying thing she's ever seen, but at least this time her legs aren't at all angles. It's almost a jump.

'See, now you look like a show jumper.'

At four, Siren is still a baby, and I don't want to do much in her first session. This is all new for her, and her concentration will be limited, so it's better to increase the groundwork sessions slowly, not to give her time to get bored.

'Come on, Ren,' I say, leading her out of the arena.

I take Siren back to the barn a different way, leading her around the other side of the property so she doesn't get used to one route. The horses are already in for the evening, and I take her past the paddocks without the worry of her being set off by galloping mares, not that she seems to be fazed by much.

'Hey, look at that,' I say to the mare as we reach a large puddle in the middle of a field alley. 'What do you think of that?'

I expect resistance - or at least hesitation - of some sort, but I certainly don't expect Siren to drag me to the middle of the puddle and start pawing the water before I can jump out of the way of the cascade she makes.

'Hey, hey, hey!' I laugh as the mare splashes water all over my trousers. 'Ren-ren,' I scold. 'Stop that, I'm soaked.'

Siren paws and paws the water, dipping her nose to the surface, and I have to tug at the lead rope with all my weight to drag her out of the puddle.

'Well, at least I know you won't have a problem with water complexes. Maybe you will be an event horse after all...'

chapter 14

I press the end of the hose into Fendi's tail, watching as the soapy water runs down it, trickling to the floor in a stream. It's Friday afternoon, and tomorrow we head to our third event of the season, and my first Pony Trial. I keep pulling my phone out of my pocket to look at one of the text messages I got the other week, confirming the entries. **Your Weston Park Pony Trial Entry LAKOTA / Indiana Humphries has been accepted into Section F No. 262.** I have a similar message confirming Fendi's entry, too, though she's in a different section, and all my ride times came through the other day. Even though the height will be no different from the Novice we contested last month, I'm still nervous, my stomach twisting every time I think about competing in a Pony Trial. Which reminds me I haven't had anything to eat today.

It's been a couple of days since we returned from the trip, but it feels like a lifetime, and in that time I don't think Sophia and I have said two words to each other. Sophia's been doing her own thing, and I've been focussing on the ponies, and on Siren. It's frightfully easy to avoid someone you share a roof with. Especially when there's a rambunctious puppy running around, drawing everybody's attention. Herbie has served as an excellent buffer, and the closest Sophia and I have got to each other was last night when we shared a sofa with Mia to watch *10 Things I Hate About You*, though in fairness, Mia and the puppy were between us. And Sophia and I both wanted to be near Herbie - even Dad, who likes to pretend he's not keen on the dogs, cradles the spaniel puppy whenever he can. There is no spat so great it can't be forgotten for an hour and a half in favour of a puppy and a 90s' rom-com.

There's also no shortage of jobs around. Looking after Otto and Fendi - and now Siren - takes up enough time as it is, but I've been pulling my weight around the stud, too. Driving the sweeper across the fields, running hay and feeds to paddocks with the Gator, being an extra pair of hands to hold foals for their first farrier session (something that takes an army), holding mares to be scanned, tidying them up to go be covered... Two mares scanned as expecting twins this week alone, and I held them for the vet to perform a twin squeeze, bursting one of the embryos with the scanner probe in a matter of seconds, while Earl walked past and made the stereotypical twin squeeze joke, 'Don't squeeze the colt!'.

And then yesterday Mia and I set up our course of show jumps on grass, loading the stands and poles onto the back of the tractor from the barn, where we stored them at the end of last season, and unloading them in the paddock Dad is allowing us to use this year. It took us hours to unstack and set up all the fences and fillers, both of us exhausted by the end of it, and of course we then spent the same amount of time riding, taking Otto, Fendi, Doris, and Harvey over the course. We also set up a dressage ring on grass, with our set of white boards and letters, and ran through our tests this morning with our dressage trainer, Edmund.

Last night I came out alone to do night check, and found Otto already lying down, resting his nose in the shavings, and I crept into the box to lie with him. I rested my weight against his shoulder, and the pony tucked his head towards me, leaning into me. I don't know how long we stayed like that, huddled in the shavings, but it was long enough that Mum came out to look for me, worried something had happened.

The water runs clean from Fendi's tail, clear and not grey as it was, and I turn the end of the hose to switch it off. Fendi is tied up in the wash stall, no stranger to the usual warm water pre-event showers, and I run my hand down her tail, stopping halfway, and swing it around in a spiral, the strands whooshing as excess water flies away.

'There,' I say. From the box of grooming products I pull a bottle of conditioner, which I spray liberally over the mare's thick tail. Otto is already washed and rugged, happily eating hay in his stable. Most of the tack is packed in the lorry, but I still have Fendi's saddles to grease. *Which I'd better do now,* I think, looking at the time on my watch. How is it already four o'clock? I've been out here since this morning without a break.

I lead Fendi to the cross ties and switch on the heat lamps above, watching the bulbs turn red. Of all the over the top equestrian technology on the market today, this has got to be my favourite. Plaiting when temperatures are lower than ten degrees is much easier when there's a giant radiator above you.

'You stay there,' I tell the mare, 'and I'll clean your tack.'

For what is, to my knowledge, the first time in history, Sophia is ahead of me today, and all her tack is already packed, while Mason is clean and plaited. Since our argument, she's made sure she's been around for Mason, and hasn't slept in or slacked off these past couple of days. I don't expect it to have anything to do with an epiphany so much as not wanting to be reliant on me. If this silent treatment goes on, I'm sure she'll have roped Mia into taking on her share of the yard duties in no time.

'Hey.'

I look up from the saddle I'm greasing to see Sophia walking towards me, something in her hand. She's not looking right at me but rather to the side, like when an actor in a movie is being filmed close-up and they're looking slightly left of the camera. Maybe I've jinxed the situation by thinking her name too many times? 'Hey.'

Sophia puts a scrunched up napkin down beside me, which unfolds to reveal a stack of flapjacks. 'Mum told me to bring you this.' A whole sentence! That's more words in ten seconds than either of us has said to the other in three days.

I focus on the saddle, on rubbing my cloth over the back of the seat, where there are a couple of scratches from me carelessly letting it rest against the stable wall. I have it set up on a stand outside the tack room, so that I can keep an eye on Fendi, and I glance at the mare before responding. I almost want to reply, *And you did it?* But I don't. 'Thanks,' I say instead.

I expect Sophia to walk away now, free of her duty, having done what Mum asked, but she hesitates, still standing in front of me, and I wonder if now's the time, if I should say something, try to apologise for words I'm not sure can be taken back or forgiven, but then Sophia looks to the right, and she starts walking that way. 'Hey, Fendi.'

The mare lifts her head at being addressed, and Sophia steps up to her, running a hand down the silky chestnut neck. 'Ah, it's so warm here,' she says, looking up at the solarium.

What. Is. Happening.

'Sophia, I'm sorry,' I blurt out, throwing my cloth onto the tub of grease as I stand up. 'You know that, right? I didn't mean what I said. I was angry and… I just snapped.'

Sophia stares straight ahead, gaze focussed on Fendi. Her perfectly straight hair is pulled back in a tight ponytail that accentuates the angles of her face, so unlike mine which earned me the nickname of Moonface when I was little.

'I'm so, so sorry,' I say again. 'If I could take it back…'

'You can't,' Sophia says simply.

I look down. 'No, I can't.'

'And you're wrong.'

'Huh?'

'You did mean it.' Sophia looks at me, the royal blue coat she's wearing the same colour as her eyes. 'You said you didn't mean what you said, but you did.'

'Maybe at the time,' I concede. 'But still…'

Sophia shakes her head, and for a moment I think she's going to walk away, but she does the opposite. 'What you said is true,' she says, closing the lid of Fendi's grooming box and sitting down on it. 'It *is* my fault Otto and Fendi went wrong, just as it's my fault Mason's starting to, too.'

'Mason's not going wrong,' I say firmly, walking up to my sister and sitting down on the concrete beside her.

Sophia nods, eyes fixed on Fendi again. 'He is. And it's all my fault.'

I almost say, *It's not your fault,* out of habit, but we're past that now. 'But you can do something about it,' I tell her. 'He's hardly ruined, nothing that can't quickly be fixed.'

'But what if it can't?'

'Of course it can. Look at Otto and Fendi.'

'They weren't fixed by *me,* were they?' Sophia looks at me, her cheeks red and her eyes glassy with tears. 'For God's sake, India, I'm not stupid. You think I don't know everything you said to me? I *know* I couldn't ride them, and I *know* it's my fault everything went wrong. Just because I don't sing it from the rooftops. I'm the one who can't ride, and I don't need to be reminded of it. By you, or Mum, or Merritt, or Alexandra bloody Evans.'

I look down at my hands, weighing options in my mind, but I realise, for the first time, that maybe the only thing I can say, the only thing I should have said, we *all* should have said all along, is the truth. 'Why don't you try to change? Why don't you just listen to Merritt - or any trainer, for that matter - and get over whatever problems you're having?'

Sophia shakes her head. 'It's not that simple.'

'Yes,' I insist. 'It is.'

'For you, maybe.' She pauses. 'I want to ride well - or, at least I *wanted* to. I wanted to be brave enough to go round big tracks, and good enough to get on any horse, and compete and place every weekend. I wanted the two best ponies in England, and I wanted to make a European team. But… I couldn't. I can't cope with being told I'm doing something wrong. It's like every ounce of confidence I have inside me shatters and my body can't function anymore. As soon as I doubt myself, I seize up. And then if I do manage to react, it's by doing the wrong thing. I get scared. If Merritt tells you to do something, you do it. And if you do something wrong, you try again. *I* can't do that. If something goes wrong, I can't breathe. I just can't hold it together. And I *wish* it weren't like that, I wish I could just keep going and move on, but I can't.'

'Of course you can. If you just try-'

'No,' Sophia says adamantly. 'I can't. It's just how I'm made.' She cranes her neck to look down the stable row, at Mason's box at the farthest end of the aisle. 'And I really, *really* don't want to mess Mason up because of it.'

'You won't, Soph,' I say, moving closer to her. 'You won't.' We sit in silence for a while, watching Fendi doze in the cross ties, one hind leg resting. But I have to ask. 'Why didn't you just say this? Why don't you just tell everyone the truth?'

'I *have,*' Sophia says, almost desperate. 'I have told you all that I can't cope with being told what I'm doing is wrong, that I panic.'

'Yeah, but-'

'But nothing! I have said that, which is why Mum doesn't let Merritt correct me - because, yes, I wasn't born yesterday, despite what you might think, I know Merritt goes easy on me.'

'I just assumed you were being precious,' I say honestly.

Sophia laughs, and it's good to hear. 'Of course.'

'Well, you can't blame me.'

'Yeah, I guess not. Maybe I *am*, in one way, but it's been going on for so long now, I just don't think I can change it.'

'You can try.'

Sophia shrugs. 'Honestly? I think it's too late. Besides, I've only got this year left in Juniors, and it's not like I'll be doing Young Riders.'

'What will you be doing, then?'

'What, in life?' Sophia smiles. 'Finishing my A-levels, going on a gap year, and then heading to uni.'

'How dull,' I deadpan, though I'm only half kidding, and Sophia snorts. 'You're really not going to work with horses?'

Sophia just stares at me as though I'm the stupidest person on earth. 'India. Come on. I'm not that delusional. It's not like I'm going to be a pro rider.'

'There are other jobs with horses,' I point out.

'What, shovelling manure?' Sophia scoffs. 'No thanks. To be honest,' she goes on, tugging at a loose thread of her sleeve, 'I don't really have the slightest clue *what* I want to do.'

'There's nothing wrong with that,' I say. 'And what about photography? You like taking pictures, and you're good at it, too.'

Sophia shrugs. 'I dunno. I don't think it's that easy to make a living out of it, and I *definitely* don't want to spend my life photographing family portraits and... *folded* babies!'

'Folded babies?' I repeat, laughing. 'What the hell is that?'

'You know.' She laughs. 'Like, newborn pics where people stick those weird headbands on babies and then position them so they look like they're folded in baskets and stuff.' She shudders. 'Ugh, I'd rather muck out for the rest of my life than do *that*.'

'There are other jobs that involve photography.'

'Wildlife and war zones?' Sophia says.

'Or events,' I point out. 'Think how much we spend on photos every weekend. Knowing how to ride probably gives you an advantage, too. I bet it wouldn't be hard to establish a name for yourself and-'

'Please, please, enough,' Sophia interrupts, covering her ears. 'I can't do any more talk about the future and jobs and *aargh!*' She fists her hands and leans forward to hit her head against her knees.

'See, it's things like this that make people think you're a drama queen.'

She closes her eyes and sits back up, stifling a laugh. 'Well, you're stressing me out!'

'Hey, it's fine,' I say, tapping her leg. 'You can always do a Mum and never get a job.'

Sophia laughs again, the two of us erupting in hysterics, and we laugh solidly for a minute, tears running down our cheeks when Fendi turns her head to look at us with an unamused expression.

'What is it, Fen?' Sophia says, wiping her eyes.

'You can't blame her for being confused,' I say. 'It's not like she's seen this before.'

Sophia laughs again. 'True.' She's silent for a moment, her eyes on Fendi. 'Though, to be clear, if you tell Mum that I laughed at what you just said a minute ago, you're dead.'

I smile. 'Deal.'

'And what about you? What do you want to do? Don't you want to travel and head to uni?'

Now it's my turn to scoff. 'No thanks,' I say, echoing Sophia's answer to my earlier question. 'I want to run the stud.'

'Seriously?' She looks around. 'You want to spend the rest of your life here?'

'Yes.'

'You'll change your mind as you get older.'

'I won't.'

'Uh-huh,' Sophia says, not looking convinced. I know everyone changes their mind about what they want to do, except I can't imagine that ever happening to me. But then, doesn't everyone feel that way? 'So you don't want to pursue riding, either?' she goes on.

I consider her words a moment before responding. 'No, I don't think so. I want to ride for my own pleasure,' I go on, thinking of Siren and how much I love spending time with her, even on the ground, 'but not professionally. I want to ride *my* horses for *me*, not train other people's or produce them to sell. I just can't imagine enjoying that.'

'Fair enough.'

I look down at my feet, the tips of my trainers wet from showering Fendi. No wonder my toes are cold. 'And what about Mason, then?'

Sophia raises her eyebrows as she looks straight ahead. 'I'm going to keep riding him and hope things don't go terribly wrong.'

'Have you really said to Merritt everything you just said to me? In that many words? Because I'm sure the two of you would have a much better understanding if you did.'

'Sure,' Sophia says, but I don't believe her.

'I'm serious. Because if you just said you don't like being corrected, and then come into lessons and throw tantrums about new bridles, then she's never going to take you seriously.'

'That was *once.*'

'So you admit it was a tantrum?'

Sophia pushes my shoulder, throwing me off balance. 'Shut up.'

I grin, so relieved to not only be talking again, but talking more like we used to. In the past couple of years, we haven't really chatted, just the two of us. We can get along in public, and sometimes have a lot of fun, too, but it's not the same, not like this. All this time of not telling Sophia the truth, of not confronting her about the ponies, of daring to say what we were all thinking, and it's really what was needed all along.

'And what about Mason? I mean once you leave this year. What'll happen to him?'

'Well,' Sophia says, voice dry, 'you seem to do so well with my screw-ups, I'm sure the two of you will get along swimmingly. And then I suppose Otto and Fendi will be going to Mia at the end of next year. She's absolutely gonna put us both to shame as far as results go. You know that, right?'

'Trust me,' I say, thinking of our gung-ho little sister, of her natural riding ability and unwavering determination and dedication, 'I know.'

* * *

'And now we welcome into the ring number 214 Indiana Humphries, and she rides Mrs Catherine Humphries's Fendigo. They come forward on a dressage score of 27.8.'

The start bell rings, and I touch Fendi into a canter, the mare moving into the hand, neck round, stride flowing. The show jumping ring is opposite a huge country house, and surrounded by rolling parkland dotted with sheep. I stand in the stirrups down the long side, sitting in the saddle before the turn to the first fence, the simple gag bit allowing me to steady Fendi with the lightest touch.

It's her third event of the year but I'm more nervous than I was for the last two, feel there's more at stake, and Fendi knows it. She also knows she's been plaited up and gone around a dressage ring, knows what phase comes after this one of coloured rails. She's switched on - *too* switched on - and revving to go, which makes my job harder. Especially when the jumps are bigger than usual and she then decides to play up and back off a spooky filler.

'Go on,' I growl, sitting deep in the saddle, driving with my legs, and the mare listens, carrying on to the jump and launching upwards, clearing the fence with way more air than she usually does.

'And that is a clear round for Indiana Humphries and Fendigo. They move forward to the cross country on that very competitive dressage score of 27.8.'

Some days, everything goes wrong. Others, everything goes right.

Both ponies pulled off super tests this morning. They were bold, expressive, but they were listening. What started off as a grey morning has turned to a bright day, the sky blue and the sun shining, neither too hot nor too cold. Perfect eventing weather.

I don't know where Fendi is in the standings, but I know it's high up, and we must be as good as guaranteed a placing if we go clear inside the time. But it's still only our third event of the season, and my first ever Pony Trial, neither of which is when you kill yourself to be a few seconds ahead of the clock.

'Three, two, one, go! Good luck!'

I focus on nothing but the track straight ahead, nothing but the jump between Fendi's ears. Not the standings, not how we look, just riding. One jump. And then another. That's all it is.

Seriously massive jumps, a voice in my head says. *Only ten centimetres higher than what you did last year,* I remind myself, though the course is more technical than I'm used to, forcing me to think the whole way around, but I'm focussed, and the mare beneath me is, too.

When Fendi gallops through the finish flags, I'm elated, but my job's not over yet, and I don't have a lot of time to think while I take her back to the lorry, untack and cool her down, no time to let the fact that I've gone double clear around my first Pony Trial sink in, because I've got to get on Otto. They are such different ponies to ride, and it's still jarring to jump from one to the other, to adapt to each, but that's what I have to do.

Otto is on fire when he sees the start box. He's always been fiery at the start of a cross country course, eager to go, but it's worse at the beginning of the season. I check my air jacket is clipped to the saddle, then trot Otto around the box as I'm given the sixty second warning. Merritt has to hold one of the rein buckles and lead him into it when it's time to go, and I barely manage to hit my stopwatch before he takes off, exploding from the start box like a prize from a cracker, dancing on his hind legs for a second before launching forward.

I let him jump the first few fences at his own pace, his speed, let him build confidence - *you do your job, bud, because these fences are huge and I'm terrified, so I'll let you get on with it* - but I have to start bringing him back after the fourth, before the upcoming combinations, and he listens much more than I expect him to. Otto slows his stride, flickers his ears when I ask something, checking with me, and I find I have more control than I've had on him before. Alex said, not so long ago, that if he trusts you, he'll look after you. *If he thinks he has a reason to,* those were her words, and they apply to most things with horses. Otto will listen to me if he thinks he has a reason to, if he thinks I'm going to do right by him. The same way he will also save my butt.

I've never liked trakehners, no matter how much I try convincing myself they're just rider scarers. 'It's just like jumping an upright,' Merritt says. But still, whoever first said they're just rider scarers had obviously never been a rider galloping into one, because they are more than scary. They're terrifying, huge logs suspended over ditches. They're bad enough at BE100 level, but this Novice-sized trakehner is huge. And in a panic, I push Otto out of his stride, urging him to take on the fence, much like Sophia did with Mason cross country schooling all those weeks ago. And I know I'm wrong even as I do it, and I wait, like a puppet - like a passenger, Merritt would say - for the inevitable. Either we take off on this stupid stride, or Otto slams on the brakes. But neither happens.

The bay pony finds a fifth leg. With no help from me he chips in another stride - *ponies are stride-adding machines,* Alex also said - and gets us safely over the obstacle, carrying on without a care.

The old Otto, the one with Alex, would have done the same.

The Otto of two years ago, or a year ago, or even of a few

months, wouldn't have.

And this ridiculous thing, this jump many would consider irrelevant, feels like more of a victory than any number of ribbons.

Otto will look after you, Alex said. *Once he thinks he has a reason to.*

And he seems to have found one.

Speak of the devil.

Alex is riding this way, on a bay I recognise as her nutty Thoroughbred mare, when I'm leading Otto back to the lorry. Mum has gone to help Sophia get ready for dressage, but even if they were both here, I'd still stop and say hello to Alex.

'There's the best pony in the whole entire world,' Alex says loudly, earning some stares from unsuspecting passers-by. 'How did he do?'

I grin - or grin wider, because I haven't stopped grinning since we galloped through the finish flags - and give her a thumbs-up. 'Double clear, first Pony Trial. I think we were twenty seconds over the optimum.'

Alex grins, too. 'Nothing wrong with that. Placed?'

'Not sure,' I say. 'There are quite a few ahead of me in the dressage, but I've seen a lot go wrong.' Even Freya, who was riding Leo three horses before Otto, didn't get around, her chestnut gelding losing his footing jumping into the water complex and giving them both a dunking. It must be the first time the combination hasn't gone double clear since Freya started riding Leo, and I felt disappointment in my gut as though I had been the one to fall when I heard the commentator through the speakers, followed by worry, but from the warm-up, while I was cantering Otto, I spotted two sodden figures walking back to the lorry park, so I know they're both all right physically at the very least.

'Well, place or not, still amazing. Can we catch up in a bit? I've got a break after this one.'

I nod. 'Sure.'

The bay mare sidesteps, and Alex loosens the contact on the reins. 'Great. I just need to speak to a friend who's show jumping at one real quick, so shall we meet near the ring about that time?'

'Yeah, okay. See you then.'

The ponies are at the lorry, cooled off, rugged, and eating hay. Fendi's only gone and won her section with her score of 27.8, while Otto's score of 33 gets him third in his. Merritt's so ecstatic she's started talking, for the first time, about Europeans this summer, saying I'm in with a real shot at making the team if I keep riding like this, something I can't quite get my head around.

It's been a perfect event, a perfect beginning to a season of Pony Trials, but I'm not thinking about any of it. Not about how my ponies were perfect, how good the weather is, how good the ground is, or even the adorably cute puppy on the end of the lead I'm holding, who makes it impossible to walk past anyone without being stopped. Instead I'm watching a horse go around the show jumping ring in disbelief, gawking like an idiot, hardly believing my eyes. It can't be, surely. But I heard the announcer, heard the name come fuzzily out of the speakers. Surely it's just a fluke, it can't really be…

'And that's a clear round for Georgia James and Loxwood. They move forward to the cross county on a score of…'

Loxwood. That's it, that's the name. I didn't mishear. That's what Pearl's foal was named, the one I never wanted to part with. We didn't name him, of course. He went to the sales unnamed, like all foals and yearlings with the odd exception. I didn't even name him myself, though I referred to him as Red because that's what he was. I only know he was later named Loxwood because of looking him up. Stalking him online, following his disappointing race record before he stopped racing full stop. I never knew what happened, if he did get re-homed or suffered a worse fate…

The rider leans forward to place a hand on the beautiful

chestnut's neck, only touching him, and I'm struck by a memory. Of a colt who used to pin his ears angrily whenever he was patted, which made us all laugh to no end. He does like having his ears scratched, though…

The chestnut gelding trots out of the show jumping ring on a long rein, back into the warm-up, neck stretched, head low, and I follow, walking along the fence line. It's him, it's really him. Isn't it? How common a name is Loxwood? Is it possible there are two, both vibrant chestnuts with a dash of white on their forehead? Seeing him like this, grown up, he reminds me of Siren. No wonder I liked that mare from the moment I saw her, and I think of the groundwork I've done with her these past weeks and wonder if maybe she'll end up looking like this, too, when she starts more serious work.

'Excuse me,' I say, walking up to the chestnut gelding - *Loxwood* - as he slows to a halt, addressing the rider. She's old to me, but young. Twenty? Something like that. My voice surprises her, but when she looks at me, her expression relaxes.

'Oh, hi!' She almost speaks as though she knows me, yet I'm sure I don't know her.

I watch as the girl swings out of the saddle and runs up her stirrups, my eyes on the chestnut. Can I stroke him? Is he really here? Can I just walk up to him and throw my arms around his neck the way someone would in a movie?

'Is your horse out of a mare called Woodland Pearl?' I babble.

'Pardon?'

'Is your horse out of a mare called Woodland Pearl?' I repeat, my voice slightly calmer this time.

'Uh.' The girl frowns, then nods slowly. 'Yeah, that rings a bell. Yeah, I think he is.' And then her eyes fall on Herbie, at the end of his tartan lead, and she looks at him with adoration, but I'm not looking at the spaniel.

I feel like my heart is about to burst into a million happy

pieces. 'Can... can I stroke him?' I say, aware that I'm not doing a single thing that doesn't make me come across as insane.

'Sure, of course. You know him?'

I nod, my eyes on the chestnut gelding. I've imagined this so many times, imagined seeing him again, and I almost expected him to recognise me, to let out a loud neigh and gallop into my arms or something, but he just stands there, probably wondering who this blubbering girl trying to touch him is. *Red.* I try the name out in my head, but I can't get it to fit him at all, not only the wrong size but the wrong lifetime. 'I - my family - bred him,' I say, stroking his neck. *It's him, he's here, I'm touching him.* Herbie tugs me sideways as he tries to go after a toddler holding a bacon bap, and I bend to scoop him up into my arms.

The girl's face lights up. 'No way?'

'Yeah. I heard the name through the speakers, then I saw him...' My voice trails off. 'I can't believe it.'

'Small world,' she agrees, scratching Herbie's head.

'Where did you get him?'

'I used to ride him out in Newmarket,' she says. 'He was useless as a racehorse, so I got him.'

'How long have you had him?'

'Um, three years now, I guess.' She lets out a breath. 'I can't believe it's been that long already, yet it also feels like I've never *not* had him.'

'And you've been eventing him all this time?'

'Pretty much, yeah. Have you never seen him?'

I shake my head. There are hundreds - even over a thousand - horses at every event, some I pick out of a warm-up at each competition without fail, others I never notice. All this time, and he's been right here, at the same events, sometimes just feet away from me. How is that possible? I guess the universe has a sense of humour.

'Would you ever sell him?' I ask. Surely Mum would say yes,

knowing how much I loved the colt, and now with Pearl gone. Especially if he's a half-decent event horse.

The girl looks away. 'No, sorry,' she says immediately, and seeing my face her expression softens. 'I'll never sell him,' she goes on. 'I'd sell a kidney and live in a cardboard box before parting with him.'

As much as I'm disappointed, as much as I want to cry at the thought of having finally found him, finally found the horse that haunts my dreams, I smile. That he's found a person who cares about him that much is all I could have hoped for all these years.

'Can I take a picture of him?' I ask, pulling my phone from my coat pocket.

'Yeah, sure.' She clicks her tongue as the gelding lowers his head, snapping her fingers. 'Hey, Lox,' she says, shaking the reins, 'pay attention, look cute. Do you want me to hold him?' she adds, nodding at Herbie as I struggle to hold on to him as well as take pictures, and I pass the puppy over to her open arms.

I snap a few photos, just enough to have proof, and I'm about to pocket my phone when I think of something. 'Pictures. Foal pictures,' I elaborate - *you're still sounding insane, India* - 'I have foal pictures of him. I could send you some or - actually, I think I have some on here…' I scroll through my phone, thumb moving as fast as it can to find the shot. I'm sure it's on here, sure I sent it to this phone because I couldn't bear to be without one…

The photo comes up, and I hold the phone out to the girl, who lets out a squeal that stops me from feeling self-conscious about my non-stop babbling.

Pearl is facing the camera, her coat glossy as she stands over a leggy chestnut colt. His expression is alert, eyes looking at the lens, the white on his forehead more prominent than it is now. The two Thoroughbreds are in a stable, standing in a big bed of straw, aglow with the evening light that shines through the sunroof.

'Oh my god. That is the cutest thing I've ever seen. Do you

still have the mare?'

I shake my head, and blink furiously to fend off tears. 'She died just a few days ago.'

'Oh, I'm so sorry.'

'Yeah, me too.' I let out a long breath, thinking of the grassy spot between rounded field corners that Dad and I have picked out to bury Pearl's ashes and lay a stone, where one day an apple tree will bloom, the fruits of which will be fed to other horses. 'She never did breed a winner,' I find myself saying. 'I really wanted her to, you know? To have one successful foal she'd be remembered by.'

The girl smiles sympathetically and sadly. 'Well, she certainly has for me. Thanks to her I have everything.'

'Hey, Georgia!'

Alex is striding towards us, on foot, and the girl, Georgia, waves in recognition.

'How's that lovely mare?' Georgia asks mockingly, and all I can think is, *They know each other? Not only has Loxwood been eventing all this time, but Alex knew him?*

'Lovely, thank you,' Alex replies, pressing her lips into a tight smile that turns into a ridiculous grin as her eyes fall on Herbie. 'Oh. My. God.'

'You two know each other?' I blurt out, interrupting the fuss Alex is making of Herbie.

Alex frowns at me. 'Um, yeah? Don't you?'

'We've just met,' I say.

'Indiana's family bred Loxwood,' Georgia says to Alex, and I think, *How does she know my name?*

Alex doesn't seem to find this quite as amazing as we do, and she shrugs as she says, 'Small world.'

'How do you two know each other?' I ask, still clueless.

'How does anyone who events know each other?' says Alex. 'Loxwood and Waffles were in Four Year Old classes together.'

'And Five,' says Georgia. 'And they're turning seven now, so…'

'You've known each other that long?' I say.

'Already?' Alex looks at Georgia. 'How many years is that? Four?'

'Three,' Georgia corrects.

Alex frowns. 'I don't understand the maths of that, but whatever. I was just coming to see you to talk about the weekend away everyone's going on… You still coming?'

Georgia nods. 'Yeah. I've got someone to cover the horses, so it should be all right. It was really nice meeting you,' she adds to me. 'And thank you for the puppy cuddles,' she says, holding Herbie out to pass him back to me, but Alex steps forward to take him before I can, his heart-shaped number tag engraved with the name *Herbie Humphries* jingling as she pulls him towards her chest.

'I have more pictures,' I say quickly, over the sound of Alex making cooing noises at the spaniel puppy. 'Of him. Loxwood,' I add. 'I have loads of foal pictures I could text you…'

'Really? That'd be great. I don't have my phone on me, but I can give you my number if you like?' I pass Georgia my phone, and she quickly types something into it. 'There. I put myself down as Georgia Loxwood so you know who it is.'

I look down at the phone, stalling. I've found the horse, after all these years, only for him to go away again. 'Great. I'll do that.'

For all the times I've imagined this moment, it never consisted of me standing in a warm-up, alone, as the horse walked away with someone else. It's all very anticlimactic. Not only does Loxwood not know me from Adam, but I could say the same thing. I recognised him, and felt emotions bubble up in my chest as I got near him, but then… nothing. A spark ignited only to sizzle out. He was mine once, in more ways than one, but he isn't anymore.

And as I watch, watch Georgia and Loxwood walk away, Alex hurrying beside them, as they exchange last-minute words - still with my puppy in her arms, I realise - something clicks in my mind.

Georgia steps nearer the chestnut gelding and rests a hand on his neck as they walk, not even having to look to know he's there.

Thanks to her, she said, *I have everything.*

Pearl mattered. She might not have been a champion racehorse or even bred one, but she changed somebody's life. She gave somebody something that matters. It might not matter to Mum or Dad or the racing industry, but she has left a legacy. She has made someone else's life.

And that will have to be enough.

It matters.

Even if the colt hasn't come back to me, the way I imagined. I guess things were never supposed to turn out that way.

Some horses find their way back to you, even if they're not meant for you. I needed to see him again to know that.

Why is it the horses we never get that are always on our mind? The failed racehorses and broodmares, and the horses I've ridden never keep my up at night, but it's the ones that never happened. The horse I spent a few minutes with at the sales that Dad didn't secure, the foals we didn't keep, that roan pony I tried before deciding on Harvey - the horses that weigh on your subconscious are always the ones you never get to know, the ones that are nothing but possibilities. What-ifs keep you up at night way more than successes and failures ever do.

Even as I asked if Red would ever be sold, it felt wrong. Forced. Like I wanted him because I was *supposed* to, not because I felt a connection with the horse standing in front of me.

He isn't meant for me. He might have been, at one time, but not anymore. He was meant for someone else. They clicked, the way Siren and I have. I think of the mare, and us maybe completing an event together one day, and the thought excites me way more than the idea of riding the horse walking away from me now. He was a *what-if,* and now, finally, I know *what* he is, and I can let him go.

That's the end of that.

I wonder if Alex realises she's just run off with somebody else's puppy, chatting to Georgia, but then they nod and wave at each other, and Alex is hurrying back this way.

'So,' she says, looking at me. Herbie has fallen asleep in her arms, his body limp, nose tucked into the crook of her elbow. 'Otto was good?'

I grin at the mention of our pony's name, the amazing rounds we've had today rushing back to me as other thoughts, of Georgia and Loxwood, leave my head. *We've completed a Pony Trial. In four months' time we could be riding at the European Championships, a Union Jack on Otto's saddle cloth.* 'He was insane. He's come third. Not only did he make everything feel easy, but he absolutely saved my butt cross country, like he's never done before.'

Alex smiles a smile that reaches her eyes. 'Tell me everything.'
And I do.

about the author

After years of living in France, Grace currently resides near Newmarket, where she works with horses full-time.

https://www.facebook.com/GraceWilkinsonWrites

gracewilkinsonwrites@gmail.com

Printed in Great Britain
by Amazon